# The Optimistic American

## Book I: Voir Dire

## By K.A. Shott

## voiced through the character of Iam Hucentmi

ISBN 978-1-7339702-8-0

K.A. Shott

To explore the works of K.A. Shott further please visit:

www.kashott,wixsite.com/livingproject

*The Living Song Project*

*The Living Song* is for **MUSICIANS ONLY!** I define "Musician" as anyone with a Musician's Soul (I trust that you know if your soul belongs to Music) in HONOR of the WWII era artists, Wassily Kandinsky (best known for painting) and Arnold Schönberg (best known for music), for they attempted to hybridize the visual and auditory arts to create a novel chromatic scale.

Both believed the union of their Crafts would offer GREATER ENERGY than the total sum of each individual aspect in isolation (aka synergy). I believe they discovered the "Method" that is essential for us to Overcome the Troubles of Our Time. I feel we MUST complete the Great Work they began so long ago so, Musician, I challenge you to create "21st Century Chromatism" to help US ADDRESS the challenges of 2020 and the critical years following it.

I hope the lens of your Musical Soul will "read" the Musical Notes in "words" but I urge you to resist the temptation of lyricism for the World has been buried beneath "messaging"; Language (written, spoken, and sung) has become as if the FIRST PIECE OF GARBAGE EVER BURIED.

But I believe (with my whole HEART) that the mathematics and logic of Music (its tonality, rhythm, and synchronization) has the POTENTIAL to break through the NOISE of a world so DEEPLY DESENSITIZED; in this time, when we desperately NEED to "hear," language has become MUTE.

Dear Musician, I know this is a heavy burden. It is your choice whether you answer this call but never forget: action and inaction DIRECTLY AFFECT collective Reality. If it helps, Beloved Musician, know that I pray for ALL who accept this challenge—for your strength, courage, and endurance.

*The Living Project* consists of three elements or components (a three-legged stool if you like): 1. "Asylum"/ *The Living Tome*; 2. "The Optimistic American: Indictment & Conviction"/ *The Living Mine*; and 3. "The Optimistic American: Voir Dire"/ *The Living Song*.

I have copyrighted the raw creative material for all three creative pieces, including the novel below, in order to protect them, legally, but I give you permission to use them, as you wish, and give you MY word that neither I nor anyone from my Tribe

4

will litigate for what you take/use from the project, *The Living Project* (or material from any one of its three elements: 1. "Asylum"/ *The Living Tome*; 2. "The Optimistic American: Indictment & Conviction"/ *The Living Mine*; and 3. "The Optimistic American: Voir Dire"/ *The Living Song*).

For all the MUSICIANS who accept this CALL TO ANSWER I pray you are blessed with Peace, Love, Light, and Wisdom for your NOBLE SERVICE and that "YOUR" music serves ALL Life—Sincerely.

K.A. Shott 5/31/2020 4:44 PM (Pentecost)

~~~

*The Optimistic American Book I: Voir Dire*

By K.A. Shott but voiced through the character of Iam Hucentmi

THE NATION: IN THE BEGINNING

The Phoenix Phenomena, or the destruction and resurrection of societies, began in America no differently than it had to all of its brother and sister societies—through a series of concurrent devastating events which included the Sleeping Sickness epidemic resulted in massive debilitation and significant loss of life resulting in massive property and asset reallocation, The Monarch systems virus (formerly, and colloquially named The Serpent) which disabled established debt in America, effectively collapsing the American economic infrastructure which, consequently, collapsed all interdependent economies, and—finally—the final transformative factor was the election of the Benevolent Leader who promised to lead the country to the other side of chaos but only if our Nation agreed to a temporary state of authoritarian rule.

The Alarmists, labeled historical zealots, mounted inconsequential protests, warned that societies had been to the end of similar journeys never enjoyed fairytale endings.

But desperation and fear made the people willing to sacrifice freedom for a promised future of a better tomorrow. Thus began the Reformation of America.

THE NATION: THE MONARCH VIRUS

the hologram, intent on speed reading the requisite four chapters of *Our New Democracy*.

## Chapter One: The Monarch Virus

The single most devastating cyberterroristic American history occurred during an election year and targeted U.S. computerized debt (or rather the deposit not actually deposited. that function to create as debt). The people called the virus The Monarch because the resultant devastation of our domestic economy affected the global economy or a butterfly effect. Programmers gladly called it The Monarch because they would accept defeat from nothing less than a king and they had been defeated. No matter was tried, including depositing of real money for a person who had no money then issuing a debt balance….that's as fast as it took for The Monarch to eradicate the entire transaction.

Some thought that by taking all computers offline, dismantling and replacing all the corrupted networks and software, that when they restarted The Monarch would be eradicated. That strategy was seen most in the media at the time. But it did not work.

The Monarch remained in force, completely irrevocable and instantly revived from its dormancy by any form of computer debt. With the U.S. economy in chaos the government was forced to act quickly and decisively with regard to reestablishing domestic debt and its repayment.

When the U.S. announced an emergency conversion to the Gold and Precious Metals Standard, claiming to possess one of the world's largest stock collection of gold, silver, and platinum, metallurgists from each of the G15 countries was given access in order to authenticate. The final report, an exhaustive inventory published and distributed to every recognized world leader, proved that, without a doubt, the U.S. held the majority of the world's precious metals.

From that moment a plague of inquiry fell upon their origins. Where'd they been all this time? What level of security had been provided where they'd been housed and who had access?

Conspiracies and rumors abounded but the only thing that mattered was that the U.S. declared they would pay either pay 0.0000001 percent on the Nation's outstanding digital debt—in gold—or they would pay nothing.

There were some wars but very few because the U.S. also declared that whoever declared war against it forfeited all claim for repayment of debt.

Though The Monarch only struck the U.S. almost every country transitioned away from digital debt out of fear.

People were afraid that The Monarch was trying to steal their retirement funds. And it did, but only when their fund manager leveraged it in order to profit from servicing debt loads—then The Monarch destroyed everything.

Conspiracy theorists claimed it was the U.S. who'd attacked itself in a clever ploy for self profit, which it adamantly denied.

Every nation was afraid: someone had successfully weaponized monetary technology. Many great minds had tried but none had succeed at anything but childhood hacks. The Monorch paled, in terms of impact on the global economy, compared to the historical and environmental payloads of Prypiat, Cherynoble, and Fukishima, what the Bikini Atols and the Nevada desert, and what Nagasaki and Hiroshima combined—there had never been a more destructive event in recorded history.

So, of course people thought it was an American invention and no one wanted them to use it on them so they all tried to play niece enough, settling the U.S. debts at its crazy 0.0000001 percent just so they could transition their own nation the same way the U.S. had.

to buy enough time to convert their own Nation's monetary back to based by Gold and Special Metals.

It really didn't matter to anyone if it was the U.S. or not—it was someone— and if they could reorganize their nation's economic system quickly enough maybe they could keep The Monarch (or other type of bug, maybe cricket) from attacking them. This is how The Monarch (though found only in the U.S.) transformed the entire global economy.

Chapter Two: The National Government Party Comes Into Power.

Shortly after the terrorist action of the Monarch the National Governmental Party came into power. He was the oldest but most fit president in the history of America—he would become known, affectionately, as The Benevolent Leader.

It was clear from the moment he was sworn into office that America would not only recover but would prosper, fantastically. You will be tested on the contents of his inaugural speech below:

> More years have passed since the unhappy day when the American people, blinded by promises from deceivers at home and abroad, lost touch with Her honor and independence. Dissension and hatred descended upon us as millions of Americans, from all walks of life, lost their homes, their pensions, their jobs, and their income security as we, the National Party, arrested by the Democratic Republic's chokehold on the Nation's throat, were forced to helplessly watch as our Nation devolved into a fractured confusion of political and personal opinions, classist economic interests, and ideological differences.

> The first thing the National Party will do is establish a new branch of government, the People's Branch, and it will be endowed with the same rights and responsibilities as those that formed our great Nation's Executive, Legislative, and Judicial because having an element of Direct Democracy is vital to our survival and the People's voices have gone unheard and unheeded for far too long. We will equip all public libraries with additional computers in order to facilitate voter participation in addition to incentive programs for people wishing to purchase persoan computers. It is our great hope that we might, finally, ease some of the fear and misunderstanding regarding computer use in the post-Monarch era. The Monarch is still a real threat but all other forms of computer use, such a media, social media, and voting are completely safe. We encourage all Americans who, out of fear and misunderstanding, practically denuded the nation of computers to rest assured that, for these purposes, computer use is completely safe…

> The misery of our people is horrible to behold! Millions of Americans are unemployed and starving; the whole of the middle class and small business have been impoverished. We are at risk of losing our nearly-three hundred year-old

inheritance, which has produced some of the greatest products of human culture and civilization...

All about us the warning signs of this collapse are apparent. Terrorism with its methods of madness is making a powerful and insidious attack upon our dismayed and shattered nation. It seeks to poison and disrupt in order to hurl us into an epoch of chaos…This negative, destroying spirit spared nothing of all that is highest and most valuable. Beginning with the family, it seeks to undermine the very foundations of morality and faith and scoffs at culture and business, nation and country, justice and honor.

All these years of Republican Democracy have ruined America; one more year of it would destroy her. The richest and fairest land of the world would be turned into a smoking heap of ruins. Even the sufferings of these past times could not be compared to the misery of America in which the flag of such dissent has been hoisted. The thousands of suffering and dead, which this inner strife has already cost America, should be a warning of the storm, which will come…

In these hours, when our hearts are troubled about the life and future of the American Nation, I appeal to you. Let the loyal National Governmental Party, let me, fight for the salvation of the American Nation.

This time the front lines are at home. As leaders of the nation and the National Government we vow to God, to our conscience, and to our people that we will faithfully and resolutely fulfill the task conferred upon us. The inheritance, which has fallen to us, is a terrible one. The task with which we are faced is the hardest to have fallen upon American statesmen within the memory of Man. But we are all filled with unbounded confidence for we believe in our people and their imperishable virtues. Every class and every individual must help us to found a new America!

The National Government will regard as its first and foremost duty to revive in the nation the spirit of unity and cooperation. It will preserve and defend those basic principles on which our nation has been built. It regards Christianity as the foundation of our national morality, and the family as the basis of national life…

Turbulent instincts must be replaced by national discipline. All those institutions, which are the strongholds of the energy and vitality of our nation, will be taken under the special care of the National Government.

The Republican Democracy has ruined the American People. During their years of power they have created an army of millions of unemployed. The National Government will, with sure determination and unshakable conviction of purpose, put through the following plan:

- Within 4 years the American People must be rescued from the mess into which they have fallen.
- Within 4 years unemployment must be finally overcome. At the same time the conditions necessary for a revival in trade and commerce are to be provided.

The National Government will couple with this tremendous task of reorganizing business life, a reorganization of the administrative and fiscal systems of America's National Government.

Only when this has been done can the idea of a continued federal existence of the American People be fully realized...

Works programs such as the P.T.P. or Pneumatic Tube Program and the L.P.P. or Lipophilic Program are but two of the new commitments this government is willing to make to help Americans secure the necessities of life and for those Americans who have fallen on hard times regardless of health or age.

These work initiatives and incentive programs are the best guarantees for the avoidance of any of the 'financial experiments' that have endangered our economy.

With regard to its foreign policy, the National Government considers its greatest mission to be the securing of the right to live and the restoration of freedom to our nation. It is impressed with the importance of its duty to use this nation of equal rights as an instrument for the securing and maintenance of peace. Peace that the world requires today more than ever. We should be happy if the world, by reducing its armaments, would see to it that, together, we all can march towards lasting peace instead of perpetual war.

If, however, America is to experience this political and economic revival and conscientiously fulfill her duties toward the other nations, one decisive step is absolutely necessary first: the overcoming of the destroying menace of terrorism, in all its forms, in America.

We of this National Government feel responsible for the restoration of orderly life in the nation and for the final elimination of our country's internal struggles, particularly regarding class. We recognize no classes. We see only American People, millions of people across the board, who will either overcome together the difficulties of these times or be overcome by them. The Republican Democracy failed. We will not.

Unity is our tool. Therefore we now appeal to the American People to support this reconciliation. The National Government wishes to work and it will work. It did not ruin the American Nation for all these years, but now it will lead the nation back to health.

The National Government is determined to make well, in four years— hopefully you will allow me eight—the the ills of ALL those years but we can't make the work of reconstruction dependent upon the approval of those who wrought destruction. The Republican Democracy and their lobbyists have had years to show what they can do. The result is a heap of ruins.

People of America, you have given us your confidence to fulfill our promises. We shall begin now. May God Almighty give our work His blessing, strengthen our purpose, and endow us with wisdom and the trust of our people. For we are fighting not for ourselves…but for America."*

Chapter Three: The Election and Executive Order creating The Greatest Compromise.

The country had never seen such an election: the Benevolent Leader won the popular vote by a landslide with unprecedented voter turnout—more than eight million more voters than his nearest predecessor—but the real miracle of his election was that the fiercely bipartisan Electoral College, unanimously chose him. Never had the country spoken with such clarity and with such timbre—America wanted to re-unite through real and lasting change

The Benevolent Leader's first executive action was to establish a third branch of Congress—the People's Branch and he charged it with the same legislative duties as the House of Representatives and Senate, and providing it with equal power because he felt that the people had an obligation to directly govern within the political structure.

It was based on the same ideals as the Great Compromise of 1787 when the government recognized that the Founder's format for the legislative branch had created an inequality of representation that threatened the cooperative stability needed to reconcile Federal with State governance.

The Benevolent Leader, in his wisdom, could see what the modern presidents failed to or refused to: the technology needed to institute direct democracy had been available for decades and the people had the right to participate in self-rule, not as an overarching model of governance but as an equal partner with the pillars that had served the country well.

It was at that point that each citizen was given the opportunity to cast their vote for every legislative proposal and to, if they chose, present arguments for or against legislation through online participation. No longer could the House and Senate ignore the people though the Benevolent Leader, in his wisdom, did allow for the 2/3rds majority rule in order to protect freedom from the tyranny of mob rule—which meant that if the people, united, directly opposed a united House and Senate, the House and Senate would win but in the entire history of the Benevolent Leader's rule there has never been such unity in any of the three parties and so, the general rules have applied.

The Benevolent Leader said, "Where once two houses were created in order that all states could cooperatively form the law with the central government, factoring for but not penalizing for each state's population, with equality—now is the time for all citizens to be treated with the equality of the states. Every state and every citizen are what we are—united in one great aim—to protect, defend, and prosper the spirit of the United States of America."

Today, participation in legislation is compulsory in order to remain eligible for a Fortaleez program.

Chapter Four: The Pandemic and the Formation of the Fortaleez.

The greatest threat to our nation occurred shortly after the election of the Benevolent Leader in the form of a flu pandemic that spread across the country. No state or district was spared. Medical staff of that era misdiagnosed it as an especially noxious form of seasonal flu because the infection symptoms of pain and fatigue persisted from between three to eight weeks.

Many died, especially infants, those of retirement age and older, those with already compromised immune systems, and a large percentage of teenagers, especially young women. Of those that survived the initial infection, 10% developed a severe form of parkinsonism. Most appeared to fully recover, returning to normal function, but also reported a sense of having been permanently changed. This was dismissed by the medical establishment as a psychosomatic effect.

As it continued to ravage America it became clear that we were facing something new. At that time the diagnostic procedure fell under the purview of the practitioner—there was no standard diagnostic guideline in place—so patient reports were filled with the varying descriptions of symptoms, making it almost impossible to search files for a standard etiology.

A group of forward thinking physicians suggested that the symptoms were reminiscent of encephalitis lethargica flu of the early 20th century but their opinions were not taken seriously because it was believed that this flu variant had been eradicated. Additionally, the 20th century flu variant, after reaching peak population infection and resultant immunological adaptation, declined and desisted but our modern flu continued to spread.

One emergency room physician, upon noticing that in addition to extreme fatigue, her patients were reporting what seemed to be nerve pain in their spines, arms, and legs as well as light sensitivity, decided to collect samples of cerebral spinal fluid.

Because of her hunch, we discovered that patients displaying hallmark flu symptoms were also testing positive for Epstein-Bar (EBV), a strain of herpetic virus but when she compared samples of her patient's EBV to historical samples, using electron microscopy, she discovered a strange formation in the interlocking protein rings of their outer shells, or capsids.

It was at that point the Benevolent Leader ordered all attending physicians to collect cerebral spinal and blood samples from every citizen, those displaying flu symptoms and those who appeared to be unaffected. He also formed a task force, comprised of our nation's top researchers, to isolate the EBV anomalies and it was their determination was that they were a previously unseen adaptation of flu variant: encephalitis lethargica.

Then they discovered something else—genetic fragments indicating mycosis which could only be explained by exposure to fungal pathogens…or mold. Our best scientists had isolated what was raging through our country, in terms of illness, but more importantly, they had discovered a living and dynamic example of cross-species hybrid, or evolution, that was capable of direct interaction with human physiology.

The Benevolent Leader began an immediate and nationwide evaluation of all building structures in order to determine which were contaminated with the mold variant threatening our nation's population. Those that tested positive were immediately evacuated and destroyed through controlled fire.

The residents were given fair market value for their property and most Americans were appeased, understanding that what was occurring was for their own health and the nation's health. The Fortaleez program was initiated to address the massive displacement of people that occurred from the Nation's attempt to eradicate this new health threat.

With houses and buildings being destroyed, the government relocated its displaced to locations in all the states, especially those in the interior, which had agreed to donate land, totaling in millions of acres, in order to accommodate temporary housing in the form of yurts, which were issued by the government. Engineers went to work immediately to build the world's most innovative cities—our Fortaleez—and everyone living in the yurts was given paid work in order to create these world wonders.

In the aftermath, researchers spent years studying the pandemic infection and determined that the disease displayed a relapsing/remitting behavior similar to some established autoimmune disorders. Though many never displayed symptoms after initial infection their samples revealed the diseases ability to remain dormant through the lifetime of its host.

In addition to physical suffering, the pandemic caused most citizens to incur significant amounts of debt, not only from medical treatment but from loss of work and the Benevolent Leader's attempted infection control policy of enforced quarantine for those displaying symptoms, whether from initial exposure or relapse.

The Monarch virus had crippled electronic debt accruement but, as a result of the American ability to adapt and overcome, by the time the hybrid flu pandemic struck debt establishment and collection was no longer a problem, which was why the Benevolent Leader developed and initiated the Debt Recovery program, which is now a component of every modern Fortaleez.

Those who'd lost everything and incurred debt due to illness were the closest to the Benevolent Leader's heart but he was adamant that no American debtor ever be denied basic and essential needs, including respectable housing with comfortable furnishings, unlimited access to desirable food and beverage, education, access to leisure both in terms of time and resource, and healthcare, including Wellness Centers established for the long term care of our fellow citizens who are aged or affected by debilitating disease.

The Benevolent Leader was able to institute the greatest era of Enlightenment ever seen in the history of the world. Though he has long since passed away—to our nation's great sorrow—his legacy continues to thrive, largely in part to his foresight in establishing the Direct Democracy Branch of government so that the dark days of elected representatives failing to uphold the nation's goodwill have been retired to an annals of history.

THE NATION: MILLIE POTAIR, LEAD SCIENTIST

Millie Potair loved her work for the nation's most esteemed scientist, Dr. Kachuka, but she loved him even more, though fact of the the latter she kept entirely to herself.

She couldn't believe her luck. While still a biology graduate student studying the early 20th century American epidemic of lethargic encephalitis, colloquially called "sleeping sickness", which occurred concurrently with the Great Flu Pandemic of 1918, she accidentally used a contaminated specimen of Streptomyces griseus bacteria that, through a previously undiscovered RNA mutation, was capable of accommodating not only the Epstein Barr virus (or EBV) but, in their combined state, could genetically graft to common fungal pathogens (or molds)—creating an entirely new species.

The discovery of such a bizarre biological trinity garnered Millie instant and global fame but it wasn't until Dr. Kachuka insisted she come to work with him at the National Institute of Health as a lead scientist that they, together, uncovered a terrifying truth: Streptomycenic EBV mold was not only the most likely cause behind the Nation's recent Sleeping Sickness Epidemic but that the only way it could be killed was through incineration.

Thus began the urgent nationwide inspection of all structures. All structures found to have mold were scheduled to be demolished, the rubble burned, and the residents were relocated to temporary housing structures that would, eventually, be replaced with the engineered small city structures known as Fortaleez.

Many people claimed that it was a cleverly disguised governmental land grab because the discovered molds had not been independently tested to determine if they were, in fact, the Streptomycenic EBV variant. No one would ever know how many were or were not. The government could not afford to test every sample and so proclaimed, in the interest of national security, that all mold was the same and required eradication.

Only twenty cities were chosen to be salvaged because the nation's top economists concluded that adequate rehabilitation of more than twenty cities from mold was cost prohibitive, that it would bankrupt the nation. They were able to economize rebuilding, with the help of Dr. Kachuka and Millie, by reclaiming cleansed building materials for the walls that surrounded every city, Fortaleez, domestic military base, and sections of the nation's entire border.

Abandoned towns and cities were left to ruin as was infrastructure not directly associated either with the chosen twenty or the Fortaleez. They, and everything other, were what would be known as the land of the Free.

CITIZEN MORIBUND WRATH

The Masculine Mystique by Moribund Wrath with Kim Shott

(extracted from The Optimistic American, to stand alone, on 7/15/18)

[NOTE: CHANGE ABRAN ALANO'S LITTLE SISTER WRITING PORN FOR MAGAZINE AND WRITING "A MAN'S RIGHT" PAMPHLET—explaining the rape culture crisis in the escalating battle of the sexes where feminist extremists are conscripting young women to declare rape in order to target young men as an act of war. Sex needs to be legally (sp consentual) the moment drugs and/or alcohol are involved because a person is willingly surrendering their control for consent or refusal by making themselves incapable of either rational decisions and/or physical resistance. The responsibility for decisions to have sex while intoxicated is theirs but even without physical evidence of rape or a legal court decision convicting you of rape they can declare you a rapist in the court of public opinion and destroy your life. Social media never dies. This is an oppressive system that the feminist extremists are propagating not to create equality, but to inflict punishment on today's men for the wrongs of past generations. It is punitive, cruel, and will be applied to increasingly more numbers of innocent young men.

How do you fight this? In a society that has become oppressive and you find yourself without the ability to fight, your only power is your refusal. Don't give them your sex. They want it as bad as you do, don't let them convince you otherwise. Make them romance you, buy you things, prove that they are worthy of your affection, that they're not scoundrels or whores who only want one thing: to get high and have sex but no desire to take personal responsibility for it. Men, just like women in the old days who were pursued by men and had to avoid sex for fear of unwanted pregnancy, because pre-birth control and pre-abortion it would ruin their lives if the men didn't marry them, you must now realize that the unwanted event is not pregnancy but being falsely accused of rape. If you are at a party and a woman keeps pursuing you when you say no and that you want to save yourself for a meaningful relationship, record their reaction, their teasing, their belittling, their coercion and report them to your schools and bosses. Only when society gets to see the ugliness of what these women are doing, will it finally stop seeing all women collectively as innocent victims and see that some women are, in fact, out to harm, to

violate, and to destroy men.]

Curling up on the couch with a drink and The Masculine Mystique by M. Wrath

Dieter Schmetterling considered himself a lucky man. He'd been a laborer

in a time when labor jobs were hard to find not because industry had been crippled by

a struggling economy but because it was cheaper to employ women and children than

a full-grown man. It just so happened, in the pre-chemical age of pulp mills, that a

back stronger than the women's and childrens' was required to handle the bolts

however, shortly after his employ, the chemical era issued in and his job, though

grandfathered, was then easily handled by women and children. For his employment

thereafter he counted his blessings.

By the time the chemicals came, a brother, uncle, and cousin (twice-

removed) were already enlisted in the service though the U.S. had not, officially,

entered into the global military conflict to be known as World War II. It was, by

1939, clear that the Chancellor of Germany and leader of the Nationalist Socialist

German Workers Party, Adolf Hitler, meant for European war. His invasion of

Poland meant World War: Treaties dictated this eventuality. Adolf Hitler had been a

veteran of The Great War, the War to End All Wars. So had Dieter 's uncle.

Whether his uncle, being only 17 years old in 1914, had been at the Battle of Ypres

(or the *Kindermord bei Ypern,* as the Germans called it, meaning "Massacre of the

Innocents") Dieter did not know. His uncle never spoke of the War. And, Dieter

truly believed, had it been left to his uncle's volition he would not have been in

WWII but the Burk-Wadsworth Act, 54, or the "Selective Training and Service Act

of 1940" had been passed by the Congress of the United States on September 14,

1940 and Dieter 's uncle, being within the draftable ages, 18-45, knew he'd be conscripted. But he knew he'd be conscripted even if he'd been older than 45 because he had a very specific skill: he was an Army sharpshooter and knew, because of this, he was required—upon necessity—to serve his country. All servicemen were. Once in, even after discharge, you were to answer the call to duty. In 1939, when Hitler invaded Poland, Dieter 's uncle knew the U.S. was going to war. It was inevitable and so he re-enlisted.

Dieter 's brother and cousin (twice-removed) both joined the Navy. They'd never seen war before. Both had been born after The War to end all Wars, as had he. But their enlistment was also inevitable because the Great Depression gave them empty bellies and hearts longing to experience something grander than poverty and they were led to believe that war would cure both ails. War would give them the chance to see the world. His cousin was due to come home the Christmas of 1941. He was stationed aboard the U.S.S. Houston, the "Galloping Ghost of the Java Coast," a Northampton-class heavy cruiser. He worked in the engine room and wrote in his last letter that sometimes he peeled oil from the whites of his eyes and even though he didn't mind it, he was looking forward to coming home. After surviving the Battle of Bali Sea (or the Battle of Makassar Strait) and the Battle of the Java Sea he thanked God he was alive. Never, in his life, had he dreamed his adventures would take him to that place. The next day was the Battle of Sunda Strait. From this, Dieter 's cousin (twice-removed) did not survive. His ship fought a gallant fight beside the Perth, the Perth that succumbed an hour after engagement and sank into the salty sea. The Houston fought, then, alone into the dark of night. Her gunners sank a minesweeper and gave the enemy some blows, but after 4 torpedoes—at midnight: at the end of what some in England called the "witching hour"—the U.S.S.

Houston rolled over and sank with her ensign still flying. Of the original crew of 1,061 only 368 survived. Dieter 's cousin was not one of them.

Dieter ' brother was aboard the troop transport ship: U.S.S.S. Harry Lee. He also worked in the engine room, but specifically he maintained the refrigeration units and distilled water. The Harry Lee took him to the grand places he'd longed to see like New Zealand, Efate, New Hebride, Hawaii, the Marshall Islands, Noumea and Guadalcanal; New Guinea, Mariana, and Guam. At Iwo Jima, after delivering her troops on February 24, 1945, she remained off Iwo Jima until March 6 acting as a hospital evacuation vessel until the time she sailed to Saipan with casualties on board. What he must have seen, on that Journey, Dieter could only imagine was horrible for after his brother was honorably discharged from the Navy in San Diego, he went to a hotel room and hung himself. He left no note.

Estelle grabbed her computer, indulging in one of her guilty pleasures, M.P. Honeycutt's blog featuring Honeycutt's latest Gratuitous Sex stories, weekly installments of the Of-Country Affairs, and HzTree & BitsOShit.

~~~

GRATUITOUS SEX by M.P. Honeycutt (pseudonym of Trella Alano when doing gig work)

"My boyfriend suggested a camping trip. I've never been particularly outdoorsy but, being eighteen years old, I was up for the challenge. Besides, he promised me I'd have fun.

After hiking up a mountain to a remote lake we found the perfect place to pitch our tent. I should say, where he pitched the tent—but I helped! At least as much as I could, considering how distracted I was when he started saying, "We're going to lay out naked under the stars tonight because we're all alone up here. You can stare at the moon while I…"

"I am no friend of riots and tumults but when people are oppressed, when their rights are infringed upon, when arbitrary rulers are put over them, when government is secret, the people become alarmed. If they have any spirit of freedom, they'll fight for their liberties and are justified in doing so." Samuel Adams

*The Masculine Mystique* by Moribund Wrath

When Dieter learned of his brother's fate, he cursed the day he'd been born wrong. Dieter was, in his heart, a pacifist. He detested war. He hated violence. He was sure there had to be other ways—peaceable ways—to solve conflicts. Many times he'd fought with his brother on this issue only to have the argument end in a heated agreement to disagree. But after the bombing of Pearl Harbor, on December 7, 1941, the dagger of vengeance pierced Dieter 's very soul, for he didn't know whether his brother lived or died, whether his cousin lived or died, he didn't know if he was the last of the next generation to stand—he couldn't stand being the sole inheritor because of an ideal—so he went to the recruiter even though his job at the pulp plant had offered him exclusion from the draft, only to find out that the military had instituted a new test. He found out that he had Rheumatoid Arthritis—he remembered the recruiter saying, "Besides, we need men in key positions that are vital to the war effort here at home too. You're still serving your Country." By then the chemical era had ushered into the pulp mill. By then, his strong back was no longer needed. And it was then that Dieter Schmetterling realized that even his strong back was not as strong as he'd believed. Nothing would be as strong as he'd believed it to be after that—and this rang resonantly clear when he learned of his brother's suicide.

Dieter Schmetterling had been born in 1921 and was celebrating his 89th birthday with a cake he'd bought from the only grocery store in the small town where he lived. His wife had long-since passed away. They'd had no children. He was, effectively, alone in the world. The cake was spraypainted with an array of foodcolor that Dieter didn't like the taste of. When he tried to scrape it off his hands began to shake so violently that he quit the attempt and ate the bright red, orange, yellow, blue, green and purple rainbow. He called his doctor and they scheduled him for an appointment the following week. He was in the last stages of Parkinson's disease.

Dieter already knew what to expect. He'd been visited by the county social worker who spelled out just exactly how he was going to live the rest of his life. She explained that he'd end up in a nursing home, that his house would be sold to cover his medical costs. She asked if he'd been a veteran of a foreign war and apologized for having to ask the question when she noticed he'd begun to cry, stating, "We have to ask because if you are, then once you've exhausted your personal assets, the Veteran's Administration will pay a certain amount for your care." Based on his reaction, she was surprised that he had not served.

She told him that he'd be eligible for Hospice care at the end of his life because Parkinson's was listed with them as a terminal disease.

"How so?" he asked.

"Well, it's not like cancer," she explained, "The disease doesn't kill you but, eventually, you'll loose the ability to swallow, then you'll have a feeding tube and usually that's when people begin eating and drinking less. After a period of time like this they usually get a cold or some kind of sickness and die."

"And if they don't get a sickness and die?  If they end up in a nursing home on IV fluids?"

"That's a hard one to call, but eventually the feeding tube is removed and at the very end the fluids are reduced and the person just fades away peacefully."

"So what you're saying is that I'll either end up sick and dead or starved and dehydrated to death?"

"I know," the girl who couldn't have been older than 25 said, with something masking as assurance, "it sounds barbaric but, honestly, from the hospice nurses I've spoken with, dying in this manner is really quite humane."

"And how can they tell?  At that point, is the person communicative?"

"Some are.  Some aren't."

"Let me guess," Dieter  Schmetterling spat, "Most aren't."

It was Dieter 's 89th birthday.  It had been years since the social worker had visited him, even though it seemed like yesterday.  She'd assured him that this might happen too due to the likelihood of developing, from Parkinson's disease, dementia. It did seem to Dieter  that it was getting harder and harder to recollect things like if he'd taken his medicine or if he'd showered that day.  He forgot when his last bowel movement was though he usually figured out when it had been too long based on the hours he spent on the pot with very little to show for a such great effort.  And his legs were giving out on him.  He fell.  He began to stay at home for fear of running into the social worker or his doctor.  He just knew if they knew how bad he was getting it would be the end for him: it would be the nursing home, starvation, dehydration— death.  Each day he woke up to he feared that imprisonment, cursing the humanity he lived in that would *help* him in such ways. He railed at them all, "As if it's not bad enough being trapped inside my body!"

He called the grocery store and asked if they'd deliver. Every Wednesday they came. He looked forward to this. He splurged and bought ice cream. He had his Social Security directly deposited into his checking account. The bank sent him new checks in the mail when he was low. He ordered his medicines online. He stopped going to church though once a-month a little old lady would come and read from the Bible with him. He was, for all intensive purposes, what people referred to as a "shut in." Television became his connection to the outside world and it was filled with terrible news: child abuse, illegal aliens, political scandals, and drugs both prescription and illicit.

One night, when his legs were bothering him particularly badly because he'd recently begun to suffer from Restless Leg Syndrome and severe foot cramping, he turned on the late night news. The main story was about a drug ring found in the big city that lay only 4 hours north of his small town. It showed the reporter pointing to the place where police had confiscated drugs estimated to have a street-value well into the millions. That night he took an extra dose of medicine, packed a bag filled with everything he needed, including a picture of his wife, and got into his car. Dieter Schmetterling had just celebrated his 89th birthday and, in the dark of night, got into the car he could still drive because he'd managed to pass the yearly driving test required in the state he lived in by perfectly timing when he took, and how much he took of, his medicine. He drove away from his house with his car's Global Positioning System set and made his way into the night.

"Four hours," he thought to himself, and that was all.

*The Masculine Mystique by Moribund Wrath*

Dieter Schmetterling lasted, approximately, 45 minutes before having to make a pit stop. The night was particularly dark. He noticed no moon in the sky as he climbed from his car and walked into the gas station/convenience store. The lady behind the register's counter had dark circles around her eyes. She instinctually pointed to the hallway.

The bathroom smelled a mix of cherry, urine and sulphur. There was a wet square of toilet paper on the ground with a shoe's tread imprinted with dirt. In contrast to the white painted door, a circle around the door's knob was a myriad of grayish fingerprints. Dieter wanted to sit down. It had been a lot of years since he felt comfortable standing up to take a piss and he worried that he'd miss and wet his pants but he wasn't going to let anything of his touch that toilet. His body tremored, so he used his muscles to lock his hips, but then the urine wouldn't come. He had to relax, which meant he shook. His water peppered the rim, the floor, the back of the toilet but Dieter Schmetterling let out a short victorious whisper: his pants remained unassaulted.

Feeling a little guilty, he decided to buy a snack. Salt & vinegar chips with a soda but when he set them on the counter he remembered the bathroom, "Just a minute," he said, shuffling off to the isle with travel toiletries. He returned with a small bottle of hand sanitizer and some diaper wipes.

"Is that everything?" the black-eyed lady asked.

"I believe so," Dieter replied.

He climbed back into his car, washed his hands, and tried to open his chip bag. Part of his trouble was that his hands were still moist, but that was not the real problem. He was loosing his coordination, his willful ability to move his body, and opening things like small bags of chips was quite difficult for him. That was the reason why, at home, he always bought big bags…and used scissors, which of course, he didn't have.

He checked in the glove compartment. At one time he remembered keeping a Swiss Army knife in there. In the convenience store's fluorescent lights he saw that he had an anthology of Vehicle Registrations arranged in reverse chronology. He laughed, "There's something to be said for tossing the new ones on top." Beneath them, he felt the knife, pulled it out, and tried to open a blade, but they were stuck and his fingers didn't have the strength or coordination to open them.

Dieter used his teeth but the Parkinson's made him involuntarily and profusely drool and soon the bag was covered with slippery saliva. Dieter threw the chip bag down, pissed off and frustrated. "The soda," he thought, only trying to unloose the cap proved at least as difficult as opening up the chips, so—still sitting in the convenience store parking lot—Dieter went back in. He bought a donut from the case, a soda from the fountain, a pair of cuticle scissors and called it good.

Back in his car, he sucked on the straw. The soda tasted "funny" to him, like sulphur. "That's the problem," he thought. "They use their water." But it didn't really matter to Dieter . He knew all about bad water. He'd worked in a pulp plant. It was all about poisonous water, especially after it had been converted to chemical processing. But none of that mattered, because Dieter was already dying, one way or the other, so it might as well be the water as anything else.

*The Masculine Mystique* by Moribund Wrath

At the next gas station/convenience store Dieter decided to fill up his car. He pushed the pump's button, "Pay Inside," and it beeped back that his decision was acceptable. Dieter Schmetterling chose the cheapest version, which just happened to be the mid-grade gasoline because his state was a corn state that contributed help in making gas "clean." As a reward, in the form of subsidy, the State's residents got to upgrade their gasoline for free. Dieter remembered when gas had Lead. He remembered its smell: sweet, thick, heady. He didn't much care for the new gasoline, though it still had original hints of smell, there was something about it, sort of like watching rubbing alcohol evaporate on skin, that bothered his nose even though he knew the new would kill him much, much slower than that which he'd grown up with.

Inside, the girl behind the counter was just the opposite of the black-eyed woman before. She was all pink-flush, blonde down, she was fresh and young with beautiful blue eyes. Dieter thought, "I bet she's downy *everywhere*." You see, Dieter Schmetterling was no saint. Not before he'd married his wife, nor after. In fact, if one were to have met Dieter as a younger man and that one happened to be a woman, it would be safe to say that a significant proportion of women would have longed to bed him. Dieter had been, in his prime, a gorgeous man and he still, in his eyes, twinkled suavity, glinted charm. He still could get young girls to blush, not out of vulgarity, but by the way he pronounced their names, with such sensuality. At least, that had been the case until his Parkinson's became worse. "Now," he thought, "All they see is my disease." And even though he liked their *sympathies*, it bothered him, deeply, this loss of amourity.

The girl piped, "That'll be..."

"Can I use your restroom?" Dieter asked.

She pointed, "Sure Sweetie, right down the hall."

To Dieter's pleasant surprise, the bathroom was immaculately clean. It smelled of cherry, full stop. "Funny," he thought as he slowly let his naked butt fall onto the toilet's seat, "It's as if the bathrooms *were* the women themselves." Letting his bladder void, Dieter decided to give pooping a try. It had been three days, he thought, since his last bowel movement and, he thought, "Who knows what the next bathroom will be like." Dieter strained. He shifted his weight back and forth, side to side, trying to dislodge what he knew must be stuck inside him. He felt his guts push out his anus. "Damn it!" he cursed. Hemorrhoids had plagued him ever since his Parkinson's had entered its final stage. "Just one little bit," he begged from God. It must have been 15 minutes when one, tiny marble plopped the water and sunk. "Ah," Dieter sighed, "Thank you God." From the strain, Dieter had broken out into a sweat. He wiped his forehead with toilet paper and stood, without wiping, in order to look upon that which had taken such great effort. He sat back down, wiped his ass, knowing that such rocks didn't really require 'wiping,' washed his hands and slowly, shakily, walked out into the store.

This time Dieter bought a candy bar, even though his doctor had told him not to eat chocolate because it made parkinsonian constipation worse, and a cup of coffee. When he paid for the treats and the gas the girl asked if he was okay.

"Oh sure," he smiled, "It's not everyday an old guy like me gets to see such a pretty face."

Her cheeks went from white to peach. Dieter took his change and, walking to his car, smiled. "I'm not dead yet."

~~~

*The Masculine Mystique by Moribund Wrath*

It had been decades since Dieter Schmetterling had driven hours at a time. He'd forgotten how boring it was to drive, alone. He'd drank his pop, his coffee, eaten his candy and chips. His belly was full and worse, because of the liquids, so was his bladder. "I'll never get there," he thought, "If I have to stop every 30 minutes to pee." Not to mention the fact that getting in and out of the car, walking to the back of the gas station/store and returning, took around 15 minutes a pop. But it was just so tiresome driving with only oneself, particularly at nighttime, with nothing to see with but eyes straining to keep between the white and yellow lines that seemed to narrow after sunset. Dieter didn't like driving at night. His optometrist had told him that as the eyes age, they saw worse at night. When Dieter asked why, he was told it was "rods and cones."

A sign indicated road construction ahead. Dieter came to the red stop sign. Orange cones cordoned off Dieter 's lane. There were no headlights. Dieter entered the oncoming traffic's side. Even though he was alone in that night, his heart beat a little faster until the orange cones signaled it was safe to return to his own lane. This made him forget about his optometrist. His bladder, however, was another matter. The problem was, not a convenience store in sight. He was, officially, in the middle of nowhere. He pulled off to the shoulder. The night was still blanketdark. He held onto his door to get up. He walked himself to the gravel using the car's hood as his cane. He leaned his butt against the fender, unzipped and let fly. "Nothing feels better than this," he thought. "Nothing better than a piss when the bladder's full." The air was heavy. "It's going to rain."

Back in the car he turned on the radio. The first station was noise. The second, third and fourth were music, he supposed, but sounded to him like noise too.

The self-proclaimed oldies station played too much contemporary stuff for Dieter 's taste. Where was Bing Crosby, Tommy Dorsey, Bix Beiderbecke? The radio belted out the refrain, "War, what is it good for?" Dieter turned it off, but thought about it. "What is war good for? Profit, I suppose. Population control. Employment. Experiments." Dieter decided to play a little game, see how many benefits of war he could come up with before his bladder made its next demand. "Sex." He remembered how that was before his wife had died. She'd never been the experimental kind, but for Dieter , that was irrelevant. He liked whatever he could get and she was amenable, as far as wives went. They'd met at the pulp mill. She was an office girl, a college girl, or rather to-be-attending secretary school.

The paper mill was her summer job. All the guys loved her. The mill was all guys because by that time the guys who'd survived the war had come home so the government went to great lengths prompting girls to get married, stay at home to raise their kids and rule their domestic realm in order to let the returning vets have their jobs back. To say it was love at first sight, on his part, would have been a lie. Dieter Schmetterling was a very handsome guy who'd had a lot of women in his time but for her, Daisy McCune, she fell for Dieter —hard. He was strong, terribly charming, and twenty-five. She was just-turned eighteen and every guy, except Dieter , was head over heals for her.

At first, her father didn't approve of Dieter . He'd hoped his daughter would either go to school and make her living as a secretary or marry higher up than a laborer. His perspective changed when Dieter informed him of the nestegg he'd managed to save. Her father consented. They were married three months after they'd met. And the fact that, 10 months later, no baby was born, put to rest the rumors that the marriage's shotgun-nature was of the oven-kind. Though it wouldn't have bothered Daisy if it had. She wanted nothing more than to have children. It would take years before she'd accept that it would never happen.

Dieter had one affair when he was forty-one. It was the early 60s, in fact, it was 1963 and a girl came to work, not in the office, but in the plant. She had long, sandybrown hair she kept tied back in a bun. She had muscular arms, for a woman, and wore blue jeans. She was tall and when he asked she said she was 18. She reminded him of Daisy though she looked nothing like her. "It was her youth," he later understood. "It was the way she smiled without worry and concern. It was abandon." Her name was Mindy Mahoney. Her father worked at the meat packing plant. Their meeting ups began in the lunchroom with the normal niceties. It took Dieter four months to ask her to meet him after their shift. He remembered that she paid for half of the hotel and when she kissed him she said, "I'm not interested in love. I want experience."

Once a week, for two months they met. Dieter told Daisy he was pulling a double shift and, having never known Dieter to lie, she believed it. Once a week and Dieter learned more about sex than he'd experienced his whole life. Positions, tongues, shifts and turns, one way—the next way—it was yoga, wrestling, a free-for-all and the fact was, Mindy Mahoney was absolutely beautiful. She was hardbodied and athletic in nature. When she held onto Dieter he knew he'd been held. She was like no other woman he'd ever known and the fact was, he was falling in love with her. He knew it. She'd lay on the bed, naked, her long hair nestled against the curves of her figure, and tell him about her dreams of going to Europe, of traveling the world over, of meeting all kinds of wonderful lovers. He knew it—because when she'd say this, he felt a pang in his heart. She knew it too and she'd laugh, "Listen old man," she'd say, "We're just having fun."

Then one day, without a word, Mindy Mahoney was gone.        Dieter asked the boss, he said she'd quit.  Dieter drove to her father's house.  He didn't care how it looked.  He didn't care if Daisy found out.  He banged on the front door like an eighteen-year-old lover, only to be met with a fat, balding man.

"Where's Mindy!" Dieter demanded.

"She went to Europe."

"When will she be back?"

"Hell I don't know.  Why?  You her boss or something?"

"No," Dieter turned, "I'm nothing to her."

He couldn't go home.  In fact, when he thought on Daisy's face, he hated her for not being Mindy so he drove around.  He found a payphone.  "Listen," he said, "I'm taking another shift tonight so don't wait up."  He drove to a bar.  Drink #1: pissed off.  Drink #2: "What am I going to do?"  Drink #3: "Screw her!"  Drink #4: "This is fucked up shit—I mean, didn't I mean anything to her?  I'm not just a piece of garbage she can throw away when she's done with me!"  Drink #5: "I want to die."  Drink #6, half-finished, Dieter went out to his car, laid down in the back seat and cried.

When morning came he drove home.  Daisy made him breakfast of eggs, bacon, toast and coffee.

"How was work?" she asked, handing him the yesterday's newspaper.

"Fine," he mumbled.

She could smell alcohol from his skin. Daisy Schmetterling knew more than Dieter gave her credit for. Sixteen years. She knew all about Mindy Mahoney because one of her friends worked at the meat packing plant as a secretary. A friend that knew of Dieter 's affair and with whom. A friend that called Daisy to tell her about Mindy Mahoney's European flight because she'd heard her dad bragging, at work, about his daughter getting out of their stinkholetown.

And it was a stinky town, between the pulp mill—which stank to high heaven—and the meat packing plant, which was no pleasant potpourri, their town was rank and people just wouldn't be right if they didn't dream of escaping it.

Daisy Schmetterling sat at the airport. She knew Mindy Mahoney the moment she saw her long soft-brown hair. She was wearing a tiedyed shirt that tied around her neck and her waist, leaving her strong back to flex in carrying her backpack. She wore bellbottom jeans, Birkenstock sandals, and a man's Fedora hat. She was the classical 18-year-old of her time. Her plane was not at the airport yet. She sat, opened her bag, and pulled out a book.

Daisy Schmetterling sat down beside her, "What are you reading?"

Mindy held the book up, "*The Feminine Mystique.* It's wonderful, so far. But I'm only on page 33."

"I see. And what's it about?"

"Well, that's sort of hard to explain."

"Try me."

"I suppose it's about what it means to be a woman. What it means to be a free woman."

"Aren't women free? I mean, we're not slaves."

"Well, I guess you could say that, technically. But we're not treated equally and that equates to slavery in my book."

"Oh, I see. So you're into those kinds of things then are you?"

"Oh yes! Definitely."

"And...do men like that? Like that you're into such things?"

"I don't really care if they do or don't. I'm my own person. They can take it or leave it."

The plane was announced. Mindy stood up and looked at Daisy. She was middle-aged, her hair was fastidiously fashioned, her clothes immaculately pressed, her shoes cleaned and polished.

Mindy looked at Daisy and her eyes got a little misty, "Listen, Lady, I don't know who you are but here."

She handed Daisy her book and, in an instant, was gone. Daisy's eyes were misting too. She read the title, *The Feminine Mystique*, and shuffled the thick book's pages like a cardplayer's deck, when a word caught her eye, "Housewife." But her shuffling shuffled past it. She went back. "The Happy Housewife Heroine." So Daisy began to read right there, right then, out of order, which was to her a no-no, but the chapter's title sparked her interest. She read the chapter right there in the airport. She watched Mindy Mahoney's plane take off, she read, "Why have so many

American wives suffered this nameless aching dissatisfaction for so many years, each one thinking she was alone?"

She cried thankful tears for Mindy Mahoney and forgave Dieter for loving her because she then understood. Mindy Mahoney had something neither of them had had—a spirit of freedom. But Daisy Mahoney determined, right then and there, to get one.

*The Masculine Mystique* by Moribund Wrath

Dieter looked at fluorescent green light of his car's clock: 2:30. He couldn't remember the last time he'd stayed awake until 2:30 in the morning, but he had gotten used to seeing that time in a day because that was usually when he would have to get up in the night to go to the bathroom and also when his legs would give him a good degree of trouble. The fact that the cramping and jumping in them had gotten progressively worse made Dieter take another dose of Parkinson's medicine, because it seemed the only thing to take the edge off. Sometimes his calf and big foot would cramp so violently, so intensely, that he could not walk. He would be stuck wherever he was, until his medicine kicked in which was why he kept a small container of pills in his pajamas and on his person at all times. One time he forgot to do this. One time he was on the toilet, the cramping hit. Dieter prayed to die it was so bad. It was like being hit in the stomach so badly one's air is knocked out, but it would not stop. He threw himself on the bathroom floor and crawled, bit by bit, to his nightstand drawer, grabbed his meds, swallowed them dry, and lay on the ground beside his bed, crying for the pain of it. Crying and quivering. It took almost half-an-hour before he could kneel. He remembered, clearly, praying for God to help him. Swearing to his Father that he couldn't stand much more.

It was 2:30. Dieter swallowed his pills with the melted ice turned water pooled at the top of staling soda. His eyes were heavy in spite of the fact that his meds were said to have a stimulant effect. There were some white lights in the distance. Dieter determined to stop and prayed for a hotel. Funny thing prayers are.

The motel was empty and brick with white paint flaking off and rusted white drainpipes. The unlit sign read, "Cozy Inn." There was a neon "Vacancy/No Vacancy" but it was dark. Dieter climbed out of his car. His joints were already stiff from sitting and he had to go to the bathroom again.

The office was dark. For a moment he wondered if the place was even open for business: it seemed that a lot of the small towns had lost theirs but the office door was unlocked. The singular streetlight lent enough for Dieter to see an old rotary-dial phone beneath a handwritten note, "Dial 0." Dieter 's finger shook as he placed it in the 0 hole. It took a great effort on his part to keep it steady enough to make it all the way around the dial until it reached the silver metal hook. He pulled it out and listened to the clicks as the dial returned itself to its resting position. It rang for quite some time before a husky voice answered, "Hello?"

"I'd like a room."

There was a long silent pause. Then the line went dead. A few minutes later the door just behind the front desk opened and a large, grayhaired hairy woman in a thin light blue satin-looking bathrobe that was too small to cover an even thinner pinkish-tan polyester nightgown trod in. As she strode her masses of flesh jiggled. She did not smile.

"Here," she pushed a small clipboard towards him. "Name and car."

"Do you need my address?"

"Name and car. I'll need a credit card."

"But I don't have one."

She pulled the clipboard back. "Sorry then. No room."

"I can pay you cash."

"No credit card no room."

"What about a debit card? I have a bank account with one of those."

She scratched the gray whiskers on her chin and wiped her nose, "Okay. But you'll have to give me a $200.00 cash deposit on top of that for room damages."

"And will I get that back in the morning?"

"Yeah sure. If the room's okay when you leave."

The room smelled dank. There was a large crack in the ceiling. There was orange mold stains on the shower curtain's bottom edge. There was a vibrating box with a quarter drop slot, "Magic Fingers." The television was small and built into a wooden frame. It was black and white. Dieter smiled. It couldn't have been better. It was just how he liked it. He deposited his quarters. The loud machine jumped the bed around. He thought of his years at the pulp mill. He thought of his wife. When it was done he got up, pulled the button of the tv into "on" and turned the dial, "click, click, click." Most of the stations were black/gray/white fuzz. One had the multi-colored bar codes and whining monotone letting people know that it was too late to be up watching t.v. Dieter closed his eyes, thinking he'd be unable to sleep, but quickly fell into wild dreams. He woke himself up, many times, that night. Kicking, punching, screaming but when his eyes opened he could remember nothing.

*The Masculine Mystique by Moribund Wrath*

Dieter Schmetterling tossed and turned that night in the hotel. The bed was fine but not his. The smells were fine but not his. The noise from the road was a constant reminder that he had someplace to go, only he didn't know exactly where.

Worry flooded over his mind like the levees of a delivering river at its pregnancy peak.

"Where am I going?" he murmured, in his sleep.

His pillow was wet with sweat when the yellow light of morning crept in between the curtains' gap. It seemed, to Dieter Schmetterling, that he'd only just fallen asleep. His lids were heavy. His leg was cramping.

"I need my medicine."

He opened his bag of pills. Blue, tan, yellow, and white; he swallowed them down in one gulp. He wondered why they bothered numbering them in addition to color code, but then remembered: law enforcement. He remembered the news. His leg stopped cramping. He got up to pee and decided, even though it would take a long time, he was going to shower. This was no easy feat for Dieter . Showering had become such a difficult task that he'd limited himself to once-a-week. The problem was, he'd forgotten when his last had been. When he lifted his arm to sniff, he detected a faint odor.

"It's time then," he said to himself. That he could smell anything at all meant the rest of the world could smell a great deal. The parkinsons, either the disease or the drugs, had affected his olfactory.

Once stripped and in the shower Dieter let himself love the water. The perfectly temperatured water running rivulets along his withering frame. He watched the drops forming amongst the gray hairs of his chest. He watched the drops gather strength in their searching for the path of least resistance that his wrinkled skin was only too happy to supply.  He noticed that there were some wrinkles the running water preferred.

He, carefully, let his head go back into the cascading waterfall.  He remembered a girl he'd known, when he was very small, who lived out, way out, and whose family was what some called 'backward.'  She was his best friend.  Her family had logged the timber from their land, planed the logs, and built a house with no electricity, no running water: nothing but a firestove, a firepit, a large black drum filled with rainwater and a well.

He remembered that she was his first love and that her name was Juliem and that every time he showered he thought of her because it was with her, standing outside amidst the forest and beneath the black drum, that the sun-warmed water showered both of their bare-naked child bodies.  He never forgot her, never.

It was checkout time, to the second, by the time Dieter  Schmetterling made his way to the office.  The complimentary breakfast of prepackaged donuts and coffee was already tucked away for the next days' customers, but the pimplefaced girl behind the desk got him his share, in spite of the hotel's rules against it and smiled when she said, "I bet you're hungry."

He was.  He gobbled the white powdered dried out dough and couldn't remember having ever been so thankful for a mouthful of food.  The coffee was bitter but Dieter  didn't mind.  He went to the girl, whose nametag read "Caroline" and said, "Thank you, Caroline."

"You're welcome.  Where are you headed?"

"To the city."

"You got family there or something?"

"You could say that."

"I see."

He gave her the key, got in his car and drove to the next gas station's bathroom, which happened to take him an hour. He bought a pack of denture-friendly chewing gum even though his teeth were all his own. He'd learned, the hard way, that non-denturefriendly gum pulled out his fillings and he had a mouthful of them. He also bought a package of beef jerky and a soda from the fountain.

Inside his car he tried to remember the last time he'd had it. He couldn't remember. He reached into the plastic bag, took out a strip, tried to bite off the tip and found that he didn't have the strength, nor did his teeth, to accomplish it. He sucked on it instead.

Oh how he preferred driving in the daylight! It was as if the whole world opened up before him and, at this thought, Dieter Schmetterling got an erection. It happened, from time to time, though he'd long given up on trying to make anything of it. When he was younger, when his parkinsons was still newer, and long after Daisy Schmetterling had died, he'd get them and try to masturbate. As hard as they started, it was but a few seconds before they passed and he'd come to accept that he needed more than a few seconds to find relief. Being thusly frustrated, he decided it best to just embrace his rigidness, to fully feel within his body, the beauty of being swollen and ready and to resign himself to the loss of it when it passed.

The world was open before him, he was erect, he was sucking on salty flesh that made him think of women.  He hadn't had such a great day in a long time.  The highway sign read, "100 miles" to the city.

*The Masculine Mystique by Moribund Wrath*

Dieter  Schmetterling drove.  The signs said the city was getting closer but to Dieter  it still felt a million miles away.  What would he do there?  What was he doing?  He did not have the answers to these questions.  He hoped the miles might have some.  But as time wore on, and the city approached, there were still no answers for Dieter  Schmetterling.

By the time he reached the city's limit it was dinnertime and he was hungry.  He pulled into a gas station, filled up his tank, went inside, emptied his bladder in another cherry-smelling restroom, and purchased two sticky-glazed donuts, a cup of stale coffee and a bottle of water that advertised, "EZ lid."

In his car, he chased his pills with bits of donut and washed the whole gooey chemical composite with a mixer of coffeewater.  He never drank coffee this late in the day.  Since he'd turned 40 he'd been, progressively, having a harder time sleeping at night.  His Parkinsons didn't help.  He suffered nightsweats, leg cramps, spasm and acting out his dreams.  He never drank coffee so late in the day because he'd be up all night from the caffeine, and peeing, but he needed to be up this night.  He was on the hunt.  Only he didn't know where to go.  So he got back out of his car, went back inside the convenience store and walked up to the counter.

"Forget something?" the young man asked.

"Yes.  I'm hoping you can tell me where this," and he pointed to the newspaper's column about the big drug bust in the city, "took place."

The young man laughed, "You don't want to go there, Pops. It's no place to be after dark."

"I'm not afraid. Where is it?"

"You got a map?"

"No."

"You can buy one. They're over there," the young man pointed to a sales rack of maps.

Dieter put the city map on the counter, paid for it, then opened it, "Now, where did it take place?"

"Why you want to know?"

"That's my business. Are you going to help me or not?"

The kid pointed to what would be, anatomically, the aortic sphincter of the city's heart. Dieter used the counter's designated pen, with an artificial flower taped to it to prevent it from being stolen, to mark the spot.

"How far is it from here?"

"Not far, mileage ways, but with traffic it will take a while."

"How long?"

"Hour maybe. Depends. Plus there's some construction, I think."

"Any detours?"

"I don't know, Man. But I really don't think you should go there. Bad shit happens there."

"Thank you," Dieter said, taking the map to his car, getting in, and smiling.

The kid had been right. There was traffic and road construction but what he failed to mention was crossing the train tracks, which just happened to be sporting a long, long train. Dieter sat. He, eventually, turned his motor off. Just when he could make out the end of the train, after waiting 15 minutes, the train stopped, then reversed. Dieter screamed, "What the hell!" But knew that was just the way it was. He watched the graffiti passing by. All kinds of loops and rounds, letters and symbols. He liked it. It made the cold utility of metal become something more important than physical transportation. "Mental transportation," he thought. He thought about his dead wife and of Mindy Mahoney. The two could not, in his mind, be separated because as soon as Mindy Mahoney left town, his wife left him. Oh, she didn't leave him, literally, just emotionally, spiritually, and sexually.

Daisy Schmetterling, Dieter noticed, had begun to read a very thick book and from the moment she'd begun doing so his life changed. No longer, when he got home from work, would supper be on the table and Daisy immaculately dressed and primped. He'd come home to, "Fix yourself some supper. I'm having a reading circle."

At first the "reading circle" consisted of the next door neighbor, Lucy Ellen McAllister but it wasn't long before upwards of 10 women filled Dieter Schmetterling's living room and were being fed nice little sandwiches that he was not allowed to touch and fresh-baked cookies that he was not allowed to eat and Mint

Juleps he was forbidden to drink. The women would sit, for hours, talking about the big book and, finally, Dieter would go off to bed.

Sometimes he thought he could hear muffled sounds in the night but when he got up to investigate, he found Daisy sleeping in the spare bedroom. That was not surprising to Dieter. She'd been sleeping separate from him ever since Mindy Mahoney left town and even though Daisy Schmetterling never actually confronted Dieter over his affair, Dieter figured out she knew and that, one day, she'd forgive him and they'd sleep together again. As time wore on, however, Dieter gave up on this hope and took to stopping at the local strip bar, once a week, on Friday nights after work to get himself a drink and some fresh food for thought.

"Besides," he'd mumble to the bartender, a young pretty girl who seemed, to Dieter, too smart to be tending bar, "She's got her READING group." The more he drank, the more vinegar he used to enunciate the word "reading."

The bartender would smile, "Do you want another one, Dieter?"

Dieter loved hearing her say his name. Her voice got sweeter and sweeter the drunker he got. "Sure, Honey," he'd slur, then turn from the bar to watch the younger girls' flesh. The bar kept its stable of fillies young. It's what paid the best. The bar owner, an old Irish guy, would tease, "Just like racing, got to keep the legs fresh." He'd wink at the bartender and she'd fling her towel at him, "You're terrible," she'd say but, in truth, she wasn't the least bit squeamish. By then, she'd seen it all and not just what the customers liked to believe in.

The girls were real people, with real problems and real loveliness, real love and terrible struggles—they were just like any other coworkers and some she liked better than others. One, in particular, was the bartender's good friend.

She began dancing after she'd graduated from Le Cordon Bleu because she happened to have a smokin' hot body. She got hired as head chef for a small French restaurant and happened to befriend the Sommelier (wine steward), who was going to college in hopes of becoming a dentist. He told her about this bar he went to where the girls who danced there got hundreds of dollars in tips every night. He convinced her to go with him. She watched the young women's bodies writhing, their tight skin sweating, the painted faces smiling and the music pumping. She watched the men fall helpless in their wills and lose control over their wallets. She was amazed at how much money exchanged from hands to hips. The table dances made loads. There was one guy who got too frisky and a big, tall bouncer escorted him out. The bartender smiled at her. She liked the way she looked, kind of like a big sister, so she went up to the bar.

"How is this job," she asked the bartender.

"It's as good as the dancers. Good dancers mean more drinks and that means more tips for me."

"And how does one go about becoming a dancer?"

The bartender told her to stand up, turn around, then sit back down. "You've got a great body. Why don't you try amateur night? Every Tuesday. The boss likes to keep new girls coming in."

And that's exactly what she did. From winning amateur night to working one night a week while running the restaurant to making the decision to dance fulltime because the pay was twice as much. She and the bartender were good friends.

Dieter liked her, especially, because he reminded her of Mindy Mahoney. She was tall and athletic. That was all Dieter needed to be reminded. It didn't matter that her hair was reddish and Mindy's wasn't anything like it or that their eyes were completely different colors. She was tall and athletic and that was all Dieter needed because, at home, his wife was having her "reading" circle and the last thing he wanted was to think about that.

The train finally decided to move on. The arms lifted, the lights and bells quieted. Dieter drove through the city's rush hour traffic and, finally, arrived at the X mark on the map just before dark. The young man, at the convenience store, was right. It was no place for Dieter Schmetterling —at least it wouldn't have been, at any other time in his life, but at this particular moment…it was exactly where he needed to be.

~~~

*The Masculine Mystique* by Moribund Wrath

Dieter had found the neighborhood of the news report. He looked at the street signs. He looked at the people. He was a definitely a minority—everyone was young. He pulled his car to the curb and almost instantly three men pressed against three of his windows, the driver's the passengers and the rear-left. The man at his window yelled, "Open up! Open up and no one has to get hurt." He could hear the door handles being jostled.

"This is it," he said to himself. It was the first time he'd admitted to himself his intention to die. He hit the unlock switch and closed his eyes.

The man yelled, "Get out of the car Gramps!"

Dieter remained as still as a corpse with his eyes closed waiting, like a man in front of a firing squad.

The young man pushed on Dieter 's shoulder. Dieter went with it. He wanted to embrace his death, not fight it.

"Oh shit," the guy yelled, "I think we killed him."

Dieter held his eyes closed. He could hear sneakered footsteps running away.

"Guys?" Dieter looked around to see his three doors standing wide open and not a person in sight. "I guess they just wanted my car. Damn. This might be harder than I thought." So Dieter decided that the best way would be to walk around with his wallet in his hands. He was sure to get conked on the head and that, he hoped, would do the job. So Dieter left his keys in his car with the doors still wide open because he figured it was better that whoever the guys were that wanted it got it without having to bust it up and he walked a few steps away before he said to himself but aloud, "I'll make it even easier." He went back to his car, opened the glove compartment, where he always kept the title and registration, and signed away his ownership of the car. He left the documents in the passenger seat and was just about to walk around in order to get conked when he thought, "I'd better close the doors because if a gust of wind comes up it might blow the title away and then those guys wouldn't be able to legitimately own the car." So Dieter closed the doors, then took the bottle of soda that he was never able to open and set it on top of the registration and title, "That should hold it down."

Dieter saw someone in the distance. He thought it might be one of the three men, "Hey," he yelled. The figure stopped for a second then ran off. "Hey," Dieter yelled and tried to move more quickly in their direction but his Parkinson's disease, being a movement disorder, made this impossible. So Dieter yelled as loud as he could, "The car is all yours!"

In an apartment, directly above Dieter, a young man watched all of this out of his window. "Crazy old fool," he said. "He's going to get himself fucked up." The young man, Abran Alano, could see guys from the neighborhood circling around in the distances. "It's only a matter of time," Abran thought.

Dieter, wallet in hand, and slowly walking along the cracked and uneven sidewalk was failing to see the men circling him and was beginning to wonder if there might be two neighborhoods with the same name. "That happens," he said aloud. Then he said, "Shit! I bet I'm in the nice one," and he turned to go back to his car only to find that the same three guys had, in fact, returned but something was wrong. They weren't taking it. Two of them were still standing outside. One was inside looking at Dieter's paperwork and shaking his head at his friends. Dieter yelled, "Hope you guys like it. Hey I've got a proposition for you."

That was all it took. The three bolted.

Abran Alano watched.

Dieter shouted, "You can *have* the car! I signed the title. All I want is your help and it won't take much, I promise. Besides, I have more to offer than just a car."

Abran grabbed his knife. It seemed too good of a deal to pass up. He could turn the car for an easy couple grand and the old man wouldn't be able to do a thing about it. He took the stairs. The elevator had never worked in all the time he'd lived there with his mother and sister. "Three years of fucking stairs," he cursed as he descended faster and faster with an ever-increasing hope that one of the other guys hadn't already gotten to the old fool's car. He was almost at a run when he hit the back door and circled round the building only to, to his utter surprise, run smack into the old man who, immediately, fell to the ground. "Oh shit," Abran thought, "now what!" He could see Alanzo, Adrian, and Cordero, the three men who'd come up to Dieter 's car, jump in and drive off, tires squealing, whooping and hollering as they disappeared around the corner at the end of the street. "Shit!" Abran thought.

Dieter felt a sharp pain in his right hip. "Oh shit," he thought, "This is *not* a good time for a broken hip!"

Abran reached out, taking the old man's arm, "Are you alright Man?"

Dieter winced, "I think it's my hip."

"You want me to call you an ambulance?"

"No!" Dieter almost screamed, then realizing that he was betraying himself tried to calm down his emphasis, "I mean…no thank you. I'll be fine."

But when Abran tried to help him up Dieter could not stand the pain and cried out. At that moment Abran's mother yelled down, "What's going on down there?"

"Nothing. Go inside."

"Is that old man alright?"

"Yes. Go inside."

Abran could feel his knife pressing into the small of his back. The collision had knocked it loose. He could feel its weight begin to shift and it wouldn't be long before it fell out onto the ground. "Shit," he thought but said, "Listen old man, I gotta go. You're alright right?"

"Fine. You go."

So Abran ran all the way back to his apartment. "I knew it was too good to be true," he thought just before he opened the door.

"Where's that old man?" Abran's mother, Melosia Alano, demanded.

"I left him."

"What! You go check on him right now. Your father, God rest his soul, would box your ears one side to the other for disrespecting an old man like that." She hit him with her dishtowel.

As Abran, slowly descended the stairs, he wondered why he did what his mother told him. After all, it was him that supported the family. She couldn't work anymore, not since his Poppy had died. Alejandro, the father, had gotten sick a few months after he'd gotten laid off from the meat packing plant where he'd worked his whole life. He'd been a scraper and hanger clear up till the time the company announced it was shutting down. Before the closure, he would brag, almost every night, about how he could keep up with the young men and, in fact, thought he kept up even better than they did in spite of age. After almost a month of being home, Alejandro began coughing and waking up in the night drenched in sweat. He stopped eating and seemed like he could never catch his breath. In spite of the fact that his unemployment was about to end and the family had no money, Melosia insisted he go to the neighborhood health clinic to be seen.

At the clinic everyone was required to pay $20.00. It was hard money to separate from for Alejandro because he knew, deep inside, he'd never make another cent in his life. The nurse practitioner ordered an x-ray. Melosia was asked to pay for it upfront because the Alanos had no health insurance. The clinic charged $50.00 for an x-ray which, they were told, was a considerably-reduced price compared to what the hospitals charged. Melosia explained that they didn't have that much. The nurse told her to bring him back when they did.

Abran was 15 years and 50 days old when his father went to the clinic. He remembered, exactly, because he'd woken up late in the night to find his mother, alone and sobbing, in the kitchen.

"What is it, Mom?"

"Nothing," she wiped her eyes. "You hungry?"

"No. I heard you crying. What's the matter?"

She told him about the x-ray. She cried and cursed. It was the first time he'd heard his mother curse—like that. She clenched her fist so hard that her fingernails dug in and made red halfmoons on the palms of her hands. Abran remembered his age because it was on that night, being 15 years old and 50 days, he became the man of the family. He had to find a way, any way, to get hold of the money his father needed and that was exactly what he did.

One week later the Alanos were told that Alejandro not only had Tuberculosis in his lungs, but that it had spread to his kidneys, lymph nodes and other areas. "But," the nurse qualified, "it's hard to know just where it's spread and to what degree." They were told to watch him and, basically, to prepare for the worst.

Within a month's time, Alejandro was bedridden and had such severe headaches that he would vomit. After one of these fits, he was so weak that he couldn't go to the bathroom by himself and he, often, had "mistakes" in bed. Melosia never complained. She cared for him as if he was her own child and even in his sickness he was sweet to her. One night, not long before his death and after a mistake, he said, "You know why I married you?"

"Because I was beautiful," Melosia replied.

"That is true. And you still are. But it's not why I married you. It's because when I got to know you you matched your name. I knew I could call, "My Melosia," and mean it, my dear sweet wife. All these years. Thank you."

Melosia cried at the funeral but not because they were too poor to buy a fancy casket. In fact, Alejandro Alano was buried in the most expensive casket in the undertaker's shop. In fact, Alejandro Alano's casket was worth as much as a full year's wages at the meat packing plant. Still, Melosia Alano cried—because she knew where the money had come from. And, shortly after the funeral, knowing such an awful truth took from Abran and his little sister, Trella, the mind of their mother.

The clinic nurse practitioner charged a "nominal" and "off the records" fee for helping the Alanos fill out the Social Security disability paperwork for Melosia stating she had Post Traumatic Stress Disorder and could not seek outside employment.

"You know," the nurse said, "It's getting harder and harder to get a disability claim."

Abran sneered, "Let me guess, for a fee you can get it pushed through?"

"No," she replied, "Even I don't have that kind of power. I just thought you should know that it could take 2-3 years to get a claim and with your mom's diagnosis they might not even do that."

"Well can you diagnose her with something else then?"

"I could test her for tuberculosis. If she had it and PTSD then I'm pretty sure she could get a claim."

"Could she have it?" Abran asked.

"You all could. It's very contagious," the nurse replied.

"Great," Abran thought but said to the nurse, "I'll bring her in tomorrow."

"Oh, and you'll need more money. I'll have to do more than just an x-ray if it's for Social Security."

Abran wanted to say, "You do more for the government than you did for my old man," but what would be the use. She was as crooked as cooked spaghetti and, for her, it was all about the money. "Fine," he replied. "Tomorrow then."

Three years Abran had been living in that apartment with his mother and sister, it had been three years since his mother had gotten her Social Security and Medicare. Melosia did, in fact, have tuberculosis and the nurse provided, for a fee, the medications she needed during the two years it took for the government to decide to help her pay for them.

"What a fuckin' scam," he thought as he walked downstairs to see if the crazy old man was still there, "I paid more to that nurse for those tests and drugs in those 2 years than what she's gotten from the gov. in these last three."

Abran Alano was 20 years old and a drug dealer and on his way downstairs to help an old man because his mother was not right in the head ever since his father died, and she was sick, and she was his mother and he loved her—and he was the head of the house.

*The Masculine Mystique* by Moribund Wrath

Abran Alano walked down the stairs of his family's apartment, slowly. Yes, he was going to do as his mother told him, he was going to check on the old man he'd left alone on the street, but no one was going to make him enthusiastic about it. Not even his mother.

Half-hoping the guy would be gone by the time he got to the sidewalk where he'd last seen him, Abran shook his head to see the little old guy still there.

"Shit," he cursed under his breath before he went back up to him.

"Hey," Dieter smiled, "I remember you."

"Yeah, well. You okay?"

"Oh sure. I'm just resting a bit."

"Well it's been like 15 minutes. You just gonna sit there all night?"

Dieter shrugged his shoulders, "I got nowhere to go."

For some strange reason this infuriated Abran, "What the hell! Why'd you come here, leave your car wide open and then when it gets stolen cry 'I got nowhere to go!' What kind of game are you playin'?"

Dieter tried to stand up but cried out in pain from the fall and clutched his right hip. Abran tried to help him up but the old man said, "No. You just leave me here."

"I can't," Abran replied.

"I told you to leave me alone. Now scram!"

"Scram? Scram! Who the hell you think you are?"

"Just leave!" Dieter yelled.

Abran rubbed the toe of his sneaker on the sidewalk. "I can't," he said.

"Well why the hell not?"

"Because my mom wants me to bring you up to our apartment to make sure you're alright."

"I'm alright damn it! I'm sick and tired of old women trying to tell me what to do!"

"Your wife?"

"No, the damn nurses!"

Abran laughed. Dieter smiled. Abran sat down beside him.

"I don't think we've actually met," Abran put out his hand, "I'm Abran Alonso."

Dieter shook his hand, "Dieter Schmetterling."

"German. Ladybug, right?"

"Now how'd the hell you know that?"

"Why the hell shouldn't I know that? Because I'm Hispanic?"

"No. Because *no one* knows what that means. German in this country is about as dead as Latin."

"Yeah, well I like learning stuff."

"Commendable. Abran, what's that mean?"

"Exalted Father."

"Oh, like Abraham."

"You Jewish?"

"No, that's pretty common knowledge for more than half of the world's religions. Besides, would that matter?"

"Does it matter that I'm Hispanic?"

"You got a hangup with this thing don't you?" Dieter cast a sideways look at Abran, noticing for the first time just how very young he was, "But to answer your question with utter sincerity, no. I do not have a problem with you being Hispanic, nor do I have a problem with any person being who they are and how they are.

That's their business and I've got too damn much else to worry about besides someone else's stuff. That's why theirs is theirs and mine's mine."

This time Abran cast the sideways look and noticed that Dieter Schmetterling did not look healthy at all and was, in fact, quite old.

"Listen, Dieter . My mom's pretty insistent."

"Well, if you think there's no getting around it."

"Afraid not," Abran smiled, stood up and put his hand under Dieter 's arm, "Let me help you up."

Dieter cried out as the young man's strength made him stand but his hip could not bear his weight.

"I'm afraid," Dieter said, trying to fight the tears that were forming in his lids, "That you'll have to do most of the work. The hip's shot."

"Do you think it's broken?"

"Who the hell knows. At my age, with my luck, probably."

"We live on the seventh floor and the elevator's out."

"Oh shit!"

"Tell me about it. Can you make it?"

"I guess we'll find out."

The going was sweet sorghum-in-winter. Every step was agony and, after an hour's work, they'd managed only one flight.

"Hey kid," Dieter groaned, already covered with sweat and braced against the wall of the landing,"You'd better just leave me here. I don't think this is going to work."

Abran looked at the time. It was getting late and at the rate they were going it was shaping up to be an allnight affair.

"You wait here," Abran looked Dieter in the eye, "I'll be right back."

With that, Abran bolted up the stairway in front of Dieter , taking two steps at a time. Another tear formed in Dieter 's eye, a bittermix of remembering when his steps were light and envy of being able to move but before he could even relish his stirring emotions, Abran was back, carrying a folding chair, a blank and a pillow.

"What the hell?" Dieter cried.

"Might as well face the facts, this is going to be a long haul and it will go a little better if you can sit down and rest a little at each landing."

"But what about the people that need to get by? These landings aren't big enough for all this stuff."

"If truckers can navigate the Freefall Freeway and Cutouts in India then the people in this building can get around one old man with a busted up hip who needs a chair. And any of them that has a problem with it can take it up with me."

For the first time Dieter looked at Abran not as a young person but as a man. "He's not," Dieter thought to himself, "the kind I'd like to get into a fight with." And it was like lightening streaking across the sky where its delicate fingers extend from its brilliance, "Maybe he's the one," Dieter pondered.

Abran, watching Dieter suddenly go quiet at his remark, became awkward. "I only meant that I'd talk to them is all."

"Abran, I've got a proposition for you."

"Oh God! You're not some fag are you?"

"Hell no! No. I was married for 50 years."

"That doesn't mean you're not gay. You see it all the time on T.V. Some guy's wife finds out her husband's a flamer."

"Well I'm not and that's not what I want to talk about at all, so can we please change the subject."

"You brought it up."

"I did not," Dieter sulked. Now the momentum was all off.

"You were propositioning me," Abran smiled, teasingly, and nudged Dieter 's arm.

"Oh get away from me," Dieter grumped, but smiled a little.

"So what's your deal Old Man?"

"Let's get up the next flight of stairs and then we'll see if I feel like letting you in on the opportunity of a lifetime."

Abran muled the chair, pillows and blanket up to the next landing then ran back to help Dieter along. Step-by-step, slow and painstakingly, they climbed and when they'd finally made it Dieter heard a beautiful woman's voice calling, "Abran?

Abran?" to which he replied, "Yes, Mother. What is it?" And the beautiful voice said, "I've made you and the old man some sandwiches."

Abran looked at Dieter and while rolling his eyes asked him , "You hungry?"

"I could eat," Dieter replied. He was lying. The pain in his hip had him on the verge of vomiting but he couldn't deny that voice anything.

"Alright Mother," Abran huffed before running up the 5 flights to her and back down the 5 flights to Dieter .

"Ham and cheese alright?" Abran asked.

"Perfect," Dieter smiled and bit into the sandwich. He thought he could, ever so faintly, smell a delicate scent of flowers and for that brief second he forgot about his hip.

Abran had already gobbled his down by the time Dieter snapped back into the reality of his body.

"You ready?" Abran chirped.

"Uh, I can't finish this now," Dieter said, handing Abran the sandwich, "Maybe on the next landing."

"Oh sure," Abran scowled, "I'll just carry your food too."

"Speaking of," Dieter said in a voice far more sheepish than he'd used before with Abran, "I could really use some water. I have to take my pills."

"Pills? You sick?"

"Parkinson's."

"Is it contagious?"

Dieter laughed, "No. It's an old people thing."

"Great. So now it's 'Abran, I need some water' and I'm supposed to go running. What a fine mess this is!"

"And one more thing."

"Oh sure, why not!"

"You wouldn't happen to know the young men that took my car would you?"

Abran grew very serious. His eyes squinted. The corners of his mouth squeezed together into a fine line and his forehead formed a hardened expression. "Why?" was all he said.

Dieter grew very shaky, sweat formed on his upper lip, and he rolled his forefinger and thumb together, "It's just that my medicine was in the trunk."

"I thought you said you had your medicine," Abran's voice was tense.

"I have today's medicine but not for tomorrow."

"So why were you trying to give your car away if you still needed stuff out of it?"

Dieter looked up at Abran, "You saw me?"

"Who didn't, you old fool!"

Dieter 's face flushed, "I'm…embarrassed."

Abran softened, "What happens if you don't have that medicine?"

"I can't move."

"It don't seem like you move too well anyhow."

"I can't move at all.  I freeze, like stone."

"Shit!"

"Yeah.  Sucks to get old, Kid."

Abran sighed, "Let me get you some water.  I'll get my sister and see if she'll come sit with you for a while.  I'm not promising anything but I'll see what I can do."

When Abran returned he had a young, beautiful girl trailing behind him.

"This is my sister, Trella," he said to Dieter .  "And this is Dieter ," he said to his sister.  "I'll be back as soon as I can."

Dieter  noticed a serious look exchange between the brother and sister.  She cried out to Abran, "Be careful," as he ran down the stairs.

<div align="center">~~~</div>

*The Of-Country Affairs* by Trella Alano

By the time he got home it was so late that the dinner of meatloaf and mashed potatos that Love had made was ruined.

"Where have you been!" she wanted to scream but noticed, by the way his sole stepped, that he'd been drinking.  She knew that one word, one single word on her part, would mean her beating would last longer and would come with greater ferocity.  Her silence was her only chance for less pain.

"Come here," he slurred as he grabbed her and pulled her close to him.

He breath reeked of his favorite alcohol, Power, and the grooves of his fingerprints were caked with the proof of the "other woman," what he'd call by name to his fellowmen: Conquest.

Love tried to free herself of Law's stranglehold but there was no escape.  Her simple act of defiance, in attempting to squirm, landed a short, powerful jab to her gut.  Her doubling over served to bend her head to his chest.

"Now that's better," he smiled, grabbing her hair and pulling it so she faced the ugliness of what was to come.  "You know you like it."

Law threw Love Of-Country to the floor.  Her head bounced only once.  "There," she thought, "Proof that my silence works."  Then he unzipped his pants and raped her so hard and so long that the next day she couldn't walk.  This time, her bruises were where no one would see them except her—and she'd grown to understand, after all the times before, that she just didn't have the courage to even try and look at the bloody mess between her legs.  She simply ran a warm bath, gathered all her strength, as she hovered her pelvis over the water, drew in a deep breath and braced herself, saying over and over again in her mind, "You can do it…You can do it…" then plunged herself into the water's sting and burning.

GRATUITOUS SEX by M.P. Honeycutt (pseudonym of Trella Alano when doing gig work)

"It was summertime when I first saw her. She worked in the local fruit and vegetable market, and didn't exactly dress up on the job. Maybe a college student working for the summer?

Her breasts were bold. That was the first thing I noticed. Bold, and bursting out of a white halter top. Her waist was tiny, and her belly button winked erotically between the bottom of her halter and the top of her shorts. Below the shorts, her bare legs were so unbelievably sexy I found it hard to breathe."

~~~

TheMasculine Mystique *by Moribund Wrath*

"You want more of your sandwich?" Trella Alano asked Dieter Schmetterling.

"No thanks," Dieter replied, sitting on the chair Abran, Trella's older brother, had brought for him.

"You cold?" Trella asked but before Dieter could answer she'd automatically covered his legs up with the blanket, then plopped the pillow on the pillow on the 2nd floor stair landing for herself to sit on. Dieter looked at the girl. He'd long-ago lost the ability to judge age. It seemed the older he got the older everyone got. Teenagers looked like adults. Middleschoolers looked like highschoolers. He looked at Trella Alano, wondering how old she was and observing that she was, in fact, beautiful. From his position, atop a chair, and her position, on the ground at his feet, he could see the strands of her dark hair as they grew from her white, healthy scalp. He could see the long, thick eyelashes as they blinked over her green eyes and the curve her mouth made below the tip of her nose, "Like a ski jump," Dieter thought to himself. She was playing with a loose string on the cuff of her blue jeans.

"How old are you?" Trella asked.

"Why do you want to know?"

"Just making small talk. Forget about it."

"How old are you?" Dieter asked.

"Seventeen," she answered. Dieter swore he could hear a tone of pride in her voice.

"I see," Dieter replied. "In highschool then?"

"Yep."

"What's your favorite subject?" Dieter asked.

She looked up at him, her face was round and moist—Dieter thought all young peoples' faces were moist and babies were moisted of all, "Boys!" she exclaimed, then giggled.

"Oh," Dieter smiled. "And how does your father feel about that?"

The playful smile immediately fled; Trella's face grew dark, "He's dead."

Dieter had half-expected as much, or divorce, because Abran didn't mention a father in the house—only his mother. "I'm sorry," Dieter answered.

"It was a long time ago now," Trella answered but Dieter could see on her telegraphed expression that he'd hit a painful spot.

Trying to change the subject, Dieter returned to the safety of the school-related topic, "Other than boys, what do you like studying at school?"

Trella thought for a few minutes. Watching her think, Dieter envisioned literal thoughts in her head wrestling each other like naked Greeks. Then she finally answered, "Art."

"Wonderful. Do you paint?"

"Oh God no!" Trella scoffed, "I'm into computer graphics." Then she sort of angled her head in such a way as to look at Dieter out of the corner of her eyes then sort of impishly added, "And I write...a little."

Abran came running up the stairs. He had Dieter 's suitcase in one hand and jingled Dieter 's car keys with the other.

Trella stood up, put her hands on her hips that she jutted out, "Let me guess," she scolded, "Stupid, Stupid and Stupider!" Abran scrunched his nose and shook his head, "Ah take off!" With that, Trella walked up the stairs, swaying her hips with such exaggeration that Abran yelled, "Cut that out!" To which Trella replied, having already disappeared, "Whose gonna make me."

Abran, breathless, plopped himself down beside the suitcase. Dieter , still sitting on the chair asked, "Whose the stupids?"

Abran smiled, "She likes to give me shit. It's all in fun you know."

"So who..." Dieter began.

"Old man, in my neighborhood you learn not to ask questions."

"Well," Dieter smiled, "Can I say 'Thank you' in your neighborhood?"

Abran saw that Dieter had not finished his sandwich and the fact was, he'd had to fight to get Dieter 's stuff with. Sure they were his 'friends' but there was a line between friends in that place—two of them actually—that cut through a big S just as neat as any friendship or kinship or colored plastic tape printed "do not cross"; in other words: money.

SCENE: Dieter and Abran on the stairs—the pitch for euthanasia, the deal. When Abran tries to help Dieter , Dieter looses his balance and grabs Abran's side, Abran cries out in pain. "I cracked a rib," he says.

"How," Dieter asks.

Abran gave him that same look he'd given him earlier.

"I see," Dieter sighed. "You're a complicated young man, Abran Alano."

"That may be true," Abran replied, "But the fact remains. There ain't no way I'm getting you up five more flights without some help."

Abran pulled a cell phone from his pocked, pushed a button, waited. Dieter could hear the rings too. He could also hear, just barely, a man's voice say, "What the hell you want!"

"Come help me," Abran answered, "I'll make it worth your while."

"How much worth."

Abran's temper, immediately escalated, "Have I ever fuckin'…nevermind," he said and disconnected.

A few seconds later the phone rang in little beeps.

"Yeah," Abran answered, clearly still irritated.

"We'll be right there," the voice said.

Abran calls his friends (the ones who'd taken Dieter 's car). One has a black eye, one has dried blood in his left nostril and the other's knuckles are scraped and bruising.

~~~

The New Covenant (needs serious work)
Abran, sitting at the bonfire, watching smiles, worries, joys and hopes crossing the faces of everyone gathered around it in the community they called, Providence, realized that they were all doomed. There was just no way they could surive, economically, based on their existing resources even when combined with their future resources from their labor when set against the cost of living. Even with his help, with modifications and gadgets—pure creativity would not be enough to fend off the govnernment's taxes.

They needed a longterm way of making some serious money. The problem was…what to do.

Abran develops a "smart" camera. It makes old people look young, fat people look thin, and thin people look healthy. The problem is that although Abran encrypts it…he is not able to keep "really" smart scientists from discovering this. And when they do, it will only be a matter of time before they steal the technology and there will be nothing Providenians can do about it—it would be a billion dollar lawsuit over decades. So the only thing there is to do is to keep it secret for as long as possible, market the heck out of it, and make as much $ as they can upfront.

How Abran gets the money is he develops a computer program that shaves off 1/3 of a cent off of EVERY financial transaction in the world, using a Pi derivative function for the computer command, and this is deposited into a corporation he sets up, "The Providian Group," which is a completely virtual company specializing in Tech research & development. The Providian Group pays all taxes, fees, crosses every T and dots every I. It is totally legit, other than how the income comes in. But 1/3 of a cent is not enough to draw any legal suspicion.

Abran sets up the company he works up until there is enough capital to construct a huge mass-manufacturing plant for the smart cameras in India. The smart cameras FLOOD the market and are DIRT CHEAP…they undercut their competitors by 1/3…they make a killing the first year. That is all it takes for the other scientists to figure out his technology.

Then Abran, via Dieter Schmetterling, sells the company to the very business that owned the scientist that figured out the smart camera. They make a pretty good deal. Upon the sale, Abran stops the 1/3 cent rerouting.

Dieter asks him, "Isn't that illegal?"

Abran answers, "You're not asking the correct question. You should ask me, 'Can anyone *prove* what you're doing is not legal?' To which I would answer, 'No.' But you and everyone else at Providence need to focus on investing this money wisely. No risky ventures. Just slow, steady growth and always, always, ALWAYS keep cash and gold securely stashed on the farms. This is the only way to truly protect your assets."

"I disagree. But that's okay." Dieter said.

"You're a risk-taker eh?" Abran winked.

"You could say that. I put my faith in God to protect our money—be it cash, gold or otherwise. And if He saw it fit that we should lose every penny—I have every confidence He would stil provide for us, one way or the other."

Abran's eyes were tearing, "I only wish I had that kind of faith."

"It's up to you. It's a choice. I remember Pastor saying that nothing in the world was tragic or fatal…"

Abran's thought about his father's death. "I think he's full of shit!"

"You didn't let me finish. He said, 'Nothing is tragic or fatal *except* not believing in, not placing our faith in, the Lord.'" Dieter's voice was calm and steady.

"You're right. I don't place my faith in religion." Abran answered.

"What about science? Do you place your faith there?" Dieter asked.

"Absolutely not. I know science like my own DNA. It's a sham. There is only so much mankind can do…the rest is dumb luck." Abran laughed.

"One person's 'dumb luck' is another's 'God.'" Dieter smiled, "But perhaps, if you really looked at it, Abran, you might realize that your life—the journey that you've been on—has less to do with luck than it does Providence."

Abran blew air out his nose, "So you're saying God used an aethiest to do His work? That somehow God led me to you people so that my dumb luck would work towards the glory of your god?" Abran seemed to almost spit out the word "God."

"It was just a thought," Dieter recanted.

Then off to work.

Excerpt from The Masculine Mystique: The Of-Country Affairs *by Trella Alano*

Scene:

       Love Of-Country is sitting on a couch inside their home. Law Of-Country (enter stage left).

Law:        I want you to attend tonight's high school sporting event.

Love:       But why? You know I don't like sports.

Law:        That is unpatriotic. Here (he hands her a VERY thick book).

Love:       (Looking at the book, she reads the title aloud) "The Art of Sport." (she hoists the book up and down) It's heavy!

                  (Law smiles)

                  It's too big for me. Can't you just tell me what it's about?

Law:        (with disgust) I should have known better. You're not smart enough to understand.

Love:       (flirtingly she reaches for him) So teach me.

Law:        (repulsed he reels from her touch) I suppose it is _my_ duty (forced pause followed by sigh). After antiquity, where those defeated in sport were put to death of banished, sport became a form of warfare, a contest of clans, that determined things such as property rights and became a way to settle disputes. And, like the Knights, the competitors wore their clan's identifying colors. (Show a frustration of having to simplify something he believes is very complicated.) This is a very basic and broad understanding that I'm most sure would be proven erroneous for many individual circumstances. (Show resignation) However, because of your lack of comprehension I am forced to oversimplify to the point of idiocy.

Love:       I see.

Law:        No you don't.

Love:       Yes I do!  You can't tell me what I do and *don't* understand.

Law:        Then why is your lack of participation, even simply as an observer, unpatriotic?

Love:       (wants to answer, to be right, but can't think of a thing—struggles but remains silent.)

Law:        I thought so.  The answer is—the Citizens have been taxed for sport. And Sport rears warriors.  And this is important because it honors tradition and celebrates our history.

Love:       But (then falls into a very small voice) we're Americans.

Law:        (Throws his hands up in disgust) I don't even know why I bother. Honestly!  (turning to the audience) 'We're Americans' she says—as if that makes any difference at all.  We're white, black, Irish, Indian, rich, poor, Catholic, Protestant, Muslim and everything in between all of these and more.  We're gay, straight, you name it. (turns back to Love) Sport is war!

Love:       But I don't like war.

Law:        (Shouting) Grow up!  You're either for us or against us.

Love:       (Shouting) For whom?  We're *all* (extra emphasis on 'all') Americans!  (calming her voice to as softly as she used when she first said 'We're all Americans) What you're saying is patriotic should be treason—it's an incitement to Civil War.

Law:        (Stunned for a moment but quickly recovering, snatches the book from Love's hands) Well...you've just proven my point.  You're not smart enough to understand the value of Sport, now get ready for the game.

      At the game a tear broke free from Love's restraint as she watch the
            frustration of

the boys grow each time they turned to the authorities for justice when acts considered foul, both real and perceived, had occurred and the authorities either couldn't, or wouldn't, enforce the law.  Love watched that frustration turn to anger and anger turn to to a hatred that welled, like a tear, in the hearts of the young men—her fellow Americans—and she saw their wells flood from fingertips to fists, from elbows to eyes with souls that, out of sheer desperation, cried: "If I had a gun I'd kill you!"  Yet their only weapons were their bodies and a ball.

Love understood, then, fullwell.

GRATUITOUS SEX by M.P. Honeycutt (pseudonym of Trella Alano when doing gig work, 2016)

"When I was a freshman in college and a shy but popular football player, I had the privelege of dating a beautiful girl who was captain of the cheerleading team. She was the all-American type—long blonde hair, golden tan, golden smile, and as sweet as apple pie.

As our romance started getting serious, I tried to make love to her but she insisted that she was saving herself.  This didn't stop us from exploring…"

~~~

HISTORY of MORIBUND WRATH

Moribund watched the sun's first sliver climb atop the horizon like a child, for the first time, climbing onto a slide.  Slides were, to her, interesting things.  They were the physical manifestation of the philosophical understanding that once certain actions are chosen one can't go back.  Of course, Moribund had always been the kid on the playground who'd get yelled at by the recess monitor for stopping herself halfway down the slide and climbing back up.  She was the one who'd, that very same day, race up the slide's stairs and run at it as fast as she could and thrust herself, through the air, in order to fly down the slide faster.  Slides were, to Moribund Wrath, interesting things.

When she finally got home she was met, in the hallway, by a Sheriff.

"Are you Moribund Wrath?"

"Yes, Sir, I am."

"You're to appear at court Friday, the__."

It was a date set, exactly, 4 weeks in the future.

"I see," Moribund said, but thought this to be very strange. It seemed to her that she was always getting served and was to appear that week or, at the latest, the following week but that was only the case if she'd gotten served too close to the end of the week prior. "Four weeks," she thought, "This is very strange indeed."

He handed her the set of papers, the set of papers that looked the same as every other set of papers from every other collector, only this time, in addition to the papers, there was a pamphlet stapled to the left-hand corner of the top sheet.

Moribund pointed to it, "What's this?"

The officer replied, "We're required to give this to every debtor. Good day Ma'am."

He, rhythmically, descended the building's stairs. Inside her apartment Moribund compared the pamphlet the old Japanese lady had given her and the one attached to the collection papers she'd just been served. They were identical.

Moribund Wrath & the P.T.P.

Waiting, again. Same courthouse. Same waiting place. Same everything except a new something. A poster:

> The Benevolent Leader wants you to know that, in accordance with the 8-year plan of the National Governmental Party, work on the Pneumatic Tube Project will begin immediately.

> Additional information will be provided to you regarding employment opportunities. There is no reason that every person who wants to, and is able to, work can't work.

> This is the first step to rehabilitating this great country.

> This is our great endeavor.

Moribund smiled, seeing the words of the Benevolent Leader. The Benevolent Leader was someone Moribund Wrath couldn't help but love. In every commercial of him Moribund had the distinct sensation that his voice was a sort of strange mixture of Mother and Father, Lover and Friend, Confidant and Confessor all wrapped into one old, yet seemingly young, man. Though, to Moribund's recollection, she'd actually never seen him speak—had never watched words from his lips or his Adam's apple, confirm that he uttered even a single syllable. It made no difference to her—or any of the other American's because the Benevolent Leader was, to everyone and for all National purposes, the perfect President. Every time his speeches were aired his firm, athletic frame spoke to him being a specimen of health and vigor. His gray hair, steely blue eyes and perfectly white teeth that smiled the most endearing smile throughout his speeches instilled in a nation mired in financial woes and upheaval a sense of fraternity, of family. It made no difference that his lips did not even attempt to mime the words of his speeches, all one had to do was look him in the eye—when he looked directly at you through your television or computer screen—and know that he was the perfect leader. Then every suspicion, distress—every anxiety simply disappeared.

Oh, and the showmanship: his speeches were lovely pieces of Art! Always the best, most appropriately balanced, mix of music playing softly in the background; music that swelled then quelled the waves of emotions his speaking points elicited but all done in a subtle and quiet way.

Even though he wasn't shown speaking, his addresses were so much better than the old days, the antique days, of politicians facing the cameras while trying to look sincere even as they lied, stole and abused the People. The Benevolent Leader could never do that—all one had to do was look at him while he stood before the ocean, looking at the sunrise out over the waves with his expression one of complete contemplation of all the deep and terrible responsibilities that he *would* master, in order to help his People. One had only to watch the speech by the ocean or the one by the Rocky Mountains and listen to his words, his nurturing voice mixed with music, to be struck by his greatness. It was as if the Nation had been given *The Thinker* but instead of a creation only dreamed about by Auguste Rodin, America had the human incarnation. Or maybe it was more like seeing a statue come to life—like seeing Michealangelo di Lodovico Buonarroti Simoni's *David* in human form, for if one were pressed to describe how he made the People feel—it would be likend to the spiritual because the Benevolent Leader's countenance made Americans feel saved.

He was as brilliant as the sun he smiled in two different speeches, one where it rose and one where it sat. He was as soothing as the moon as it rose—there was a speech about hope for that one. And when the moon passed in front of the sun—his speech addressed the solar eclipse as a metaphor for the New Government's eclipsing those systems of the past.

Moribund remembered that one specifically because she thought, first, how beautiful the visual capturing of the eclipse was and that she especially liked the acoustic guitar accompianment, "But," she thought, "That logic doesn't make sense. The eclipse produces no permanent change. The moon is still the moon, as its specific distance and weight and the sun is, in no way, affected." But as she thought about it a little more she conceded, "Perhaps he meant that brief moment when the eclipse affects the lives of people, animals, plants and such here on earth." She decided to leave it at that. She was trying to be an optimistic American.

Besides, the Benevolent Leader had done something no one had done before: he was loved as if he *was* Love. He made the People *feel* genuine affection not only because of his words but because of his actions. The New Government created so many new programs, provided for so many of the People's needs, and seemed that every endeavor it took on was a success—combined with the absolute American-nes of the Benevolent Leader—it made all Americans feel like Americans again. And the Nation, slowly…ever-so-slowly…began to recover from the dark, dark days that had gone before when industry's greed had snapped the spine and political corruption had severed America's spinal cord. It was as if both had studied the "ice pick" technique patented by Dr. Walter Freeman: they had lobotomized the Nation in hopes that their rape would go unnoticed—therefore unpunished—but the ice picks driven into the brain of America did not perform as they'd predicted. Altered? Yes, America became altered because of their surgical skill, but complascent, manageable, controllable—it was only a period of time before the "doctors" saw their "patient" would tolerate them no longer. The Benevolent Leader was no doctor, he was a Medicine Man, a Healer, and—compared to those "politicians" and "corporations"—he was a true Leader.

Still, if Moribund Wrath were really honest—I mean really, really honest with herself: something about it all sat wrong. What? She didn't have a clue.

Studying the words of the poster, "Pneumatic." Moribund knew what pneumatics was, only she couldn't, for the life of her, figure out what it had to do with a large governmental project. Some of the old banks still used them…some museum organs. It puzzled her. In fact, she paid attention to nothing else but that poster and was so engrossed in her pondering that the attorney was forced to call her name, twice.

Inside the same small room, at the same metal desk, with the arrangement unchanged, Moribund didn't listen to a word. She figured it was her turn to be 'tolerant' to the, then, female attorney who was representing a different creditor—one of the other big banks she'd owed money to for years. Moribund simply stared out the window. In only a week's time the outside had changed from late-winter to early-spring. She remembered being inspired by this, as a writer, to clean up her novel's transitions. She aspired to make them as subtle and effective and Nature, so seemingly effortlessly, always did. And yet on that late-winter/earl-spring day she really wasn't even thinking much on that, just noticing it really. "Pneumatic Tube Project."

The woman attorney's voice increased in volume, "Excuse me. I asked you a question."

"I don't have any money."

"You need to provide proof. Everybody says they don't have any money, even when they do."

Moribund lifted her foot, even though she was wearing a skirt and hadn't been able to afford underwear for as many years as she'd been unable to buy sock, to show the woman the sole of her shoe. The woman averted her eyes in disgust before Moribund had gotten her foot high enough to show her the hole.

"See," Moribund nearly beamed, "No money."

"People are clever. They play dress-up on court days."

Moribund smiled, at least the woman was honest. "Listen," she said, "Lady, I don't have any money but you're right. I played dress-up today. I happen to be wearing my very best clothes because, in spite of what you might think of me, I actually do care how I look when I come to the bastion of justice. I try my best to be as presentable as I can. I even washed my pits in cold water because my electricity got turned off, which means no hot water. So when I tell you I don't have any money. I don't. Simple as that."

"Then how do you live?"

"Cheap."

"I mean, how do you pay your rent?"

"My building's almost condemned. It's cheap too. I get Social Security."

"How much to you get a month?"

"You got to be kidding me!"

"You have a legal obligation to pay your debt."

"Lady, you have no idea. My Social pays my rent. That's it."

Moribund opened her mouth. Her teeth had gone bad. Black spots on the yellow teeth and white, sticky paste on the once-pink tongue. "I'm 35 years old. You don't have to tell me. I already know I look 70. My Social pays my rent. I get food credit from the government, which affords me bread, most times, and that's about it. I got nothing you want, Lady. Nothing."

"You need to provide proof." She slid a piece of paper across the desk to Moribund. She wouldn't even dignify her with handing it to her, directly. "Here is a list of acceptable proof items and an address to where you can mail them. Good day."

The woman rose, grabbed her attaché, and left Moribund, who was still sitting, alone in the courthouse's room. Moribund thought, "Justice sure is blind."


A knock on her apartment door and her remaining still behind it, hoping they'd think she wasn't home. She could tell that the person was a debt collector by how long they waited, listening—long enough for the drawings of the oranges and apples on the grocery boxes Moribund had stacked beside the door to remain in her vision even after she'd covered her eyes with her hands in an attempt to chase them away. The boxes, filled with bits of writing, important documents, and unopened mail, stood ready for moving at a moment's notice because even Moribund knew debtors didn't get advanced eviction notices.

The knock came again like a raven and Moribund remembered asking her mother about her name.

"Blame your first name on the doctor who drugged me and a nurse because I'm positive I said 'Moira'. I can still recall the image I had of you, all grown up with long brown hair wrapped tidily into a bun when I told that stupid nurse your name. Then your father and I get your hospital birth record and it read, Moribund Wrath. Of course, Wrath was fine—that was all on your father. Your father told me that he chased down the nurse and she said, "Your wife said Moirabunned and that didn't make any sense, I mean who'd name their child a made-up name? So I figured she meant the real word and the closest thing I could come up with was, Moribund, but if that's wrong you can change it at the courthouse." Which we never did and that's how you became who you are."

The pounding of her head, the knocking memories, wakeful dreaming: she remembered lying down and peeking through the gap between the door and the floor. The hallway revealed the uppers of a man's pair of shoes. She noticed the seams between the stitched soles and the leather were failing; his white socks could be seen through the holes. Then, without notice, the shoes pivoted forty five degrees with a precision that made Moribund sure that the shoe's man must have been an enlisted man, once; everyone was something once…before everything had gone so wrong…and, eventually, enough shoes came and forced Moribund to appear at court to address her debt.

Rainwater pooled in the courthouse's worn stone stairs no differently than those hayloft ladders of old barns; even stone wore down from too much traffic. The placard bolted to the wall read, Magistrate, and the wallpaper featured wheat stalks. The humming from the overhead fluorescent lights drew her gaze upward; Moribund wondered if anyone else thought they looked like the old metal ice cube trays—or if anyone even remember such things had existed and this made her think of existence, in general, and she wondered if anyone remembered anything or anyone for more than passing moments.

The noise of the steam-heat radiator's "iss" and "iz" drew her eyes back to the ground, to the linoleum and the cast iron staircase railing, an ornate design of what looked like mythical lion-like creature's whose tongues warped into ivies, Fleur de Leis, and Oak leaves—there were crosses too—and then there was the judge who said that she was lucky that the Benevolent Leader had a kinder way to deal with debtors like her. And then there was being transported, like cattle, to the first sets of Fortaleez.

*Moribund Wrath & FORTALEEZ*

Another day a different sandwich, Moribund Wrath was getting pretty sick of waiting in line and she wasn't the only one. William Henry Little was growing day-by-day increasingly sour. But who could blame him? It had been something like 3 weeks since he'd seen his wife and children, though the passage of real time was hard to establish.

Moribund, having lived so long in destitution, had long-since forsaken the luxury of purchasing calendars and had learnt, the hard way, that floating newspapers around rubbish heaps were not reliable either. Just because garbage was added daily, didn't mean it had been added chronologically. So Moribund Wrath used the sun and moon as her calendar. They never let her down. By her estimate, she'd been in Fortaleez for just about 3 weeks. And, from what William Henry Little had told her, he'd been there just about the same length of time.

William's suffering was growing, this much was obvious to Moribund by his temper was growing shorter the longer he stood in line. Moribund tried to comfort him by saying that they were doing all they could, being in line everyday from sunrise to sunset, but this didn't help. Moribund was shocked to hear Marie's words come out of her mouth, "Don't worry, William, they don't start enforcing our work contracts for at least 6 weeks." As soon as the words escaped her lips she thought, "Was it 6? I recall something like 2-3 weeks. But then didn't someone say 8 weeks? I even think I heard 12 weeks somewhere."

William could see that his friend was trying to make him feel better, "I'm fine, Moribund. Don't worry."

"I'm not worried," Moribund quipped, as if William had just flung an insult at her. "I never worry."

"Okay. Don't fret."

"I don't fret either!"

"Fine!" William Henry Little flung himself around. He was in no mood for semantics.

He was in a foul temper. Sure, he had all the creature comforts: a nicely furnished house, a helper who happened to be a young, attractive young woman, lots of the best food he'd eaten in longer than he could remember and luxuries including the best gaming systems and television. He was living the life he'd always dreamt of living but could never have afforded to but without his wife and children his life felt as if charred ash sprinkled on a desiccated tongue; Moribund could not relate in the slightest.

CITIZEN VAE BELKNAP

Vae Belknap had never been happier than when the Benevolent Leader proclaimed the abandonment of all cities not deemed of critical value either in terms of size, strategic location, or National historical significance, leaving only twenty to protect and maintain because even though it had been done to conserve resources and to enable the Marines greater protective and defensive efficiency, Vae Belknap—all the virologists—knew that it also created more precise disease vectors from which to study.

Her wish of all wishes was to study how, or even if, their population had experienced the Sleeping Sickness but after the Benevolent Leader's Great Relocation, which included the New Treaty establishing that in exchange for all tribes receiving additional land that they would, thereafter, have complete sovereignty, which meant that the Nation abandoned all creation and maintenance of infrastructure other than that of the Cities and Fortaleez in exchange for weekly aerial drops of essential and nonessential items as well as guns. This translated into the

Reservations becoming tourist spots for the very wealthy…and all that came with it and Vae Belknap, though would be well-paid would never—not in a lifetime—earn what would allow her such privilege. Besides, she'd always liked her creature comforts and those were hard to come by on government wages.

A different man's voice began. *It sounds a bit chirpy, like a bird, but it's pleasant*, Vae thought until he revealed it would be history he'd voice. *I can't. Imprecise. Soft science will have a lot to answer for if the quantum physicists are right.*

But before she could switch the program off he said, "That's why the Benevolent Leader, in the face of extreme criticism, commanded that airdropped supplies be regularly delivered to those living Free proclaiming, 'I am the leader of America. I will protect, defend, and provide for the needs of all Americans. End of story.' He knew that the Nation was deeply wounded, you all remember The Phoenix Phenomena, and that the Cities had to be culled because it was the only way to stabilize the National income. We forget that it wasn't just our buildings and homes we lost but our countrymen—our Nation's manpower. It was a crisis that threatened everything but because the Benevolent Leader focused on fixing our Nation's complicated, heck impossible, problems he depended on the American spirit, to be good neighbors, but relied on science and—thank whatever you thank—our lead scientist, Dr. Notoc Kachuka discovered the technology we now use in every L.P. Program, the transdermal extraction of human fat.

CITIZEN NOTOC KACHUKA

THE CREDIT COLLECTOR:

Regna Kachuka was the son of Indian immigrants. He was fifty years old, had worked for the same company for twenty-eight years, had been married for twenty-five years, and had one teenaged son.

His parents, unlike many, cut all ties to their old world. The day they became citizens of the United States, while Regna was just-formed in his mother's belly, was the happiest day of both their lives. No couple could have had blood more red, white, and blue than the Kachuka family. When they would see other Indian people they avoided them. To say they were racist would have been correct except that it wasn't as much race as it was country affiliation. The Kachuka family did have one Indian family that they would associate with and that was only because they, like the Kachukas, were hardcore Americans. Even any vestige of language accent was ferociously gutted out, like one might attack crabgrass in a lawn. There were times when Regna's mother might slip a syllable and his father would pinch her arm, hard.

So Regna grew up knowing nothing of his cultural heritage. He grew up with the same American dreams that every red-blooded American dreams of: a good-paying job, a nice house with a 3-car garage filled with 2 nice cars and a riding lawnmower for the large yard, a pretty wife and a smart, athletic child. By these standards, Regna was the epitome of American.

Regna graduated from the state university with a Bachelor's degree in Business. He was in the top 5% of his class. He ignored the students that teased him by saying his success was because he was Indian. Regna could safely say that he'd never felt Indian a single day of his life.

The university annually held a career day and the booths ranged from the U.S. Marine Corps to multi-billion dollar corps. One company caught Regna's eye. It was a collection agency and the president of the company was running the booth. One might think that this would make the company less appealing. Maybe it meant that the company wasn't doing well or wasn't very big and maybe that's why that particular booth wasn't frequented much, especially by the high-powered students who enjoyed being in the top 10%. Regna, on the other hand, was curious.

It took less than seven minutes before he was signing a contract and it was a good contract. Seven minutes was all it took for Regna to see the company's specs and to learn that the man he was speaking to was, in fact, one of the Country's leading attorneys in Collection Law. Regna knew this was true because he looked up the man's file on his handheld computer. Seven minutes and Regna was guaranteed to make more money in a year than his father had made in ten. 7, Regna determined, was a good and important number.

By the time Regna graduated he'd already passed, with flying colors, the probation period for the law firm of Chuck Littowa, Inc. and he was already the company's lead ace. Chuck, the man Regna had met on career day, believed in incentive. He kept a board up on the wall and every agent had to jockey for their position. Like a pack of wolves, or jackals, there was a pecking order and those who, consistently, stayed on top—like Regna—got first pick of the prey. Prey, in these terms, could be anything. It was up to the pack leaders to decide in what form they took their flesh. Some chose to get the customers who would be less hostile, the ones who were still paying their bills, the ones who had jobs. Some, like Regna, liked the challenge of stamping the word 'impossibility' out. He was hailed as a genius because no matter how deadbeat the person was, Regna always got some money out of them. But when the juniors would call him a genius to his face, he'd say that it was the simple rule: people are good and that makes them want to do good. "If ," he would tell them, "They believe being a debtor is bad then they'll believe paying a creditor is good. I just make sure to remind them to be thankful we live in a new era where they're no longer viewed as the criminals they once would have been and imprisoned just like murderers and rapists. Then I tell them that this little mix-up can be resolved by setting up a reasonable monthly payment plan." The juniors, usually, just shook their heads in awe. It takes a certain philosophy to have the guts to say those things. It takes a purely American philosophy and if there was a more pure American than Regna, one would be hard-pressed to prove it.

~~~

The Credit Collector

When Regna's hand touched the metal of his front door's handle a sigh of contentment escaped him at the simple weight of his happiness. He flung the door wide, smiling and, only half in jest, cried out, "Honey, I'm home."

Regna's wife came rushing to the door, the same way she'd done every day they'd been married, as if from a scene straight out of Hollywood, kissed his cheek, said, "Welcome home. How was your day?"

To which he'd, politely reply, "Good. How was yours?"

To which she'd reply the same way, minus the question she'd already asked.

Regna's wife was a beautiful woman.  She was from the Midwest, had blue eyes, blonde hair, a nice figure that she worked hard to keep and good, American values; she wasn't a big thinker and hated politics.  Fashion was her passion and she was socially active with church, her two secret societies, and supporting her son's school athletics, music, art, and academics.

Sure, it was hard for her, she'd admit, moving away from her hometown but she was more than happy to be where she was—where Regna could make a really good living and where they had a beautiful home.  And this was her son's last year of high school so she'd been, subtly, dropping hints to Regna that, perhaps, they might take some time to travel.  She felt, as time grew longer, an increasing desire to escape…but she quickly put such thoughts out of her head because there was much to do when her husband came home from work.

It was true that Regna insisted on them retaining a fulltime housekeeper and gardener because he didn't want her to be overworked when he came home.  He wanted her fresh, entertaining, beautifully dressed, her hair styled, makeup applied— he wanted her to be his goddess.  But this didn't mean that she had no work.  Regna insisted on one other thing: that she cook his every meal and that she cook them brilliantly.

This was not so easy of a task for May Kachuka.  Perhaps some might assume, maybe even Regna assumed, that a girl growing up in the Midwest would naturally be a good cook.  But May's experience, and maybe it was simply the small town she'd grown up in, was that her town must have been 'progressive' because girls did all the things boys did, which meant there was very little 'free' time for learning to cook.  May had even lettered in cross-country running, band, choir and academics.  She'd gotten a full academic scholarship to study psychology at the university where she'd met Regna.  But after she'd met Regna, and he'd made his intention to marry her clear, May decided it was better to focus less on psychology and more on domesticity.  She was somewhat surprised to find so many cookbooks in the stacks at the university's library but thankful all the same.

Haut cuisine was Regna's thing—and barbeque.  May failed to see the difference between haut and BBQ because the BBQ recipes she'd found, and the ways in which the different meats were processed seemed, to her, just as labor intensive, and maybe even more so. Her culinary duties were breakfast and dinner. Each week she prepared a menu for Regna's approval. She'd found that he enjoyed this, tremendously. He told her, once, that it gave him yet one more thing, in addition to her beauty, to look forward to coming home to.

She liked to think on that, especially when she was struggling with a recipe that just would not come out right and her stress level increased, incrementally, with each batch that went into the garbage knowing that Regna was not only expecting a certain meal but also anticipating it. It made her thankful she'd been an athlete; she knew how to make adrenaline work for her but sometimes, in the black of night on one of those nights when she'd had to battle so fiercely to pull off another meal, she trembled. Like a small earthquake, a tremor. In those nights, while Regna snored rhythmically tucked amidst the Egyptian sheets of their California King bed, May felt herself coming a little unhinged. She'd go to the kitchen. Her battleground had been swept clean of all remnants of war. It smelled of Lysol. There was a small t.v. on the countertop, beneath the cupboard filled with her son's childhood sippy cups. She could throw neither the cups or it out. Her son was graduating. He'd been accepted to M.I.T. He'd received a full-ride scholarship to study biotechnological engineering. She took one of his sippy cups from the cupboard, the one where he'd scribbled his name, Notoc, with a permanent marker and then the paper was encased in plastic. She traced the backward 'c' with her index finger. A tear escaped. She reached for the t.v. and switched it on to the Home Shopping Network. She uncorked a bottle. She lifted the sippy cup to her lips, taking a drink, and thought, "I shouldn't." But did.

The Credit Collector

It was unusual, at Regna Kachuka's house, for the house phone to ring. It was especially unnerving to Regna when the phone calls began interrupting the service of his supper. May could not jump up, answer the phone, and serve him his meal all at once. So the phone ringing in the middle of his supper was becoming increasingly disruptive to the welcomed order Regna enjoyed in his home.

When Regna asked who it was and why they were calling at that hour, May quickly replied that it was different fundraisers and that she, somehow, must have gotten onto a mailing list and that there might even be a fundraising 'season.'

"Maybe," May quickly added, "It's because I gave money to the shelter…or to the cancer people." Regna accepted this but grumbled, "That's not good business you know. They should consider that if they make their organizations unpalatable, by calling at inconvenient hours, then people will be less willing to give them money." May replied, "Yes, Dear," and resumed serving him.

One night May was halfway through the desert service when the phone rang. Regna and their son, Notoc, both noticed that when she jumped up from the table she seemed edgy, like a cat hearing a loud sound. When she came back to the table she said, "Oh, I forgot. I promised I'd give to the homeless cat society."

Regna laughed, "You'd better be careful, May, you'll break the bank."

May looked as if she'd been wounded straight to the heart. She stood up, tears in her eyes and ran upstairs to their bedroom. Regna looked at Notoc, who shrugged his shoulders. Regna left his half-eaten desert and while he climbed the stairs tried to figure out what could be bothering her. "Maybe she'd going through the change," he thought. "She's about that age, maybe a little young for it, but it wouldn't be exceptionally early. Or maybe she thought I was criticizing her giving to charities. She should know better than that, but maybe she thought I was questioning her judgment."

Regna knocked on the door. He could hear May crying but the door was locked.

"Let me in, Honey. There's nothing we can't work through."

It was no use. For the first time in their marriage she seemed intent on keeping him out. But he figured it would pass. "She'll come around," he thought as he went back downstairs to finish his desert. "I bet by the time I'm finished, she'll be back." But she wasn't and, that night, another first happened: Regna slept in the spare bedroom.

This did not go over well with him at all and by the time morning came, the time when he had to get ready for work, he was as fired up as a summer hornet only to find May as sweet as sugar. She'd even made him a special breakfast of Eggs Benedict, fresh berries with clotted cream, fresh-squeezed orange juice and Turkish coffee. As upset as he was with her, he couldn't stay that way—it was obvious, by the work she'd done that morning, that she was making up.

But after he'd eaten, he tried to talk to her about what was upsetting her; she put her finger to his lips, "No talking," and led him upstairs.

That morning she made love with him like she hadn't done in decades. Every nerve thrilled him. It was as if she was young and free again and it made him feel the same way. "If this is menopause, I'm in for a wild ride," he thought as he showered for work. While he drove, images of the morning kept flashing before his eyes. "My beautiful wife," he thought. "I'm so lucky," he thought. The day seemed like it flew by and the work of getting deadbeats to pay their bills didn't seem near as tough as it usually did. He thought, "This must be what it feels like to hit a ball in the sweet-spot." Everything was in perfect order. He drove home, whistling. He never whistled not that he couldn't he just didn't, but he felt like it. It felt like a day for whistling. He was looking forward to seeing his beautiful garden, his beautiful wife, and the lovely meal he just knew she'd prepare for him on that exceptionally perfect day.

That morning, while Regna was showering, the phone rang. "Is this Mrs. May Kachuka?"

"Yes," May replied.

"Mrs. Kachuka, I'm calling on behalf of Capital One because it's been over 90 days since we've received a payment on your account."

"I don't think that's right."

"I have here that you sent a payment…"

May could hear Regna in the shower. Was he…whistling? She smiled.

"…3 months ago. You used a credit card. We can make this account current today. Would you like to use the same credit card to bring your account current?"

She said, "Sure," but knew it wouldn't work. That card was already maxed out.

"It will just take a moment to process this.  Will you hold?"

"Sure," May replied, but when the music began she hung up and unplugged the phone—all of the phones.  "Regna and Notoc won't notice," she thought, "They both use their cell phones anyway."

As soon as Regna stepped out of the shower, still dripping wet, May ran to his arms and kissed him.

"I love you, Regna," she said.

"I love you too, May.  What's gotten into you?"

She was crying, "Oh I don't know.  You know.  Silly things women do."

Regna knew it.  It was the change.

After Regna had gone to work, Notoc told his mom that he'd gotten a summer job at the organic grocery store a few blocks away.

"I have to make some money before I go off to college," he said, kissing his mom on the cheek.  She started to cry.

"What's wrong Mom?"

"Oh, nothing.  I just…well.  You're going off to college.  I guess…I never really imagined what it would be like having you go away."

"It's not like I'm dying or something.  I'm just going to college, Mom.  Gees, I'll be back."

"Yes.  Yes, I know.  I'm just being silly."

But Notoc hugged her and kissed her again.  He hated seeing his mom upset because she hardly ever was.  She was a rock.  She was the one who always had a smile and kind word.  She'd picked him up by his bootstraps many-a-time when he'd get worried or stressed about school…or life.  She was the first to give a hug and the last to deliver an angry word.  He couldn't say the same of his father, but even he wasn't too bad.  "Overall," Notoc thought as he rode his bike to his first job, "I've had a pretty wonderful life."

Finally alone, May plugged the phones back in. Instantaneously, they began to ring. She imagined a symphony where the ringing came from bells and that the sound the rope made as she tied the knots she'd learned in Girl Scouts round her ankles and the sturdy 2nd story deck railing, that didn't have to be too sturdy because, lately, she'd lost some weight from the very little weight she normally wore, sounded like a jazz drummer using brushes instead of sticks and when she let herself drop over the edge, safe from view from the neighbors who all worked in the city—it was a bedroom community—but also safe because Regna had insisted on a privacy fence built as high as was legally allowed, when she hung, upside down, with her skirt over her face, she heard a train, "Chush, chush, chush," in her ears. The ringing, the brush slides, the train's drone and all safe within her skirt, like the blanket tents she'd hung around her room as a little girl, she took the boxcutter she'd held tight in her hand, tight as life itself because she knew if it dropped that her whole plan would be foiled. She held that boxcutter as carefully as she'd held Notoc on the day he'd been born, as tightly as she'd made love to Regna that morning, so tight because it was her last chance to be free. She used her full strength, the athlete in her for all those years, against her own flesh. That first strike badly damaged her wrist but she would not give up. Even though she was only able to use her forefinger and thumb she mustered all those years, all the stress and worry, all the anxiety and fear together.

She gathered it all up into those two fingers and screamed, "FREEDOM!"

They unleashed their wrath on the soft skin of her virgin wrist. Then the boxcutter fell to the ground far below.

It did not take gravity long to drain May of her life. Her upside down skirt fluttered in the wind.

As Regna drew near his home, after having the most marvelous day, there were two police cars, a fire truck, and two ambulances. His first wave of panic was, "Something's happened to Notoc," but when he saw Notoc he realized it had to have been May, "Could she have had a heart attack? She's too young isn't she? But it seems to be happening to people earlier and earlier." These were his thoughts as he ran up to Notoc and the paramedic who was with him.

"What's going on," Regna cried.

"Are you Mr. Kachuka?"

Notoc fell into his father's arms, crying, "Oh Dad! Dad! Dad!"

"What's going on!"

"Oh Dad, Dad it's just too awful."

For the first time in his life, Regna felt a new feeling. It was fear. "What's happened?"

The paramedic led Notoc to one of the ambulances and sat him down. A police officer came up to Regna, "Are you Mr. Kachuka?"

"Yes. Yes! What's going on here!"

"I'm sorry, Mr. Kachuka, but your wife is dead."

The phone was ringing inside. He must have fainted because Regna found himself inside the same ambulance where Notoc had been taken a few moments earlier. Notoc was holding his hand.

"It's going to be okay, Dad," he said.

Notoc felt, somehow, proud that his son had become man enough to comfort and care for his father but when he tried to sit up, the paramedic said, "No. You just lie there for a few minutes and then we'll get you up real nice and slow."

A police officer came to the ambulance and told Notoc to wait outside. Regna noticed the loss of his son's hand and that he was suddenly cold.

The paramedic put a blanket over him, "Don't worry. It's just shock."

Regna seemed to remember learning about shock, somewhere but where he could not remember. He couldn't remember anything except that people could die from shock.

"Mr. Kachuka," the police officer continued, "Where were you today?"

"I was at work. Where's my wife?"

"I told you, Sir. She's dead."

"But how?  Was she murdered?"

"We don't know yet.  And what time did you go to work?"

The first emergency vehicle to leave was one of the ambulances and it had left just shortly after Regna collapsed.  In it contained the body of May Kachuka.  It was being rushed to the hospital for a forensic autopsy because, in the words of the scene's police, "Never, absolutely never, had they seen anything like it."

The second vehicle to leave was the fire truck but, closely behind it, went the second police car and, eventually the final ambulance.  The remaining police car remained: the policeman questioned Mr. Kachuka and his son.

The phone rang…the answering machine picked up.

After a long time the last police officer left too, but not without stating, "I probably don't need to say this, thanks to all the TV shows, but I need for you guys to stay in town.  So if you have any plans for trips or traveling, you'll need to cancel them, at least until we get this whole thing sorted out."

The phone rang…the answering machine picked up.

And then it was just Regna and Notoc.  They went inside the house.  It seemed too unreal.  It seemed just like it always did.  It smelled clean.  It looked neat.  Neither of them realized that May had dismissed the housekeeper and groundskeeper three days earlier.  They did notice, however, that there was no dinner ready and no "How was your day?"  There was simply a big, empty house.

During his questioning, the police officer showed Regna a note.  He asked him if that was May's handwriting.  Regna said he thought it was but couldn't be sure.  In fact, he hadn't really seen much of May's handwriting.  When they'd been dating they used computers to write little love notes.  Naturally, email didn't involve handwriting and May was very neat so even her shopping lists were tucked either into her purse or somewhere else the whereabouts he didn't have a clue.  She didn't use checks, she preferred debit.  So Regna suggested to the police officer, in order to be sure that it was her handwriting and not a murders', to compare it to her credit card signatures.

To this, the police laughed and said, "Thank you Mr. Kachuka. You've been a real help."

The phone rang…the answering machine picked up.

When Regna asked to see the note, the police officer asked him what he thought it said. Regna said he didn't have a clue. The officer must have believed him because he let Regna read it through the Ziploc bag it had been placed into.

*My Loves,*

*You have been a good husband. Notoc, you have been a good son. This is not about you, it's about me. I have not been honest and now, I fear, I have brought ruin onto all of us. Please forgive me…I never meant to. I just couldn't help it. In my top dresser drawer is the key to the lock. Then you will understand. I LOVE YOU BOTH so much! And I'm sorry.*

*May (Mom)*

When Regna asked about the key the police officer told him that it was in evidence but continued, "Do you know what it's a key to?"

"I have no clue," Regna replied. "I don't think she has anything here that is padlocked."

"We couldn't find anything, but that doesn't mean it's not here, so keep your eyes open and let us know if you come across something that can help us."

After Regna replied, "I will," and shook the officer's hand in goodbye, the phone rang. This time Regna answered.

"Hello," the voice said, "Is May Kachuka available."

"Excuse me," Regna's voice quivered.

"Is Mrs. May Kachuka available?"

"May I ask who's calling?"

"Are you Mr. Kachuka?"

"I am but who are you?"

"This call is an attempt to collect a debt." Regna hung up.

The phone rang again. Same person. "Mr. Kachuka?"

"Yes."

"I'm sorry, we must have been disconnected. Are you listed on Mrs. Kachuka's accounts as a representative?"

"Listen you Motherfucker, she's dead, I'm a debt collector myself and might I say that your technique SUCKS! So don't bother calling here again because you're not going to get a motherfucking thing out me and you certainly aren't getting it out of her. Understand!"

There was a slight pause, "Did Mrs. Kachuka happen to have a life insurance policy?"

Regna slammed the phone down. It rang again the moment it touched the receiver. He had never, in all his life, been so enraged, "Listen, I swear to God if you don't stop calling..."

"Excuse me," it was a woman's voice. Humiliated, Regna apologized.

She replied, "That's okay. Is this Mr. Kachuka?"

"Yes."

"Hi. I'm representing Capital One and this is an attempt to collect a debt."

This time Regna didn't hang up. This time he learned that May owed over $20,000.00 to Capital One, that she was 3 months delinquent on her account and had been receiving over-the-limit fees and late fees with an interest rate of 35% .

The woman said, in a very kindly sweet voice, "Mr. Kachuka. We can take care of this today. All we need is to bring Mrs. Kachuka's account below the over-the-limit balance and then she can continue to make her regular monthly payments. Do you have a credit card you'd like to use tonight so that we can clear this up?"

Regna said, "You're good."

The lady laughed, "I don't know what you mean."

"I'm in the business and, believe me, you're good. You'll go far. But my wife is dead."

"Excuse me."

"Yes. I came home from work, from doing just what you're doing right now, and found her dead."

"That's terrible Mr. Kachuka. I'm so sorry."

Regna began to cry, "Thank you. What was your name?"

"Juliana."

"That's nice. Thank you, Juliana."

"Uh, Mr. Kachuka?"

"Yes."

"Did your wife happen to have a life insurance policy?"

"Yes. But it won't pay out for suicide."

"I see," she said.

Regna could hear computer keys typing in the background. "My condolences, Mr. Kachuka. I'll make a note on her account."

"Thank you."

When Regna hung up the phone it rang again, it was Capital One. When Regna told the woman that he'd just gotten off the phone with Juliana who'd said she'd make a note on the account regarding his wife's suicide and that they should stop calling him, the woman replied, "I'm sorry Mr. Kachuka, there isn't any note on her file. Can you bring this account current tonight?" Regna hung up, then unplugged the house phones in order to have enough quiet to call his boss on his cell.

He was given two weeks bereavement leave and his boss' condolences. Regna plugged the phones back in. He knew they'd ring only ring for a few minutes longer, that night. The government had passed legislation regarding credit collection calls. There was a season for everything. It was time to talk with Notoc.

After the police had left, Notoc went to his room and shut the door. The last time he'd seen his mother alive kept playing in his mind, over and over, like a recording skip. He remembered the feel of her pressed against him when she hugged him goodbye. He remembered her voice, he remembered what he thought was everything but was just as sure that he'd forgotten something. Some small thing that he should have noticed that would have let him save her life. He just knew it was his fault. That's when the grief overwhelmed him. He curled into a fetus, he wrapped his body into as tight a ball as his spine would allow, he wept and rocked himself back and forth, he cried, "Mother…Mom…Mommy," and wished he'd die then too. For all the life they'd shared he thought, "She knew more about me than I knew about her." And he hated himself for that. "Why didn't I take more time to know her and now she's gone!"

Regna knocked on the door.

"Go away!"

"I need to talk to you."

Silence. Regna checked the doorknob. It was unlocked so he entered. Notoc, startled by the intrusion, sat up, wiping his tears, and said, "I said go away. Can't you hear or don't you care about my wishes."

"I need to talk to you."

"You don't care. You don't care about anyone's feelings or wishes or you couldn't do what you do. That's why Mom's dead!"

In his entire career, a career being cursed at and hated, he'd never been cut so deep, "Notoc. That's not true. I loved your mother and, I believe, she loved me."

"Then why is she dead!"

"I don't know but I will find out."

"That's right. You're the expert on digging things up about people aren't you?"

Suddenly it dawned on Regna that Notoc might know something about May's credit. "Notoc, was Mom getting collection calls while I was at work?"

"Why should I tell you?"

"Because it just might help figure out what happened."

"Yeah. Sure. Fine. You figure it out."

"How long?"

Notoc was seized again. He curled into himself like an armadillo under attack; the attacker was the thought that maybe, if he'd told his dad earlier, about the collector's calling…

"Notoc!"

"What do you want from me!"

"I want you to tell me how long this has been going on."

Notoc sat back up, "All I can say is that since school let out for summer, it's been going on. All day. Every day. That's part of why I got the job at the store. I just couldn't stand that constant ringing anymore. And every time Mom got off the phone she'd be upset but would pretend she wasn't."

"Why didn't you tell me?"

"I figured you knew."

"But I didn't!"

"I figured you were the one responsible for putting her through that. I figured you knew and you got to go to work, escaping those hounds, leaving her here all alone, outnumbered and weak, to fight them off."

Regna pulled Notoc to him, "Oh! I could never. NEVER! I love your mother. I love you. I just can't believe what I'm hearing. It doesn't make any sense to me. I mean, I give your mother plenty of money for everything she wants. And I can't, for the life of me, see what it is she's spent so much money on."

"How much money?" Notoc asked.

"I don't really know. One company has one of her cards at $20,000.00 and that same company, a different account, has her at $15,000.00. There could be other accounts with the same company and there could be other companies with multiple accounts. It's impossible to know without having the account information." Regna turned to Notoc, "You wouldn't happen to know where you mother kept her statements would you?"

Notoc shook his head.

"Will you help me look?"

Notoc nodded. They went, first, to Regna and May's bedroom. Every drawer was emptied, every box was emptied, every square inch was emptied, the bed was lifted, the box-spring was overturned: nothing. They went to the office and searched it just the same. They searched the entire house and finally ended up in the kitchen. Every canister was emptied. Every box of food was opened and emptied. The cupboards, one by one, were emptied until Notoc found the sippy cups. He saw the one he'd made for his mother when he was small but when he pulled it from the cupboard he noticed that the seal, the one that kept the writing paper inside it dry, had been broken. The center of the cup spun free so he lifted it out to reveal a small strip of paper on the bottom. "U-Store, #7."

Notoc showed his father. They ran to the telephone book, flipping so fast they passed the Us, frontwards and backwards, several times before settling into the middle, then their eyes raced the U columns to find "U-Store." They didn't even speak. They drove. It was downtown and in a bad neighborhood. There was a security camera and a buzzer box. Regna pushed the button.

A voice called, "Can I help you?"

"Yes. I'm looking for #7."

"The name?"

"Kachuka."

"Ah yes.  Come to the office."

"Where's the office?"

"To your left."

The gate opened.  They went in.  The office was small and dingy.  Wallboard was everywhere and it reeked of smoke.

The fat lady said, "Who are you?"

"I'm Regna Kachuka, May's husband and this is my son, Notoc."

Notoc tried to smile.

"So you're her husband then?"

"Yes."

"Good.  She owes me 3-month's rent.  You gonna pay it?"

"How much is it?"

"$600.00."

"What!"

"Yeah, you heard me, $200.00 per month for a unit that size and that's a deal let me tell ya."

"But I don't have that kind of money on me right now."

"You can't use a debit like your wife?"

"No.  May kept the checkbook and debit card.  Listen, I have $200.00 and I'll go to the bank tomorrow for the rest, okay?"

"Okay."

The woman put her cigarette in an ashtray and made out a receipt.  "She's been late a lot lately.  What's going on?"

Notoc couldn't stand it anymore, "Listen, she's dead okay. Is that good enough for you!"

The lady wasn't too surprised. She lived in a bad neighborhood. She'd seen a lot of things. "So you guys here to pick up her stuff?"

"Uh, sure, I guess."

The lady looked out the window at Regna's car, "You gonna need bigger than that," and she laughed.

Notoc thought, "I'll kill her;" he'd never, in his life, hated someone as much as he hated that lady with all her fat and her stink and her disgusting callousness.

"Can you tell me how to get to #7?" Regna asked.

The lady gave him a map, the place was that big, and #7 was clear in the back. It took Regna and Notoc 10 minutes to find it and they thanked God that it was under one of the few streetlights in the area. They could see, clearly, "#7" and they could also see that it was padlocked.

"That's what the key was for!" Regna cried.

He called the police from his cell phone. A woman and a male officer came with the key. Regna asked about the officer who'd asked him so many questions at his house.

The woman laughed, "Listen, we don't work ourselves 24-7, he's swing and this is graveyard."

"I see," Regna replied.

The officers opened the storage unit. It was the largest unit U-Store offered and it was filled, to the gills, with unopened Shopping Network items.

The lady officer, watching Regna's shocked expression, asked, "You know about all this?"

Regna shook his head. That's when he noticed, on the left side of the unit, pressed right up against the wall, stacked apple boxes. The top one didn't have a lid on it. It was filled with the statements, the bills, from credit card companies. He called the police over. They proceeded to open each box. They were all the same: piles and piles of credit card debt. The lady officer said something to her partner, who came over to Regna.

"Listen," the young man said, "You and your son go home. There's nothing you can do here. We're going to take these boxes and we'll let you know what we find out."

"What about my wife's body?"

"It shouldn't be long. This sort of changes things, I think."

Notoc noticed how young the male police officer was. He didn't look any older than himself. This struck him. That one so young could be facing so much sorrow, chaos, and destruction as part of his occupational duties.

Regna and Notoc drove home in silence. It was already becoming the next day. The police had put tape around the crime scene and told Regna and Notoc not to go out there but Notoc couldn't help it. He had to see. He wanted to see. He climbed under the yellow plastic. It made him think of all the times, in track, watching other people cross the finish line. From the deck there was nothing noticeable. The rope had been taken by the police but Notoc looked to see if he could find where the rope had rubbed the wood. There was nothing. Then he looked over the edge. The grass below was dark. That was all that was left of his mother. Dark grass.

He went downstairs. He climbed under that tape and lay next to the dark grass. He lay on his side so that he could look at it, at eye level, so he could watch it occasionally dance when the wind struck it right. He reached out and touched it. It wasn't sticky anymore. He plucked a blade and cried on it, hoping to hydrate life back into the dead blood. But it was no use. What remained of his mother was elemental: iron, salt, sugar. He lay there thinking about the nature of things until his father called to him. For fear of being caught, he dashed through the police line. For his mother, when he broke that plastic, he threw his hands into the sky.

The autopsy found the cause of death to be self-inflicted/suicide. The police released May's body and her personal things to Regna. Regna made the funeral arrangements and Notoc worked to putting back all the things they'd emptied. The phone rang incessantly. Regna called the phone company and disconnected the phones so he could have peace and quiet while he worked on the apple boxes only to find that May's financial situation was just about the worst he'd ever seen.

She'd had 30 credit cards, all were maxed and over-the-limit because she'd stopped paying on all of them 3 months earlier. He discovered that she, now he, was more than $200,000.00 in debt. He received notice in the mail that, based on the circumstances of May's death, her life insurance policy of $500,000.00 was not going to pay out.

Regna sat and, with pencil and paper, made two columns. In the first he figured what he still owed on the house, his car, and all other expenses including May's debt. In the second he figured what his income, and potential income was. The discrepancy stabbed Regna in the heart. He felt sick. He ran to the bathroom and vomited. He'd never be able to pay it off, never. And he knew, because it was his job to know, that based on what he could afford to pay and the interest rates of May's credit cards, he had—effectively—been sold into bondage.

Later, when Regna went to Notoc's room, he had a bottle of Scotch whiskey.

"You want a drink?" he asked his son.

"No thanks, Dad. Never touch the stuff."

"I see. Good. It's bad. I'm just having a little."

Notoc had never seen his father drunk. Once in a great while he'd see his father have a drink, but usually it was because something good had happened at work. This time was different.

"Are you okay, Dad?"

"Well," he said, sitting on Notoc's bed, "Not so really."

Notoc laughed at that. He thought he noticed something, like a fragment of an accent.

"I need to tell you," Regna continued, "Why you're named Notoc."

"Because we're Indian."

"NO! Don't ever say that!"

"Why not," Notoc stood up tall, "That's what we are."

"Your grandfather would turn in his grave."

"Then let him!"

Regna smiled, took a drink, "You know, when you act like that I see your mother in you."

"What? She was never outspoken like that."

"She was…in her own way. She was when it came to you. She was relentless."

"How so?"

"Anyway," he poured another drink, "You were named Notoc after my great-great-great-great—great grandfather."

Notoc laughed, "Dad, I think you'd better slow down on that," but when he tried to grab the bottle Regna clutched it to his chest.

"I said my great-great-great-great-great grandfather and I meant it!"

"Okay, Dad, take it easy."

"Your grandmother, God rest her soul, told your mother in strict confidence, his name because when your mother found out she was pregnant she insisted that my son…my son…" Regna looked up at Notoc and smiled, "…my son know who he was. Of course when she'd asked me about my family history I had nothing to tell her."

"Why all the secrecy?"

"Because your grandfather absolutely forbid anything to do with our," Regna even whispered the following, "Indian background."

"But why?"

Regna harumpfed, "That's just the way it was. Anyway…your mother didn't care. She said she loved me and that meant loving where I came from too so she went to Grandma's, sat down in the living room and refused to leave until Grandma told her a few things, including a family name." Regna looked at Notoc, "That's how I know even this little bit about myself, it was your mother and her strength. Otherwise you would have been named Bill or John or something American like that."

"Dad," Notoc said, quietly, things have changed. It's okay to be Indian."

Regna grew quiet, as if the words haunted him. "Things have changed," he repeated.

"Dad, you were telling me about my name."

"Oh yes, Notoc. Notoc Kachuka was, well, different. He was what some might call, 'touched.'"

"He was a nutter? You named me after a nut job?"

"He wasn't a nut! He was just, uh, special."

"Ah Dad! Special's just another name for retarded. Great! That's just what I need on top of everything."

"He wasn't retarded, he was fucking brilliant okay! He was so fucking smart that no one could understand him and back in his time, in India, mind you and of our caste—which was the lowest of the low—things were hard for him."

Notoc sat with his father. "Okay. I'll have a drink too."

"Really?" Regna beamed. "Here you go."

Notoc gulped it and coughed, wiping his mouth and trying not to gag. Regna patted him on the back.

"So," Notoc asked, "What happened to him?"

"He was murdered."

"What!"

Regna took another drink. "Yep. No one knew who did it, but one day he was found with his head bashed in with a rock."

There was a long pause. Notoc took another drink then said, "I think I preferred thinking of my namesake as being retarded." They both laughed.

The next day Notoc went to work at the organic grocery store. Regna, who had a bad hangover, was milling through the apple boxes when Notoc called out, "See you later, Dad. Do you want me to bring something home from the store for dinner?"

"That would be fine. Have a good day."

That evening, when Notoc rode his bike up the driveway he noticed that his dad's car was there but the garage doors were all closed. He carried the red pepper hummus and pitas he'd brought for dinner, into the house and called to his father but there was no answer. He went all around the house then finally he opened the door leading to the garage. He stood in the doorway, frozen and numb. His father had hung himself from the rafters.

Notoc's father had left his affairs in tidy order. Unlike with his mother's, Regna's death made everything free and clear: Regna's mortgage insurance did not have an anti-suicide clause so the house belonged to Notoc and Regna's life insurance policy, which also did not have an anti-suicide clause, paid him a large sum of cash.

The first thing Notoc did was to rehire the house and grounds keepers. He quit his job at the organic grocery store and dedicated his last months of summer to studying all sorts of things. He was driven, in those few months, to make sense of what had happened to his mother and father.

The Credit Collector

Fall came quickly for Notoc. He was off to Cambridge, Massachusetts. He was beginning his freshman year at M.I.T. to study biological engineering. He'd requested a single room in Bexley Hall. He got it. He requested that white dry erase boards be placed on every wall of the dorm room. He got it. He requested that all academic holds, including overload restrictions, be removed so that he could take any class he wanted and as many as he chose. He got it.

To say Notoc Kachuka was a genius was to say the Mozart was an excellent pianist: both are true yet are so grossly inadequate as to make them of little value. Notoc Kachuka had scored 36 out of 36 on his A.C.T. (American College Testing Program), he scored 2400 out of 2400 on his S.A.T. (Scholastic Aptitude Test) Reasoning Test, and he took the G.R.E. (the Graduate Record Exam) as well as the Subject Exam in Biochemistry, Cell and Molecular Biology only to score perfectly on both tests even though the G.R.E. was designed for people desiring to go to graduate school after having 4 years of college. He was 18 and had just finished high school.

At first there was some skepticism like perhaps Notoc Kachuka was a cheater. Maybe, like a card counter in gambling, he'd figured out the testing systems, which would mean that his perfection was route and not genius. But when Notoc interviewed at MIT, that theory was quickly dismissed. It was dismissed almost as quickly as the offer was made that should Notoc require anything, anything at all, to just speak to his advisor and the school would make sure it happened if it was, at all, within their legal abilities.

The first thing Notoc did was to sign up for his classes:

Biophysical Chemistry and Biophysical Chemistry Techniques,

Molecular Principles of Biomaterials,

Materials and Processes for Microelectromechanical Devices and Systems,

Design of Medical Devices and Implants,

Introduction to Biological Engineering Design,

Foundations of Algorithms and Computational Techniques in Systems Biology,

Biomaterials—Tissue Interactions,

Cell Matrix Mechanics, and

Molecular Principles of Biomaterials.

Other than his Intro to Bio Engineering Design, which Notoc took for fun, the rest of his course load was graduate level. And, considering a full load for the average really intelligent person at MIT was 4 graduate courses, Notoc was taking double. The professors and graduate students were less than enthusiastic. To them, it felt a bit like showboating, and they made the argument that education wasn't just about who could get the best scores but it was a process and it had a standard operating procedure and that there was value in jumping through the proper hoops. Even though the head of the department was in agreement with them, he was unable to do anything about it. He'd been informed, by those superior to him, that Notoc Kachuka was to be given full access to whatever he wished.

After this defeat some of the professors but most of the graduate students reacted with the attitude of "Fine, let him take the courses. He's going to fall flat on his face." Unfortunately, for them, this did not prove the case. In fact, rather to the contrary, he was, academically, the leader. So they resorted to other techniques, like making fun and ostracizing. This had no effect on Notoc whatsoever. Notoc Kachuka had three interests: learning all there was to learn at MIT, training at Zesiger, and understanding two, and only two, art pieces.

The second thing Notoc Kachuka had done when he got to MIT was to take the 90 minute Sculpture Tour. It was the first time in his life he'd seen many of those artist's works, but it was the art of Henry Moore and Alexander Calder that absolutely haunted Notoc. He just knew that there was some truth in them and that if he worked hard enough they'd reveal to him a key element to his understanding. Notoc found this part of his education at MIT the most challenging. The courses were interesting. Fun even. He enjoyed them immensely. He learned mostly from books and his room in Bexley showed it.

The white boards, as the semester wore on, remained white and the few graduate students who, out of curiosity, ventured to his room wondered why they were there at all though none dared ask. The fact was, Notoc had a sort of threatening aura about him. Maybe it was his eyes. Not the color, for to many it seemed they could not recall the color of his eyes, but the intensity. It was unnatural that a boy of his age, just 19 years old, should be so piercingly bright. When someone spoke it was as if every word was being processed by a supercomputer or by an alien. The grad students called him ET. Notoc understood. He was different. And his parents had taught him that being different was a deadly thing, which meant he was deadly. He was like a ghost, dead but amidst them, and so he understood their attempts to deal with his presence by making jokes or fun. They had to cope with him as death…just as he'd had to cope with his parents' deaths. In fact, Notoc envied them. He wished he could have used the coping mechanism of humor, but that was one thing inaccessible to him. He was serious. He was focused and he was a genius.

The head of Notoc's department was required to report his progress to the Dean, who was then obliged to report it to National Security. Notoc's room was searched. There was nothing but stacks and stacks of texts. When asked by two men in nice suits about the whiteboards, Notoc replied that when he first came to MIT he was under the impression that he'd be working really hard to keep his grades up and so he wanted the whiteboards in order to do his calculations.

"But," he continued, "Since I've found the coursework here to be entertaining versus challenging, I have no need of the whiteboards other than for, as you can see," Notoc pointed to a poster of a girl in a bikini and a poster of Mt. Everest with the slogan, 'No goal is too high when you've properly prepared yourself for it through hard work.'"

The men confiscated his computer. They asked if Notoc had any other electronic devices, "Like a cell phone or MP3," one of the men clarified. Notoc smiled, "Nope. Since my parents died I don't have anyone who needs to get hold of me. And, I might add, it's amazing how expensive they are."

Later that night, long after the men left, Notoc drew the curtains. He fastened the Velcro he'd attached to the edges so that no light could penetrate his room—or escape. He taped all along the edge of his door. Then he removed the light switch cover to reveal the secondary switch he'd installed. The room was filled with black light and his calculations came to life.

The Credit Collector

A few weeks after the government men had taken Notoc Kachuka's computer, two different, smartly dressed men, returned it and apologized for the inconvenience. Notoc ran a complete diagnostic. It looked clean. "But," he thought, "I smell a rat." Notoc copied, by hand and with a ballpoint pen, the computer files into composition notebooks. It didn't take him long. He was a fast writer. Then he configured a rerouting application that actively searched biomedical journals every 15 minutes. To Notoc, that computer was dead. Even though he couldn't find the rat, he knew that his computer had been tampered with and so all of his work, from then on, would be done by hand and most cloaked by the light of blackness.

Just what Notoc was working on was a topic of conversation amongst the graduate students. There was a faction, small to be sure, that was convinced that Notoc was a government spy sent to monitor all of their works. Amongst the more rational, this was viewed not only as paranoid but a little crazy. Neither conditions being altogether foreign to the people who succeeded in bioengineering.

The standing joke, whenever an obviously mentally handicapped person was seen, the students laughed and pointed, "There a bio-en."

To which another would reply, "Or mathematician!"

This made them split their sides. There was, to the credit of a branch of psychology, a measure of truth to this, obviously, idiotic observation: highly creative and/or highly intelligent people as a cohort had been found to exhibit a statistically relevant higher percentile of mental illness. The genius/madman scenario made famous by literature and art had been proven, by science, to be—by degrees—true. And many of his colleagues believed Notoc fit this bill.

Notoc's first semester ended with an unsurprising 4.0, straight As. By the end of his second course-heavy semester with difficult subjects, Notoc had taken all the classes he wanted to take so he scheduled an appointment, by special request, for his department head and the Dean to meet him at his residence—at night.

This was highly unusual, procedurally, but both agreed and met Notoc in his room. Both looked at the empty whiteboards, the stacks of books and composition notebooks then looked at each other.

"Listen," Notoc began, "I am through with MIT. You have been great to me and have given me all the freedom I needed. But as you know, I have taken the most difficult courses you have to offer and they were not difficult for me. In fact, at the risk of sounding egotistical, they were rather easy. Please believe me that I'm not trying to be disrespectful it's just that I must continue with my own work. It is of the utmost importance."

The Dean, unaccustomed to being spoken to in such a manner, especially by a first-year student, was insulted, "What makes you think that this school is not challenging enough for you. You've only just started. Maybe this course of study is too easy for you. Did you ever think of that!"

The head of Notoc's department pulled on the Dean's sleeve. The two met by the door. The head whispered, "I know for a fact that my department is the most challenging in the school."

"That's a little presumptuous, don't you think?"

"No. Just true."

"What about physics, mathematics, Lasers for crying out loud!"

"No. Ours is the most rigorous I assure you." Then the head whispered to such a reduction that the Dean had to, literally, bend an ear to the head's lips, "Ours is the program the government is interested in. In other words, if a student shows promise in mathematics or physics, they are referred to our program. Most of these recruits fail out because it's so hard. Some do make it but, in the end, all of them will work for the government."

The Dean, trying to save face, grumbled, "I know about *that*!"

They both turned to Notoc.

"Is there anything we can do for you, Notoc?" the Dean asked.

"You can let me have unrestricted access to testing laboratories."

"I don't think we can do that."

"And," Notoc continued, "I don't want anyone to have access to the laboratory but me. I don't need any assistants and if you can't do this for me I am sure I can find a university that can."

The Dean pulled the head's sleeve and whispered, "What do we do?"

The head said, "Notoc, you are very bright. But having a laboratory is more than just academics. It can be a liability to the community and so we must know what you are up to if you want us to seriously consider your request."

"Okay," Notoc closed the blinds and sealed the door. The Dean and the department head both looked at each other. There were always urban legends about students who'd gone mad and slain their teachers. The Mad Genius Syndrome. But as soon as Notoc switched off the light the head of the department scurried around Notoc's calculations like an excited white lab mouse in a maze. And, just like the mice, he found himself almost immediately lost. When he asked Notoc to help him come through his own understanding in order to exit the Labyrinth Notoc, being the consummate scientist, said no. The head of the department, in manners resembling a small child on their birthday after seeing the pile of wrapped boxes on the table just waiting to be opened, grabbed not only the Dean's sleeve but entire arm and shook it, so violently, up and down that the Dean, forcefully, pulled away.

The head chattered, "We must give it to him! We must! This is absolutely fantastic!"

The Dean stared wide-eyed because of the head at the black-lit equations and had not even the slightest clue what it all meant.

The government was called in. They photographed Notoc's walls. They confiscated Notoc's computer again in addition to his composition notebooks. Three days later Notoc was given his own laboratory.

For Notoc, having government officials searching and seizing became routine even though they never came at regular times. One morning he'd come to his lab and find his computers gone. One afternoon, in the middle of working out equations, they'd come wearing their nice suits and neat haircuts, including the women, and carry off his computers. He laughed every time because he knew what, obviously, they didn't. That the greatest computer, the fastest and most competent computer with regard to multiple computations, was something that they could never confiscate: his brain.

Still, Notoc liked to have fun with them. One time he hacked into the restricted H.A.A.R.P. files and used some of their schematics for the ionosphere on a simulated brain. He even created bogus spreadsheets, graphs, and tables with half-expectation to be called before an investigative board to explain his actions. Not a peep. The computers were returned to him, as always, with all his data completely intact. Of course, sound waves were part of his research and brains were too, only it had nothing to do with projections and bulged space…it had to do with fat.

Notoc Kachuka was on the verge of making the greatest scientific discovery of all time…maybe even *for* all time. There was only one problem—his theory was missing something and this frustrated Notoc beyond belief for there had been nothing, nothing in the world, that had stumped him before. So he turned, first, to Alexander Calder.

Watching the sun apex the metal, how the two seemed to connect each other in traveling while remaining unconnected in body. He watched the sun's strange shadows, impermanence, move through the through permanence of the sculpture's skin. He noticed that in one the metal had degraded like arthritic change in a joint. He remembered watching a documentary on Alexander Calder's "Circus" but it wasn't the childlike posturing of the man that impressed him, it was his ability to use pneumatics, metal and his own energy by blowing, twisting, turning, to create something that could actually suspend belief. Notoc knew there was an answer to his own work within this art…he could feel that it was just out of reach. So he turned to Henry Moore.

It was a beautiful afternoon. Not too hot, not too cold. There was a slight breeze. It was pleasant. There were bugs, birds, and butterflies. There were lovers. Students, teachers and others, he took them all in. He was formulating his equations about living organisms when he arrived at Moore's *Three-Piece Reclining Figure.* He walked around and around it. Circling it, like the sun. Taking in every angle. He lay upon the ground. He crawled beneath and squinted to the sun. He climbed on top of the foot. He climbed on top of the mid-section. But he wanted to stand on top of its head: to see what the sun saw. Did he dare? It was forbidden, he was sure, even though students were always climbing on it and there were plenty of students and people all around. But he had to. He had something to figure out and perspective might be the key.

He was fast. He was an athlete. He knew he could make it, so he tried. Climbing to the metal's head proved more difficult than he'd imagined because the metal was quite warm. His sweating hands slipped. For every bit he went up he slid. What he thought would be a matter of seconds grew into an increment that began to draw a crowd. Some people started yelling, "Hey, get off that. You can't do that." Notoc knew he had no time. He thrust every bit of his energy into his limbs. He clamored. His legs swung round its neck like young school girls on the playground bars. He heard, "Listen guy. Get down from there." Notoc didn't look back. He could only see the top and how close it was. Notoc refused to use his energy to reply. He was almost there and he needed all the energy he had. Notoc tuned the world out. Everything was silent. He'd made it. He was standing on top of the *Reclining Figure's* head. He was on top of her. He looked up at the sun, directly, knowing it could change his vision…and then he looked down. It was then, that he saw more clearly than he'd understood *The Big Sail*: disparate things that are physically unconnected are not detached Physically. Physics was the Uniter in spite of every instinct, even ocular, telling the world it was divided. Finally, he was satisfied. However, climbing down proved a bit problematic for Notoc.

He hadn't accounted for the curvature upon descent. He hadn't accounted for the fact that he'd spent all his energy, physical and psychological, in ascent and discovery. Notoc, accepting his depletion, simply plunged to the ground only a foot or two in front of the campus police officer. The police officer who'd told him to get down. Notoc noticed how young the officers were, with their guns, and remembered thinking that same thing the night his father had called the police to his mother's secret storage unit.

The officer wrote Notoc's name in his notebook but before he left he added, "You know, you shouldn't be climbing on the sculptures."

Notoc replied, "I know. But I see other students doing it."

The officer scoffed, "Yeah, but that doesn't make it right. Besides, do you have any idea how much they had to sink into that one," he pointed to Moore's

Figure, "just because students like you climb all over it?"  He didn't wait for Notoc to reply, "A lot!  So keep off okay."

Notoc answered, "Yes."

But none of that mattered to Notoc: he had found what he'd been searching for.  Finally, his work would be complete.  From that moment on the pace Notoc assumed could only be described as fierce.  He worked day and night.  He slept in minutes not hours.  He never left his lab.  He didn't shower.  He drank from the sink…and other things too.  He didn't eat and would have collapsed had it not been for the government men who'd come to confiscate only to find Notoc in such a haggard and desperate condition that they phoned their supervisor for further instruction.  The Dean and the head of Notoc's department were contacted but when they tried to enter the lab Notoc screamed and ran towards with his arms flailing like a madman.  The government officials looked as if they were going to intervene, but the department head waived them off.  Tugging the Dean's arm and motioning to the officials, the four men quickly exited to the hallway.

"He's mad," the Dean cried.

"Perhaps," the head replied, "But sometimes mad is good."

One of the officials spoke up, "But sometimes it's bad."

The other confirmed, "This is true."

"Yes," the head said, "But what if, as I suspect, he's on the verge."

"You keep promising us this," the Dean cried, "But where are the results!  We can't even make sense of his data.  I half-think he's a lunatic not a visionary."

"We shall see," the head said, but even he appeared unsure.  "The one thing I know is that we must take care of him.  If I'm right, his body needs us to keep it going long enough for that brain to change the world."

"What do you need us to do?" the first official asked.

"Bring food, drinks, toilet paper, and some buckets.  From what I saw, in those brief moments, at least we can empty buckets."

"What kind of food?" the second official asked.

"All kinds. Junk, health, booze, water, soda, get as much variety as you can. He's going on pure instinct, so we need to make sure to give him what he needs even though he doesn't know he needs it."

"Coffee?"

"Don't be silly! Where the hell is he going to brew…oh never mind…yeah, get those cold bottled coffee things. Oh, and caffeine pills."

"What about sleeping pills?" the first official asked.

"Are you fucking crazy! No! No sleeping pills. We want him to work his fucking brains out okay! Okay! Now get all this quick. We don't have much time."

The officers came back, with the addition of ten more officers, with more food, drink, and booze than a regular person would be able to consume in a month. In all, the cost was probably close to a middle-salaried worker's monthly income. There were several bottles of 30-year single malt whiskey, brand-name vodka, and Champagne. There were foodstuffs and cheeses from around the world. There was caviar and oysters. There was SPAM and deviled ham, crackers, boxed cereal and boxes of milk needing no refrigeration of various flavors including 'Rootbeer Float.'

Just before the officials attempted to enter the room with the supplies the head of Notoc's department pulled them aside, "Listen, you must be as innocuous as possible. Put the things just inside the door as quickly as possible. Don't make eye contact. Don't attempt to get his attention. Just put the stuff down and get out. Are we clear?" They nodded in one fine-suited motion. The door was opened, the boxes deposited: it was like watching the 50-yard dash. And, to the head's ease, Notoc seemed not to have noticed a thing.

After the drop off, the ten official helpers left. The original two remained and sat, with the Dean and the head of the department on the floor of the hallway. It was now official. Notoc could not leave without being interviewed. It was obvious, he knew something and they needed to know what that was before he could be free to do as he willed.

But, after another hour, the Dean turned to the head and said, "Listen. If anything happens just call me. I need to get some sleep."

The three men sat in silence. The officials, it seemed, were trained in not talking. The head would have invited polite conversation but didn't for fear Notoc might hear them and it would interrupt his work. So the three sat. And sat.

Until finally, that niggling feeling the head had had that Notoc hadn't noticed the food drop off drove him to announce, "Listen, I'm just going to check on him. To make sure he gets something to eat and drink, okay?"

The officials nodded and remained.

The head slowly opened the door. His first venture into Notoc's lab had been so fast that he hadn't really had the chance to take it all in. This time, seeing Notoc across the room, scribbling on a board, talking to himself in low grunts, erasing and re-writing, obviously consumed, the head saw and experienced that place. The smell was best described as foul. That's what he noticed first. He covered his nose with his shirt collar. The room was all but dark except for the desk lamp Notoc had turned onto the board. The head wondered if Notoc was dangerous. Every so often there was a news story about a student who kills their teacher. This was the first moment he felt afraid. Yet something compelled him to move, continually, toward what would either redeem or destroy him. Closer and closer he drew, so close that he could see how Notoc's hair was sweated into masses and his hands were shaking as he wrote.

So close that when his voice spoke out, "Notoc?"

He almost hoped it would not be heard, but suddenly Notoc lunged toward him, grabbed him by his collar, lifted him up, bringing him eye-to-eye, as Notoc screamed, "Is this what you want! This!"

Notoc pointed to the board. The head looked and looked but could not see.

Notoc grabbed his head and shoved it against the board, pressing the head's nose into his fresh ink, "There! Can't you see it! YOU, the brilliant YOU! You can't see it!" Notoc broke out laughing. "You're all pathetic!"

He was screaming and laughing, hysterical, dancing around the head like a child at a party. The officials rushed in, but the head waved them out.

"Notoc," the head said, in a quietly deep voice. "You must eat now."

As if cast out of a spell, Notoc turned to the head. "You're…right," he said, then collapsed.

The head called to the officials who attempted to call an ambulance but the head forbade it. "He just needs something to eat." And so the head gave him a mouthful of very fine whiskey. It was miraculous! He perked right up. Like smelling salts and began ravishing everything the men had brought. Even the buckets, because it wasn't long before all the food came right back up. He'd gone long enough without. It would take him small bits to come back. So he had more whiskey and, over time, recovered enough to allow, rationally, the officials to clean out the sinks he'd been using as a toilet. But that was as far as it went. When the head suggested he go home and take a shower, get shaved, take a rest, Notoc grew fierce.

He would not leave his work unattended and no one, not the head or any government official, was to touch anything "Or," Notoc said, "I'll kill myself. And you will never know the secret because the final key is in here." And he pointed to his head.

Now the officials knew Notoc wouldn't kill himself. It was their job to make sure he couldn't. And they also knew that if the key was in his head, they'd either get it out the easy way or the hard way. But they also knew that Notoc didn't need to know that information just yet. There was still time for voluntary disclosure.

Meanwhile the head assured Notoc that no one would interfere his work and that his fatigue and malnourishment were making him paranoid. So Notoc agreed to take a bucket bath, in the lab, brushed his teeth, and put on deodorant: the officials had preemptively prepared for personal hygiene.

The whiskey was the first thing gone and not purely because of Notoc; the head liked good whiskey too. The officials were offered, but they refused 'being on duty' and so forth. The vodka loosened Notoc's lips. The head discovered the Notoc

Kachuka had done exactly what he'd predicted: he'd changed the world. He'd discovered a way to confiscate biological fat, transdermally.

Almost immediately, Notoc's lab was a buzz with the world's top scientists and secured by the Country's most vigilant. The newly-elected DemocraticRepublic government wasted no time nor spared any cost for the studying of Notoc's discovery. In fact, every animal testing facility in the country was put under lockdown and commanded to study Notoc's hypothesis. Gene studies: out the window. Toxic metals, pesticides: out the window. Even social science studies were shut down because their funding was siphoned to support Notoc's work. So, within a relatively short period of time, and across the nation from all the labs, and with acceptable variation, Notoc's hypothesis was proving correct. Within record time, human trials began and to speed up the process, the government released Federal funds for paying the humans subjects at twice the normal going rate. No one was turned away from the research. HIV, tuberculosis, alcoholic, drug addict, everyone qualified because their fat was as good as anyone else's. And, again, within record time, the human trials proved Notoc's hypothesis correct. The government pushed hard to have the hypothesis notarized into theory. Some scientists pushed back, but they simply either acquiesced or faced blackballing when it came to further research funding.

Notoc's *Theory of Fat Confiscation* was released to the world in a timely manner: at the TED (Technology, Education, Design) convention, in California, in Spring. It was, for Notoc, one of the loveliest places he'd ever been but not because of the warm weather, or the glitz of stores, but because his eyes gazed upon the most-lovely girl he'd ever seen. Then TED became not about fat but about discovering who she was. It did not take him long to find out, she was an animal behavior anthropologist who, ironically, was also from MIT and he uncovered this knowledge because she was slotted to speak immediately after him on the second day.

Following a lineup of hard-hitters: Jane Goodall, Stephen Hawking, Bill Gates, Temple Grandin, and Daniel Kraft, Notoc flat blew them out of the water. There was no technology after he spoke. There was no concern for autism, mosquitoes, or the small space between animals and man. Even the topic of bone marrow harvest, which Notoc found particularly interesting, fell mute. It was as if the world stood still—and very quiet. It was as if they could not quite take in what it meant but understood that it was going to change the world. There was both awe and an aura of doom, though no one could specifically identify why they felt as they did. This did, for Notoc, run contrary to what he'd expected.

His whole goal was to save his country from its greatest threat: obesity. Painfully, to him, it was obvious that physical education, nutrition awareness, and all the fancy gyms and personal trainers in the Nation were failing. Childhood obesity was threatening the very core of America for many reasons such as co-morbidities and inability to serve the military in times of need. He was, he felt, blessed by God to discover a way for fat to be extracted, what he called confiscation, because it was the sewing of what had been reaped. A land grown fat from prosperity. A land too rich. A country that was entitled to seize what had been appropriated to the public: too much biological wealth. Notoc had more plans regarding this, but they were secret. For now, at TED, in his 18 minutes, he explained how he'd successfully developed a non-invasive technique for removing fat transdermally, or through the skin.

"The first thing I had to develop was a hybridized iron molecule." Above Notoc's head flashed a giant, 3-D model of the element he coined, *Fe-Regna*, or FeR. "As you can see, instead of the traditional Fe configuration there is a minute interstitial space. A tube, if you may, that is the result of reverse polarity magnetism made possible by the hybridization process. FeR is not able to participate in normal iron uptake therefore it circulates in the bloodstream and is, eventually, excreted. Studies so far have not shown any deleterious effect of FeR. The interesting thing about this new element is that the very thing that allows its creation, polarity, is exactly what facilitates its ability to adhese to cell walls when in the presence of alternating magnetism. Once this adhesion is secured," another image flashed above Notoc's head, showing what looked like little nuts (like those plumbers use in conjunction with bolts) all lined up along a transdermal blood vessel. Then a slow-image film showed how the circulating FeR, after receiving the electromagnetic stimulus, immediately collected on the wall, like children in a schoolyard upon hearing the recess bell. "Once the FeR is established in the bloodstream, a series of high-frequency sound waves are administered to the skin surface which caused the subcutaneous fat to warm and become more soluble. This also increases the blood flow to the surface area covered with FeR, which, ultimately, increases fat uptake."

Another film section showed this process. "Finally, through a series of proprietary chemical reactions, the fat, preferentially 'clings' to the chemicals outside the body versus remaining in the bloodstream." Another film showed radiographic-stained fat cells, literally, exiting through the skin via the FeR.

This was his entire speech. It was less than 15 minutes. The entire room was silent. No camera clicks. No murmurings. Notoc, holding his head in a fixed position, moved his eyes around the room. The lights were bright. He couldn't see well but he knew the room was full. It was always full. It was deafeningly full of quietness. His voice broke, considering he was not even old enough to drink, beneath the strain, "Thank you," he said and exited to not one applaud.

In the wings stood the woman he'd seen, the woman he'd longed to know. She looked at him with horror in her eyes. Her dark eyes, her dark hair, her beautiful profile. He wanted to ask what he'd done that was so wrong, but the MC (Master of Ceremonies), after recovering herself, announced her name, "Misha Goldstein on the anthropology of canine behavior."

For the life of him, Notoc couldn't imagine what he'd done that had, obviously, offended her so he waited in the wings and listened to her speech. She spoke eloquently about the history of dog behavior and what potential impact this understanding had for contemporary dogs and society. It was not the hard science that Notoc admired, but he thought it quaint, mainly because he felt, with his very being, her loveliness.

When she finished her speech, Notoc gave, he was sure, the audience's most earnest applause. He clapped so hard his hands stung. He even though he may have bruised the hamate bone from his enthusiasm, but it made no diffrence to Misha. She wouldn't even look at him as she stormed by. But Notoc wasn't one to be dissuaded easily. Misha noticed the officials following her, because they were following Notoc, and this did not improve his likeability. She began to walk more brusquely. Notoc increased his pace. The officers responded likewise. She looked over her shoulder. She began to run. Notoc pursued. The same for the officers.

"Wait," Notoc yelled. His time in the lab, discovering, had left him weakened.

Misha turned and faced him, a good room's-length away, "Leave me alone you creep!" Then she dashed. Her athleticism impressed Notoc even more.

The officers, in unison, asked if he'd like them to apprehend her. It was tempting. He wanted to. He didn't have the strength to say no.

That's how Misha and Notoc met, in a room, surrounded by government officials and nothing but contempt issuing from her eyes for him. But Notoc knew that if only she'd visit with him for a little bit, if she'd just listen, she'd realize that he wasn't a bad guy. What he didn't know, what he couldn't understand, was that Misha being the one person he longed to love, could never love someone who forced against the will, of her…or of her people. Yet, it was clear to Misha, after having been sequestered for 10 hours of listening to nothing but Notoc talking about his parents, their deaths, his research, that if she didn't go along with Notoc's agenda, she just might never be freed. And in spite of the fact that every fiber of her hated him for creating this situation for her, she needed freedom more. She acted. She asked questions. She feigned interest. And when he asked if he could call her, she gave him her phone number. The officials checked its validity on the spot. He accepted it with all smiles and hopefulness. He just knew, if she only took the time to get to know him, she'd like him. She was let go. She flushed her phone down the toilet, and—to the embarrassment of the officials—seemed to disappear off the face of the earth.

The Credit Collector

Having returned to his laboratory at MIT, Notoc was kept under lock and key while he worked on a way to harness the fat he'd extracted in a form that could be easily applied to large numbers of people. This was not an easy task. The first, most obvious, collection system for dripping fat was simply a bucket. This not only proved messy but wholly ineffective as the fat simply glided over the skin until it amassed into rivulets and this, overall, was determined to be a rather disgusting procedure. A squeegee approach was applied next. Though it had better results than natural pooling, the overall 'disgusting' factor, as reported by the candidates, remained too high for it to be a serious consideration. The head of Notoc's department suggested using a towel to "mop it up" and to this Notoc heartily laughed, but only for a moment. Then he kicked the head out and began his second journey into the creative madness of science.

Having begun to recognize Notoc's genius 'signals,' the head had the government officers, who now never left Notoc's side, order up food, booze—the gamut just like before—to prepare for a long siege. It turned out that extracting the fat transdermally, even though this was itself a genius breakthrough, was the easy part. The collection system flat had Notoc stumped, that is, until the head suggested mopping.

Notoc thought of mops. Cotton. Absorbency and fats. Saturation, glycerol, binders—carboxylic acid. He drew configurations of fat with carbons, the OH (hydroxyl), Cis and Trans, Alpha and Omega and suddenly he thought of soap. It was at that moment when something utterly unexpected occurred: Misha.

After having been thoroughly searched by the government officials, Misha Goldstein was allowed exactly five minutes to speak with Notoc Kachuka. The only problem was that in those first five minutes neither of them seemed to know what to say to the other. Those five minutes were spent with "ums" and "uhs" and awkward silences that seemed to last forever. That was, until the government officials came to escort Misha out of the lab. Then, to Notoc's understanding, the time had flown by and more, he was unwilling to let her go. "No!" he shouted at the officials. Even though they tried to force Misha out, Notoc forced harder, "I won't work if she doesn't stay." It was the magical phrase, like Ali Baba's 40 thieves' "Open Sesame" (or in the original vernacular, "Simsim"). Unfortunately for them both, the extension did little to improve their interpersonal communications.

An hour went by. Misha got restless and started looking around the lab. She could see that her presence, or maybe what she might observe, seemed to be agitating the government officials.

"Don't worry about them," Notoc assured her, "They're pretty harmless once you get to know them. That one, on the left, is Jeff. He was a football player until he blew out his knee so he went to medical school."

"And he's doing what now?"

"Working for the government."

"Why all the security?"

"You heard my lecture at TED. You know exactly."

"That's what I've come to talk to you about."

This, visibly, hurt Notoc. For in his deepest wishes, he'd hoped she'd come to see him.

"Listen," Misha continued, "You musn't continue this work."

"Are you crazy!"

The officials took a step closer to the couple.

"Shhh," Misha cautioned.

Notoc obeyed. The officials relaxed their stance.

"I know you don't know me but I can tell you that what you're doing can do harm."

"What I'm doing," Notoc spat, indignantly, "is providing a win-win situation. Fat people will become thinner and healthier. Have you had your head in the sand? What is the most pressing pandemic in our country? Obesity! And not just because of all the resources obese people consume but all the secondary health costs. It's ruining our country."

"Yes. You're right, but have you considered the larger ramification?"

"In fact, I have. And, if I could only figure out how to store the excised fat…" Notoc was getting so involved in his own thoughts that he, accidentally, kicked over Misha's purse. A menstrual pad fell out on the floor but before Misha could put it back Notoc grabbed it, "That's it!" and without thinking, in the excitement of "Eureka!" he kissed her and cried, "Listen Misha, I don't have time right now. I think I've figured it out so you'd better go."

This was all the officials needed to hear but before they'd reached her, Misha cried, "Let me help you!"

Taken aback, Notoc asked, "How?"

"Well," Misha stammered, "I don't know exactly, but two great minds are better than one."

If it hadn't have been for the fact that Notoc liked Misha, he would have quickly set her straight on her misconception. He waived the officials off and Misha and Notoc began a series of complex chemical equations involving sodium and potassium hydroxides, sphagnum, and cellulose.

Two days ensued where Misha was just as feverish as Notoc. Notoc was, duly, impressed not only by her insights but by her stamina. He'd never met another person who could become so enthralled with science as he. And he'd never, in a million years, have thought Misha would prove his theory that all the world's population, relative to him, were idiots particularly because of the lecture she'd given at TED. But there she was, in his lab, proving herself to be his match, scientifically, his set, enthusiastically, and the game, love: love.

When the frenzy had settled, Misha Goldstein and Notoc Kachuka had designed a thin papyraceous-looking textile that attracted fat, absorbed fat, but completely dissolved in, and bound itself to, water. Neither of them could have known that in a different MIT lab another brilliant scientist was perfecting the methylation of human fat and, unbeknownst to all but a few government officials, a group of sworn Patriot scientists, sworn to absolute secrecy, were developing a cost-effective method for refining it.

The Credit Collector

Notoc and Misha worked together for one whole week, day in and out all the night through. The first night, after solving the absorption problem, Misha lined up four chairs.

"What are you doing?" Notoc asked.

"Making a bed."

Notoc went over to the government officials. In less than 30 minutes two rollaway beds entered the lab complete with sheets, cased pillows, and comforters.

"Nice to have friends in high places," Misha said.

"Would you like some whiskey?" Notoc answered.

"Sure."

The two lay beside each other with the lights off and in quiet other than the occasional shift of a foot, or cough, or sneeze of the officials. It must have been almost morning when Misha whispered, "Are you asleep?"

"Not a chance," Notoc replied.

"What are you?"

"A scientist."

"No. I mean what nationality are you?"

"American."

"Oh give me a break!"

"Okay. My grandparents were Indian."

"What tribe?"

"Indian Indian."

"I see."

"What about you?"

"Isn't it obvious? With a name like Goldstein?"

"No, not really."

"I'm a Jew."

"Oh. I see. I've never understood that."

"What do you mean?"

"I mean the cultural-religious unity/separation. I am Indian but I might be a Jew but not a Jew at the same time."

"True. But, being a Jew, I still don't understand it. I'm not a good Jew."

"Why?"

"Because my parents were communists."

"Is that allowed?" He smiled, then poked her arm.

"Don't be an ass!" There was a long silence. "By the way, how did you come up with FeR?"

"We go from communism to Iron in span of two sentences!"

"I'm a non-linear thinker."

Notoc laughed, "I can see that. Well, FeR wasn't that hard…" Notoc was setting up the moment, making her wait, "…for a GENUIS!"

"I see modesty is a strength for you."

"Never heard of it. Anyway, I was looking that Calder, you know Alexander Calder, the great sculptor?"

"I know Calder, alright. FeR?'

"So I'm looking at the Calder here on campus, looking at all that metal, seeing how it stands in relation to itself, but that was only the first key. The real understanding came from Henry Moore's piece and only when I was standing on top of its head."

"King of the world kind of thing?"

"Actually, yes. I realized that Iron is the King, biologically speaking."

"What! What about calcium, potassium, sodium and ionic transmission?"

"Oh those are important too, in fact vitally important—as minions."

Misha laughed at the way he pronounced minions more like mini-ions than onions.

"Yes," Notoc continued, "Iron was the King and all the others were slaves."

"Okay, Notoc. Let's just agree to disagree."

"But that was only the beginning. It was from the Moore that I came to fully understand how interstitial space is, or can be, irrelevant based upon structure or, better-phrased, sculpture. That's what FeR is. It's a chemical sculpture. And because of it's unique shape, it functions in an amazing way."

"Another topic. TED." Misha piped.

"Okay. What about it?"

"Did you hear who got the TED prizes?"

"I couldn't care a less. Who?"

"You won't believe it! Woowoos! That's who. They're the ones that got all that money for their research. Whackos with no hardcore science."

Notoc laughed, really laughed.

"What are you laughing at?"

"Well," he said out loud but thought to himself, 'Don't say it…keep it to yourself," then blurted out, "Look who's talking."

Misha rolled over, turning her back to Notoc.

"I'm sorry Misha, but it's true. I mean the anthropology of dogs. Come on!"

Misha rolled back over and sat straight up, "Oh yeah, well my research is being used this very moment by the same government goons who are at your lab right now so whose work is all-important, not just yours!" she cried.

"Really?" Notoc was surprised. "Work on dogs has government funding? Do you get all these things too," Notoc pointed around the room to the food, booze and supplies.

"Well," Misha softened, "Not exactly."

"Do you have guards watching you twenty-four-seven?"

"No."

"Then my work is more important. New topic. What would you have done if you'd won the TED prize?"

"Eliminate idiots like you!" this time Misha smiled and poked Notoc. "Did you have to fill out the card asking you what you'd request, the Wish, if you'd won?"

"Yep. You?"

"Yep. What did you say?"

"I wrote, 'That the whole world, voluntarily, excised debt. You know, treat it like the cancer it is and cut it off from the body of humanity.'"

"That's what you wrote?"

"Something like that."

"I bet that's *exactly* what you wrote. So you're a poet too, huh. A regular Renaissance man."

"Something like that."

"But that wish is kind of a wasted wish isn't it? I mean, The Serpent is all over the news. It's basically done what you asked for."

"True. But the World didn't do it voluntarily. That's the difference."

"Yeah. Do you suppose the creditors have figured a way around it yet?"

"Never!" Notoc boasted.

But they had.

The Credit Collector

Day after day Notoc and Misha worked together, perfecting the absorption system of the fat-collection material. The problem they were encountering was saturation. If they applied their absorption "paper" only to the areas where the released fat pooled the paper quickly became saturated. To use this as a collection procedure would mean that either the person or an employee would have to remove the saturated swatch and replace it with a fresh one approximately every five minutes for the entirety of the collection process. The collection process, Notoc determined, could be safely operated on an obese person for between 30-60 minutes per day, depending on the level of obesity, without jeopardizing the person's vital, fat-based biological processes such as brain function. With the collection swatch, this would mean removal and reapplication of between 6 and 12 swatches, per person, per procedure therefore making it functionally unfeasible. Misha suggested creating paper suits out of the absorption material. This was their first true collaborative event. The government officials brought in sewing machines and conventional thread. "Of course," Notoc added, "The thread is not viable. It will not properly digest." Misha understood what he was saying. So before they began sewing, they worked on developing a digestible adhesive. Obstacles. That was what Notoc and Misha's days were filled with. Their nights, however, were a different matter. That was when they lay together, separated by the two wooden ledges of their canvas cots that pressed up against each other, and talked.

On one of these nights Misha asked Notoc, again, about his name.

"My name is part of a history I know nothing about. My father was American. That was it. Just like my grandfather."

"What about your mother?"

"She was as American as you get."

"What do you mean?"

"Blonde, blue-eyed, beautiful."

"I see."

"What do you mean?"

"Aryan."

"It's not a Jewish thing alright."

Notoc turned his back to her. It was nighttime that confused him, that irritated him, but mostly that frustrated him. "What does she want from me," he would ask himself at moments like this, with his back to her like a castle's fortification. "Why does she always have to push!" he'd feel his heart beating faster like a heifer running for its life from a mountain lion. "All I want to do is to get to know her," he'd rant to himself, "and all she wants to do is fight." Then, with all his thoughts vented out, he'd roll back over—usually to find she'd turned her back to him and knowing that there was only one thing that would unstop, like a plugged toilet, the massive obstruction between them.

"I'm sorry," Notoc said.

Sometimes it would work right away and Misha would roll back over. Notoc discovered that these easy victories were because she'd been thinking, while her back was turned, of the things she wanted to say to him the next chance she got. Other times Notoc's "I'm sorries" would be met with cold silence and no matter how many times he repeated them, she maintained her defenses in tact. Notoc, eventually, realized that these binds were the deep, heavy, dense plugs—the ones that could not be easily undone nor were, really, of his construction. And, being always the intellectual problemsolver, he came to understand that these issues required snaking. A slow, twisting, turning of a firm but flexible sort with length and duration that was able to reach down to where the problem was. Notoc, having spent many nights by then with Misha, realized that his quip about Misha's heritage would require this technique.

"Misha," he said, "I'm sorry that I what I said hurt you. But, honestly, my mother's physical characteristics and my family's emphasis on being American had nothing to do with being anti-Semitic."

Her back remained turned. A different twist was needed.

"Okay. Well, if you define anti-Semitism as condemning a race of people based on physical characteristics then, perhaps, my father and grandfather's views were anti-Semitic in nature because they were anti-Indian."

He waited. He watched the profile of her ribs rise and fall. She was crying. But her position remained unmoved.

"Alright. Maybe my mother's physical attributes being "ideal" meant that, subconsciously, my father was a Nazi. Is that what you want me to say?"

Misha, violently, rolled over and faced him, "Is that what I WANT you to say! How could you think I want you to say any such thing!" and she flung herself back to her original position. Her ribcage was heaving, only not with tears but breaths of anger.

"I give up!" Notoc yelled and turned, summarily, his back, once again, to her.

The government officials did not budge, not even an inch, for they'd gotten quite used to the fightings between Notoc and Misha. And, having gotten used to them, knew that this fight was not over. The next hour, however, was still and for this they were thankful especially for Daniel Shays, the former football player, who happened to be on duty this particular night.

Daniel Shays was a large man. He'd been an offensive lineman and one of the largest of them. In his prime, he'd not been pure muscle, but close. After his knee gave out, he leaned out. There was no need in life to carry around so much weight, he determined. So he stopped eating so much, started running more, decided to invest the money he'd made playing sports into an education that would slate him for a government position. And, it just so happened, one of his former coaches knew a guy who knew a guy that hooked him up for a tryout. He got on the fast-track because his athletic background had taught him tactics and, before he knew it, he'd been assigned to one of his department's most promising ventures: Notoc Kachuka.

But Daniel Shays wasn't a science-kind-of-guy and he found his days at the lab pretty uninspiring. Most times he daydreamed of glory days, of crushing bones, of battling his enemies head-on and with victory either confirmed or denied with every hit. This job, Daniel decided, had its victories too—only sometimes it was hard to tell the differences between them and defeat. And, Daniel came to understand in himself, that conflict between muscle was much-preferred to what he witnessed between Notoc and Misha. It was true: Daniel had never had a meaningful relationship—though his former occupation had the perquisite of attracting fine mating specimens—but, after watching the two scientists, he decided that a nice, quiet girl was the girl for him. And this decision, he realized, was the direct result of the stalemates, the dead silences, that happened on nights just like this.

The morning came early and with the announcement by Misha that, once the collection system was viable, she was "out of here." Notoc, having slept very little replied, emphatically, "Fine." Daniel sniggered. His relief was due at 8:00am and he suspected it was going to be a 'rough' day in the lab.

There is a certain irony in science. Sometimes the most obvious answers prove terribly elusive. Misha requested an industrial-sized roll of tissue paper and a box of sewing pins, which both arrived in short order. She'd printed off a suit pattern from the net, laid it out on the tissue paper, pinned the pattern in place, cut and began sewing, on the machine, a tissue paper suit.

Notoc, on the other hand, was researching adhesives. The synthetics interfered with the biodegradability of the absorption paper, which meant elastomers, thermoplastics, emulsions and thermosets (expoxy, polyurethane, cyanoacrylate and acrylic polymers) were out of the question. The natural adhesives weren't proving much more friendly. Animal glue, from horse teeth, was not only difficult to procure but the organic material preferentially reacted to the dimethyl sulfoxide (DMSO) in the transdermal fat proprietary blend which meant that the fat cells didn't even make it to the collection site. Notoc found this also to be true of the albumin of human blood both in regard to ethicality and reactivity with the DMSO. Casein, a protein from milk, was ethical and it didn't react as strongly with the DMSO so it was proving to be one of the most promising candidates until Notoc discovered that something about it was altering the acid-base state of the chemical environment thereby preventing the transdermal fat reaction.

Misha was sewing away. She'd even started humming a tune. The worse Notoc's experiments went, the more her voice irritated him and the casein study was his final straw.

"Don't you ever shut up!" he cried, throwing a beaker into the sink, where it shattered into noisy, tinkling pieces.

Misha stopped sewing her fourth suit. The three she'd completed were strewn across a table, each with different features.

Notoc stormed over to the food. He tore open a candy bar, shoved the whole thing in his mouth, then grabbed a bottle of vodka, and washed the sweet goo down with its fire. Unfortunately, it was a nutty candy bar with oozy caramel and the vodka's heat made his throat involuntarily swallow hard. The nutty gloop stuck in his throat and he found himself choking but before the government officials even had time to figure out what had happened, Misha had put her arms around him, thrust her fists into his solar plexis, and Notoc vomited.

"Drink this," she said, handing him the bottle of vodka.

"No thanks. I'm not in the mood now."

"That wasn't a request." She pushed the bottle into his hand and tipped its bottom up. Notoc drank. She made him drink again. And again. After the fifth swig she relented.

"Listen," she said, sitting beside him, "I'm sorry but I don't think you understand me at all."

Notoc laughed, "Yeah." His head was beginning to tingle. "I'm getting that."

"But," she looked him in the eye, "I want you to."

It was the first time Notoc felt there was hope for something more, something greater than science. His heart flopped, he dared not speak for fear of ruining the moment, and his throat gulped.

Misha smiled, grabbed his hand with hers and said, "Let's get this adhesive issue worked out."

That was it. Notoc Kachuka was officially, head-over-heals, in love with Misha Golstein.

The rest of the afternoon the two worked in synch with each other and it was beautiful, like dancing, the way they countered each other's leads. Notoc explained what he'd done and what he'd encountered. Misha added that it was her belief, and love for animals, that the bioadhesives resulting from them were not viable because they were unethical.

Notoc didn't argue, though his mind did for a brief time.

"We need," Misha asserted, "to consider the nature of our absorption system in relation to the trandermal fat process. I think the key is that the cellular basis for the swatches we've created, so far, are purely vegetable."

"Yes," Notoc confirmed, "But vegetable adhesives aren't near as durable as animal."

This was when Misha led Notoc away from the chemistry and over to apparel.

"See," she said, lifting up the third suit, "I believe we can design a suit out of our absorptive material that would collect the fat but require very little adhesive. In fact, the only adhesive required would be right here," she pointed, "at the collar."

Notoc looked at the article Misha held up. To him it looked like a giant ball. In fact, it looked a lot like a garbage sack with a drawstring at the top.

"So you're saying that a person would put this on?"

"Yes."

"And saturate it with fat. And then take it off?"

"Yes and the only area that has to have adhesive is this seam where the drawstring is."

"And what about the drawstring?"

"Make it out of the same absorptive material."

"Why not make sewing machine thread out of the material then?"

Misha dropped her head, "I tried. But it wasn't durable enough to be sewn with."

"Which means we're back to the adhesive issue."

"Yes."

Notoc left Misha with her suit and without a single word as to whether he approved or not. Disappointed, but ever the scientist herself, she returned to chemistry. Eventually, left no other choice, they resorted to starch with borax. It dissolved easily in water, but because of the sodium tetraborate decahydrate Notoc had to adjust his proprietary blend to accommodate the equation and this did not make him happy—at all.  And it wasn't a quick fix either, *but there was just no other way.*

Sometimes a lifetime of science can be spent in microscopic adjustment.  The grand breakthroughs almost seem easy, the "Eurekas!" that the world sees as important matters not nearly as much as a chemical tweaking here and a dose-adjustment there.  Human relations are like this too, at least, that was what Notoc was discovering on one night, in particular.

"Misha," he asked, "Why don't you want me to do my work?"

Misha sighed, "It is an ethical paradox."

"How so?"

"Because it creates a terrible conflict of interest.  You're delivering to a government that is entrusted to protect the best interests of its People, a system that enables them to harvest the fat from its people."

"But that's not what my work is designed for."

"True.  That's why it is an ethical paradox.  But you and I both know that great science works for both good and evil."

"But this will help people suffering from obesity."

"And this will help the government or you wouldn't have government officials and sponsorship.  Haven't you even once asked yourself what *they* might want it for?"

"That sounds very conspiracy theory to me."

"Maybe so.  But it makes me sick that the only way we can collect your fat is using soap technology."

"So?"

"Nazis!  Jews!  Have you no sense of History!"

"Oh God, here were go again."

135

"Leave God out of it. I'm talking about human fat used to make soap."

"What?"

"Oh my Gosh! Notoc, how can you not know! How can you be so blind. It's frightening, you're frightening, really…to not know."

"I'm sorry OKAY! I'm not some bleeding heart liberal that makes our government out to be the Boogey Man. I happen to think that my government does a lot of good for a lot of people."

"That's true. And the Nazis did a lot of good for a lot of people too."

"I thought you were a communist."

Misha sighed. It signaled the end of the round. Notoc knew he'd effectively ended the conversation that was, for him, taking him places he didn't want to think about. "Besides," he rather palely added, "We've got work to do so we'd better get some sleep."

That night a thunderstorm clapped throughout the sky. Lightening danced from cloud to cloud. The large windows of the laboratory were like the old-fashioned drive-in movie screens to a heavenly display of light, power, and the potential for destruction. Every so often the windows would shake. Every so often, Misha clung to her blanket and cried softly and to herself, thinking about her grandparents and how they'd died because of the pogroms their government descried yet did nothing to eradicate.

She whispered, half hoping Notoc was asleep and would not hear and half longing for him to understand, "The Communist movement was filled with Jewish intellectuals because commune-ism is based on the ancient Jewish laws of Sabbatical and Jubilee, which is why it was so fiercely anti-capitalistic. The Christian capitalists violently opposed commune-ism because of its condemnation of worshipping money. But it wasn't the Christians or capitalists that killed my grandparents. It wasn't even the fact that they were sentenced to forced labor and starved to death in a Siberian Gulag, that's not what killed my grandparents. What killed them was having to witness how God's laws had been corrupted in order to create a fascist dictatorship."

There was a long silence. Misha sighed. "He's asleep," she thought.

"How did your family survive?" he asked.

"My grandparents knew it was only a matter of time before they were arrested. My grandmother, being old herself and never having had children, never suspected she'd get pregnant, but she did. They hid it from everyone. Her only goal was to have the child survive. They used every connection they could and made an arrangement with a young Russian couple. The day my mother was born the Russian woman took her. Two weeks after that my grandparents were arrested."

"When did this happen to them?"

"1953."

"So that would make you…"

"Yes, Notoc. I am quite a bit older than you."

"But you don't look *that* old."

"You see, Notoc. Things aren't always what they seem."

"But how did you come to be in this country?"

"That's another story. For now, it's time to sleep." And Misha rolled over, secretly glad to have shared her story with at least one other human being.


The Credit Collector

Notoc Kachuka and Misha Goldstein turned out to be an amazing couple, with regard to the scientific mind. When one stumbled the other picked up and ran. It reminded the government official, Daniel Shays, of his football days.

Daniel had always been athletic, even as a kid. His mother would scream at him because he'd come home cut up, bruised and banged. Whether it was rock fights with the neighborhood kids or climbing trees, the worst thing in the world for Daniel Shays was doing nothing. In fact, that's what he hated most about his job with the government: too much standing around doing nothing. Of course, he'd been trained to understand that the life of an agent was 99% bored out of your skull and 1% balls to the wall. But that really hadn't been his experience. Notoc Kachuka and Misha Goldstein weren't his first assignments, nor were they his first scientists. He'd been working for the government for almost a decade and in that time he'd learned the nuances of laboratory security.

"Labs," he'd say to a newcomer, "Are the hardest things to guard. There are too many variations and unlimited access to weapons of all kinds, including chemical and biological. It's a dangerous job so don't ever let your guard down."

In fact, he'd only gotten to say that speech once. Daniel Shays was, typically, the "new guy" because the teams worked like totems: it didn't matter how many years you had…only that someone had more than you and they got to straddle your shoulders while you bore their weight, their superior's weight and so on until the head, represented by the Eagle with talons filled, on one side, with the arrows of State and the other filled with the Olive Branch of the Hebrew Bible that carried God's message to the People that He'd taken mercy upon Humanity after destroying the world for its iniquities. Daniel Shays stood beneath all of this and his strong shoulder, like Atlas, bore it all.

But Daniel Shays had noticed that his knee, the one he'd injured in football, was bothering him more and more the older he got. And Daniel Shays was definitely getting older. He could tell by the way he felt when he got out of bed in the morning. His back was stiff. His shoulders creaked like old wood stairs. He noticed bits of gray hair patching up by his temples and wires coming out of his ears. It was at those times that watching Notoc and Misha caused a twinge in him. A longing to find a mate because in spite of the fact that Notoc and Misha fought, a lot, he could see that that's exactly what they were. Though he was pretty sure that they were beginning to realize it as well, the day Notoc approached him he became absolutely sure.

It had been a rough afternoon. They'd long-since worked out the problem of fat absorption materials by creating a lightweight cellular suit that completely degraded in water and chemically disassociated from the fat. That was a long and arduous project but immediately afterwards the head of Notoc's department came and said that the government wanted them to create a seat, like a transportation seat, capable of collecting fat as well. This project was proving quite difficult. Mainly because, as Notoc immediately pointed out, if the person is not in a controlled environment and wearing the specialized absorptive clothing then what would happen to the fat after it came out of the body. The head of the department told him not to worry about that, to just create the seat that could, theoretically, go into a car…or a train.

"Whatever," he said.

The head of the department was not stupid. He'd become aware of Notoc's relationship with Misha, even if they hadn't, and so he said, "After all, Notoc. You really don't want to stop working on this project do you? I mean, if you've done all you can then the lab will be closed and everyone will go back to doing what they do. If you know what I mean."

Notoc glared, "I don't. But I am interested in this project. I've committed my entire being to this project."

"No need to get excited," the head said, "Just work on a seat model, that's all."

"Fine," Notoc replied but after the head left he couldn't help sensing that his time with Misha was coming to an end. It hardly seemed possible. The amount of work they'd done was enough to be a lifetime, and yet they'd only shared months. It wasn't a fair trade. Notoc determined, after the head's visit, to be more assertive with Misha. The problem was, he didn't have a clue what to do. So, one day, he went up to Daniel Shays.

"I need your help," Notoc said.

"Yes Sir," Daniel replied, "What can I do for you Sir?"

"Oh nothing like that. I just need some…advice."

The government agent standing beside Daniel smiled but kept his stare facefront.

"What can I help you with, Sir."

"Please don't call me Sir."

"Yes Sir. I mean, Dr. Kachuka."

"I'm not a doctor yet, officially."

"Yes Sir."

"Just call me Notoc, okay."

"Yes. What can I do for you, Notoc?"

After this exchange, Notoc seriously questioned whether or not the man could be of any help to him. Notoc stared at him, at his blue eyes, his nose, which had obviously been broken at some time or other, his cleft chin. He figured he was, by masculine standards, a goodlooking man and, by reason then, would have considerably more girl experience than Notoc had had, considering Notoc hadn't had any.

Feeling awkward at being stared at by the scientist, Daniel Shays, coughed.

"Oh, I'm sorry," Notoc said. "I just don't know if you can help me or not."

"Tell me what you need help with and I will tell you if I can help you."

"Okay. I want Misha to fall in love with me."

He couldn't help it. It was totally involuntary. Daniel Shays smirked and huffed at the same time. Notoc's eyes grew whitewide. He was not only horrified but incredibly embarrassed. But when he tried to walk away, Daniel Shays grabbed his arm so forcefully that Notoc had no choice but to stay.

"I'm sorry, Sir, I just am not accustomed to someone saying what they mean."

Notoc laughed, then, "That's right," he quipped, "You work for the government."

The other agent's eyes were watching them both. The other agent was a dark man, not because of his skin, because it was morbidly white—almost ashen—but because of his spirit. He oozed an aura, if one believed in such things, of crude oil. He was hard as coal and even smelled a bit sulfuric. His name was Schei Loch but everyone called him S. Schei Loch was a strange name for a strange man. Daniel

Shays had made the mistake of asking him, only once. He said he was a descendent of a great philosopher. And that was all. Daniel Shays never asked again and, secretly, hated having to work beside him though once, when they'd been stationed in a different lab, with different scientists and shortly after Daniel had begun working for the government, Daniel was glad for S. One of the scientists had gone mad, had lunged for Daniel with a scalpel, screaming "Freedom! Freedom!" Daniel watched, in amazement, the speed with which S silenced those screams. The speed and silence haunted Jeff, at night, in his dreams.

"So let me," Daniel said to Notoc, "understand you correctly, you want Dr. Golstein…"

"Is she a doctor?" it suddenly struck Notoc that he didn't know if she was a student or faculty.

"I believe so," Daniel said, "But I could be wrong. I thought you were a doctor too."

"That's right," Notoc said. He felt a little relief from the shock that she might be more accomplished than he was.

"Anyway," Daniel continued, "You want her to fall in love with you?"

"Yes."

Daniel scratched his chin and looked at the young man in front of him, "What makes you think she hasn't already?"

Notoc beamed. He really and truly beamed, "You think so!"

"I don't know. You guys sure fight a lot."

"True. I didn't think that was love. I thought that was hate."

"Oh you can tell the difference."

"How?"

"Hate is violent."

Notoc thought for a moment. "Okay. So say she loves me too but I want to, you know, move the relationship to the next level."

Daniel laughed, again, involuntarily but Notoc was more at ease.

"Yes," he preemptively answered, "I've never been with a girl okay. I was a little busy trying to save the world. Besides, I'm not even 20 years old yet."

Daniel laughed again.

"Is that old?" Notoc's face grew red.

"It's old. But good. At least you don't have VD."

"Oh God no. Hey…but what about her!"

"That's right, buddy. You got to think about those things."

"There are blood tests."

"How about condoms."

Notoc grew more uncomfortable than he'd been up to this point. Daniel recognized it, "Listen, they're not hard to use. They've got instructions."

"Yeah. I'm sure. It's not that. It's just. Everything's going so fast. I mean, do I really have to think about that? I just want to kiss her."

Daniel really laughed this time. Even S smirked. "Then go kiss her," Daniel whispered, pushing Notoc back into the lab room like a trainer pushes his fighter back into the boxing ring at the end of rest between rounds.

Notoc stumbled, a bit. Misha was bent over a microscope. He walked up beside her. "What'cha doin'?"

She looked up, glaring, "Why are you talking like that?"

"Just tryin' to have some fun."

"Well don't. We have way too much work to do."

And with that, the day evolved into fats, metals, and quarrels all while Notoc Kachuka tried, in every conceivable way, to figure out how he could facilitate, warrant, initiate the act of kissing Misha Goldstein.

The Credit Collector

Notoc Kachuka and Misha Goldstein were hard at work in the laboratory while Daniel Shays and Schei Loch guarded them one shift out of three, five days per week. The other guards, to Notoc's thinking, were nons. Non-entities. Non-persons. Personæ non gratæ. Schei Loch was one of the nons too, but it seemed he part of the matched set with Daniel Shays and Notoc had taken a liking to former football player, especially after he'd shared his confidences with him regarding Misha.

To say that their relationship was progressing beyond anything other than friendship would have been flightful fancy on Notoc's part. Misha Goldstein was, in fact, pure professional. Except at night. At night, without the lab to fortify her, without science as her underpinnings, Misha Goldstein seemed less formidable to Notoc's hopes of her.

They'd been sleeping in their cots, side-by-side for almost a full run through of the seasons' lineup. Spring, Summer, Fall, Winter had already cycled through and, once again, the birds were beginning to sing in the ever-earlier awakening of the sun. Spring was Notoc's favorite time of year. It was the season before his whole world had crumbled beneath the weight of that hard hard summer.

"What is your favorite season?" Notoc asked Misha one night.

"I don't care."

She was in a dark mood. She had them, Notoc noticed, regularly and, being ever the scientist, determined it was related to her monthly cycle. That's when he thought up a brilliant plan!

"May I rub your back?" he asked.

"Why?"

"You've been working hard and I couldn't help noticing you putting your hands on your lower back today."

"Mind your own business," she snapped.

"I am. You are my business. Without you, my research is sunk so let me rub your back and then you will be able to work better tomorrow."

"So you're saying that my work sucked today, is that it!"

Daniel smiled, thinking, "There they go—again."

But Notoc would not be deterred. He was going to risk it all, that night, that beautiful Spring night because he just knew if she'd let him rub her back, let him ease her suffering even a tiny bit, that there would be hope for something more between them. Yet, he couldn't help his hand's apprehension. He so feared that she'd take offense, as it seemed to him he was always offending her, and that she'd recoil from his touch in anger, or worse, disgust. But there was no other way. He had to try.

Slowly he reached past the wooden threshold of his cot, past the wooden threshold of her cot, and gently touched the small of her back. She moved away from him, but remained silent.

He raised his eyebrows, to himself, in the dark. "Okay," he thought, "That's not a total denial." So he reached again, touching his hand to her lower back. She lay still. If a heart monitor could have been hooked up to Notoc's body it would have been out of sight! His hand trembled. Misha noticed this and smiled, to herself, in the dark. He rubbed, gently, her clothing. He could feel that her muscles were, indeed, very tight and cursed himself for not knowing more about things like massage and seduction because everything had become subsumed to the study of biophysics and chemistry.

He wanted to pull her shirt aside, to touch her skin, but did he dare? He wanted to, oh how he wanted to, but was afraid of going too far too fast and he didn't want to spoil the progress he was making. But the longing! Just to touch his skin to hers, he ached to try. That's when Misha did a most unexpected thing, she rolled over, facing Notoc, and pulled him to her, pressing her lips to his. As unbelievable as it might seem, it was Notoc's first kiss; it was, however, obviously not Misha's. She touched her tongue to his tongue, gently, at first, then deeper. She sucked his lower lip into her mouth, for a fraction of a second, then darted her tongue to his as if to play hide-and-seek, or "Tag, you're it." She put her hands on the sides of his head and kissed his forehead, the bridge of his nose, his eyelids, his neck. Notoc's breath came short and quick. Something was coming over him, a sort of animal instinct, he felt desire for her with such conviction that he feared he'd be unable to stop it— should she opt to stop it—so he grabbed her hands from the sides of his head.

"Listen," he said, "I think we'd better slow down."

"Do you know," she laughed, "What my name means?"

"That you're Jewish."

"Not Golstein. Misha?"

"No."

"It means Bear. It's originally a masculine name, Mishka."

Notoc was still breathing heavy, "That's very interesting."

Misha smiled, "Yes it is. But do you want to know why?"

"Sure."

"Bears usually like to be alone, but in the Spring they look for their mates. The males, who are substantially larger and stronger than the females, will keep their distance from the female they want for as long as it takes her to feel safe enough to accept him." Misha entwined her fingers with Notoc's, "Come with me," she said and led him to the lab's closet.

Schei Loch motioned as if to check but Daniel Shays ran interference, "Leave them be," he said. "It's been a long time coming."

In the closet, like teenagers playing Seven Minutes in Heaven, Misha let Notoc touch her skin, let his skin touch hers, and let Notoc discover what it meant to be a man.

The Credit Collector

For one month, Notoc Kachuka forgot about his parents' deaths. For one month, Notoc Kachuka forgot about saving humanity. In that month of developing a functional fat polarizing, extracting, and storage "chair," Notoc Kachuka and Misha Goldstein fell in love.

The whole atmosphere of the lab changed. There was no more fighting. Daniel Shays, one of the government officers, was pleased. Shy Locke, the other government officer was not.

"They need to be focused on what they're doing," he told Daniel one night, "not monkeying around."

"Oh lighten up," Daniel quipped but when he looked at Schei Loch his face was stone serious. Daniel took a different tack, "They're doing their jobs. They can't work 24-7. They have to have some time to regenerate, let loose, think of other things. Otherwise their work will suffer."

Shy Lock's expression remained fixed. "It's no use," Daniel Shays thought, "He's as cold as ice." Daniel Shays had often wondered how it was that he'd come to this job. He wasn't like Shy Locke. He cared about people. Sure, he was big, strong and agile. If he had to run someone down or take them out, his body was made like the proverbial shitbrickhouse but it wasn't his body that worried him. It was the way Locke and most of the other guys he worked with looked at life, at people, at their jobs, as if nothing was more important than a directive. As if the only thing that mattered to them was following orders. It made Daniel think about the few times he broke rank while playing sports. The gameplans were clear. The team studied them like a Bible. The game films were gone over with eagle eyes to show each and every player who stepped out of line and cost the team. Being an offensive guard, he knew what his job was and he did it good. His coaches loved him. He was what they liked to call a "workhorse." He didn't ask questions he just got the job done.

Then, one game, something happened that changed everything. Daniel saw something that no one else did. Of course everybody, fans and coaches alike, saw that the quarterback had blown it and all of them were instantly screaming like maniacs but in that split second those things were not of Jeff's concern. He was grunting against his opponent when he saw the ball reflected, almost like an afterlife experience, as if in slow motion or a film reel of an outer perspective, he saw the ball reflected and a hand's back, the hand of his enemy, touch it. To him it was clear as a star in a black sky but closer, so much closer, so close he could just reach out his own hand and grab it. He remembered, like his life flashing before his eyes, being a child and reaching for the stars, reaching for the moon, it was like that. He reached for it and felt the ball's skin on his skin and it felt as if it was his skin, as if it belonged inside his skin, so he pulled it close, pulled tighter and harder than all the weights he'd lifted in his life and without knowing what was happening, like being born, his legs kicked, he screamed and thrust his head into the small window of light his eyes could only just make out. He ran as fierce as a workhorse towards the gap. He ran with the might of a Belgian, a Percheron, he ran and pushed through the obstacles that came before him and would not listen to the whistles telling him to stop. He knew he was right. He knew the rules. He knew he was right and he was running with it. Then smash and black and he looked up to see his coach's mouth moving but he could not make out the words. He felt everything all of a sudden. Out of pure instinct he reached for the source of the pain, his knee, his coach was screaming mad. Then, like the wind, his expression changed. He was smiling. He was slapping Jeff's shoulder. Daniel was carried off the field. His career was over in a splendid display of physicality and everyone cheered that the lineman, after reviewing the replay, had had the sense to know the legalities of the game and had the courage to exploit them in what would prove to be a strategically important game for his team.

Daniel reached down and rubbed his leg.

The game had cost him all of his medial collateral ligaments (superficial, medial, and posterior oblique), his anterior collateral ligament as well as his patellar tendon. Literally, his lower leg was torn off at the knee. Some of the best surgeons worked on Daniel Shays over what ended up being multiple surgeries. Many of them said they'd never seen a knee so damaged in spite of the fact that Daniel hadn't sustained a single break in his bones. This, he'd learned, was not a good thing. That maybe if his bones had been a little weaker, they'd have broken in order for his soft tissue would suffer less trauma. But he had the bones of a workhorse and ligaments and tendons just weren't meant to experience what Daniel Shays's had on that night.

The only problem was, Daniel had no idea what had actually happened to him that night.

The minute his teammates showed up at the hospital Daniel asked them. "It was weird," he remembered thinking, "Because they wouldn't look me in the eye." They flat refused to talk about it. They told him everything else about the game but the minute he tried to bring the subject back up, they either changed the topic or said they had to go and left. His favorite coach came.

"What happened Coach?" Daniel asked.

"You did a great job is what happened Kid!" and he smiled even though his eyes betrayed him. Even *he* wouldn't talk about it.

After Daniel got out of surgery he decided he wasn't going to be put off any longer. He demanded to see the tape. Afterwards he remembered thinking, "That was a mistake," because when he saw his leg do what it did, he vomited. Legs just aren't supposed to go in that direction. And when Daniel Shays saw that tape he realized that he could never play football again. There was no way. In fact, it was at that moment when the panic hit him that his doctors might be right, maybe he'd never even walk again without a cane or a crutch or a horrible limp.

Daniel Shays looked at Schei Loch again. He noticed that the lower left corner of his mouth drooped down. He noticed that the man must be getting on in years. Then he turned face-front to watch the two lovebirds creating.

One month of Notoc Kachuka floating on clouds. One month Notoc walked up to Daniel Shays, never taking his eyes off of Schei Loch because he not only disliked the man but distrusted him, and said, "Can I speak with you?"

Schei Loch looked directly at Notoc.

"In private," Notoc qualified.

Daniel looked at Shy Locke. Schei Loch was, in fact, the superior officer. Schei Loch nodded.

"Okay," Daniel smiled.

Knowing that he would not be allowed to actually leave the confines of the lab, Notoc led Daniel by the arm, cattycorner to where Misha was still at work on the project.

"Listen Jeff. I like you." Notoc whispered.

"I'm glad to hear it, Sir." Daniel replied.

"Yes, well, the thing is. Misha and I are together now. If know what I mean."

"I do, Sir."

"Good. Well, it's been exactly a month and I would like to do something really special for her."

"What did you have in mind?"

"That's the thing. I don't have a clue!" Notoc raised his voice on the word 'clue' but then self-corrected back to a whisper, "All I know is that she's the most wonderful person in the whole world, that I can't live without her, and I want her to know that I completely adore her and want to spend the rest of my life with her."

"Wow, Sir. That's a lot. Don't you think you might be a little, say, overenthusiastic? I mean, do you think she feels the same for you?"

"I do, Jeff. That's the point. I do. I really do. And I was thinking, well, I was thinking that I'd like to propose to her."

"Wow!" this time it was Jeff's voice that rose too high.

"Too fast?"

"Fast," instantly slipped out so he qualified, "But only you know if it's too fast."

"It's not. I just know it. So here's what I want you to do. I want you to go and buy the most beautiful ring you've ever seen, today, when you get off work, and I want you to bring it to the lab."

"But I need to go home and get some rest because I'm on again tonight."

"I know. But I can't leave the lab and I really want to give it to her today. You see, not only is it to celebrate our being together for one month but," Notoc grew very quiet, he looked back to see what Schei Loch was doing, he grabbed Jeff's shoulder and pulled him down, covering his mouth and Jeff's ear with his hand while whispering in the quietest of quiet whispers, "We've finished the project."

This time it was Daniel Shays who looked at Schei Loch who was, at that particular moment, watching Misha working.

"What about the money? I mean, I don't have that kind of money just lying around."

"No problem," Notoc smiled, "In fact, I've been thinking about this for a little while now. I've got quite a bit of money but I can't get to it from in here. If I can call the bank telling them that I am doing highly-sensitive work that I can't get away from and I'm authorizing you, as a government official, not only verbally but with a handwritten and signed letter that is witnessed, say, by Misha, then they'll have to give it to you."

"I don't know. You said it's a lot of money right?" Daniel asked.

"Well, I think it's a lot money. I suppose those kinds of qualifiers are subjective."

"What are we talking here?"

"Half-a-million cash."

Daniel laughed, "Yeah, I'm pretty sure they're not going to let me have that."

"Not even though you're a government official?"

Daniel laughed again, "You seem to think that matters to bankers. But I don't think it will."

Notoc's happy mood almost instantly grew gray.

"Hey," Daniel poked Notoc's arm, "I'll try. Okay? No promises."

Notoc's happy mood returned, "And if you get the money then you buy a wonderful ring with it okay?"

"Yeah, one step at a time. Here's my phone, but don't let Schei Loch see you. Go in the storage closet. No one will hear you in there, if you talk quiet. Do you know the number of the bank?"

"By heart," Notoc piped, but suddenly thought of the last time he and Misha were in the closet and for the first time in his life he got very self-conscious. "Jeff," he asked, "You, uh, can't hear things when Misha and I are in the closet can you?"

Daniel smiled, "Nope. Never."

"Whew," Notoc replied, "That's good. I would have died a thousand deaths."

And with that, Notoc made his way to the closet and Daniel made his way back to his position beside Shy Locke.

"What did he want?" Schei Loch asked.

"To know if we can hear what he and the girl are up to in the closet."

"And what did you say?"

"I told him we can't hear a thing," Daniel replied.

Schei Loch laughed, "Liar."

It was, to Jeff's recollection, a singular occurrence both Locke's laughter and his lying.

Notoc came out of the closet and waved to Daniel to come.

"Hey now," Shy Locke's face grew serious, "I don't like this."

"Don't worry," Daniel replied, "It's probably some 'advice.' He seems to think I'm his friend."

"Just remember," Shy Locke's ice returned, "He's not your friend. He's your responsibility and if you get too close, he'll be your liability. Understand?"

"Completely, Sir." Daniel answered, "I won't be but a minute and I'll explain that he is not to act so unprofessionally."

"Very good," Schei Loch replied, looking again at Misha who had since stopped work and was reading a technical manual.

Once Daniel was beside him Notoc slipped Daniel his phone back, "All set. They said it would be fine."

Utterly surprised, "They did!"

"Yes. The full amount. They'll send a form along with you that you can take back to the bank tomorrow. Just paperwork but the manager was wonderful. I explained that I was working on a top secret way to help people around the world to stop suffering from obesity and that I was under government lock and key. She was very sympathetic."

"Oh Notoc," Daniel was beginning to regret getting involved, "You shouldn't have done that."

"Why not? My discoveries will be world news in a matter of minutes by the end of next week, I should think. So what's the difference if I told her a tidbit. I mean, it's not like I told her any specifics."

"Yeah, but you're not supposed to have any contact with the outside. What if she tells the press. Then I'll be fucked, man. Seriously fucked!"

It was the first time Notoc had heard Daniel swear, "I'm sorry Jeff. I didn't really think of it that way. Hey, don't worry. When you go in there just tell her that she mustn't tell anyone. You're big and impressive. You totally look the government part. She'll be intimidated I'm sure and then she won't say anything."

Daniel sucked in some air, "Okay. But you can't talk to me anymore. Locke is getting suspicious."

"Okay. Here's the handwritten note. And you'll come back this afternoon with the ring right?"

"Yeah, and your change," Daniel smiled.

"Oh yeah. Hey, whatever is left over, you take 10% for yourself. Finder's fee."

"Really?"

"Absolutely. None of this could have happened without your help," Notoc smiled ear to ear. "And I can't hardly WAIT until tonight."

Notoc almost skipped across the lab's floor to Misha, whom he grabbed around the waist, swung her around like the old movies of countryfolk doing square dancing, and laughed, and smiled, and kissed her and yelled at the top of his lungs, "Misha Goldstein, I love you!"

Daniel resumed his position, explained to Schei Loch that Notoc had wanted some advice in the 'bedroom' arena, qualifying it by saying, "You know, sometimes I forget that he's just a kid."

Schei Loch sneered, "Some kid. Freaky geniuses. I can never stomach them. Too eccentric for me. Give me a president, a foreign dignitary, the Treasury and I'm good. I know the deal with them. Watch the doors—all of them. But these guys," Schei Loch nodded his head in Notoc and Misha's direction, "I can't make heads nor tails of them."

Things were changing. Schei Loch never divulged personal information. This bothered Jeff. It really did. After that Daniel didn't speak and neither did Shy Locke. Three hours of total silence between them, but that hardly created a silenced environment because Notoc and Misha were like springtime squirrels, chasing each other about, running into closet, making love, running out of the closet, eating food and drinking champagne, running back into the closet.

Three hours later Daniel and Shy Locke's replacements came.

"See you tomorrow," Daniel said to Schei Loch as he got into his car.

Schei Loch did not reply, he simply nodded and drove away.

Notoc had written the name, address and phone number of the bank, as well as the manager's name, along the top of his handwritten note ordering the bank to release the entire funds of his account to Agent Daniel Shays. Daniel decided it would be best to call and verify that was possible before driving all the way across town. He was pleasantly surprised to hear the voice of what he envisioned to be a beautiful young woman, the manager, affirm that the funds were ready and waiting for him.

"Great," Daniel said to her, "I'll see you in about twenty-five minutes."

"I look forward to it," she replied.

The bank was beautiful. Rich dark wood, plush upholstered furniture, green shaded banker's lights and Persian rugs. It was one of the most luxuriant banks Daniel Shays had seen. He walked up to the only girl sitting before an open cashier's window.

"I'm here to see the manager," he said.

"Oh yes," the girl smiled with lips glossed and colored by rosy pink shimmers, "She's expecting you."

Off to the right a woman in a forest green dress suit, matching high-heeled pumps, and fiery red hair waved him to enter her office.

"Hello. You must be Agent Daniel Shays," she said, holding her hand out to him.

He took it and was surprised by the strength of her handshake, "Yes. And you are Chloe Simpson?" Daniel made an obvious attempt to make sure she saw him look at her nameplate.

"Yes. Please sit down," she smiled.

Daniel obeyed.

"I have a form for you to fill out and I have a form for you to take to Mr. Kachuka to fill out and return to the bank. Will that be a problem?"

"No Ma'am."

She smiled, again. "Good. And you have the handwritten letter?"

"I do," Daniel said, handing it to her.

"Very good," she replied, looking it over. "Now, while you fill out your form I will get the money for you."

"Okay."

Daniel watched her walk out of her office, walk over to the cashier girl, watched them both look back at him, all smiles, and at that moment he turned away and filled out the "Assumption of Liability" form.

When Chloe Simpson returned she had in her hand a bubblewrap-lined 9x13 inch envelope, "Here you go," she said.

"Is that all?" Daniel was taken by surprise at the smallness of the package.

"Yes. It seems like it should be bigger, but it's all about the increment and Mr. Kachuka was very specific about how it was to be."

"I can believe that," Daniel smiled.

"You know," Chloe changed her demeanor to slightly-less professional, "You look very familiar."

"I get that a lot," he smiled.

"Would you like to go out to dinner with me tonight?"

"I can't," he answered, automatically, without thinking and he could see that she was sort of shocked by being turned down so abruptly. "I mean I can't tonight. I have a previous commitment."

"I see," Chloe's professional demeanor was back on, "Well, the form is in order. Thank you Agent Blook. You may go now but remember, you must have Mr. Kachuka return this form to the bank as soon as possible," and she handed him another piece of paper.

"I mean," Daniel stumbled, "I would really like to go out with you another night. Would that be okay?"

Chloe Simpon's eyes squinted, "That depends on whom your commitment is to."

Jeff, after a moment of blankface, realized what she was saying, "Oh no. It's nothing like that. It's a professional favor. Something for work."

An even-less-professional demeanor came over Chloe Simpson, a mixture of flirty seductive and coy all at once, "Then you can call me," she sort of purred and handed him a card with her personal number handwritten on the back.

"I will," Daniel tried being seductive back, though that had never been his strong point, "I promise," and then he did something he'd never done in his whole life, he reached out for her hand…and kissed it.

The Credit Collector

Daniel Shays left the bank with a skip in his step and a song whistling his lips. He had Notoc Kachuka's cash, a mission of love to accomplish and the hope of a future date with the beautiful banker, Chloe Simpson. It had been long enough since Daniel had been with a woman that the simple thought of her sent chills up his spine so he ducked into the first jewelry store he could find. The sign read, "Gill & Sons Fine Jewelry."

An elderly man with a cheerful voice said, "May I help you?"

"I'm looking for a ring," Daniel Shays replied.

"Then, my boy, you've come to the right place."

Daniel Shays liked being called a "young boy" and smiled, "Price is not the issue it just has to be special."

"I see. Is your fiancée a traditionalist or a modernist?"

Daniel Shays laughed, "Oh, it's not for me. I'm buying it for a friend."

"I see," the old man's eyes narrowed. "That's strange."

"You don't even know the half of it," Daniel smiled, "But I'd have to say, knowing what I know about the girl, uh, traditionalist."

"Very fine. I'll be back in a moment."

When he returned his slow, steady gate brought a tray of three rings set atop it. He gently fingered the first, putting it on his own pinky finger, "This one is a very old diamond set into a modern white gold of traditional pattern."

Daniel looked at it, "What do you mean 'a very old diamond'?"

"We specialize in antique diamonds."

"What does that mean, exactly."

"They're used," the old man smiled, "But I only purchase the very best."

Daniel looked at the ring again, "How much would this one cost?"

"$45,000.00."

"What!" Daniel cried.

"I thought I would start out with the least expensive of the three rings."

"For a *used* ring!"

"Oh no, Sir, never! Our rings have never been worn. They are each designed pieces of art, each unique. We guarantee you will never find another ring like the ones you see at Gill & Sons."

"For $45,000.00 I should think not."

"Do you wish to continue?" the old man asked.

Daniel thought about Notoc Kachuka, thought about Misha Goldstein, and reminded himself that it was not *his* money he was spending.

"Okay," Daniel said, "Let's talk about this one," and he pointed to the ring on the man's finger, the cheapest of the three.

"Very good choice," the old man replied, pushing the tray off to the side, covering the cast-off rings with a deep marine blue velvet drape, and pulling from beneath the counter, a jewler's loupe.

"This diamond came from the mine at Nothern Cape town of Kimberley in South Africa where the Vaal and Orange Rivers meet and which was controlled, primarily, by the company De Beers. Regarding political history, Kimberley was the setting of the Second Boer War. The diamond mine was closed in 1914, although three of the five holes did not close down completely until 2005. Here," the old man pushed a photo towards Jeff, "is a picture of what remains of it."

Daniel looked at the most beautiful blue-colored hole in the ground he'd ever seen.

"It is called 'Big Hole,'" the old man smiled.

"It is that indeed," Daniel smiled back.

"Now," the old man continued, "To business. He turned on a small light, held the loupe over the gem, and let out an authentic gasp.

"What's the matter," Daniel asked.

"Oh nothing," the old man looked at him, "I just always experience the glory of it in that way."

"I really don't understand jewelry."

"This is not jewelry, my young man. This is Art. Let me show you."

The old man spent the next 45 minutes explaining to Daniel the ways in which a diamond's art could be understood and the sculptor's artwork that had been the basis of its setting. He provided the artist's signed schmatic drawing for the ring's setting and the provenance of the diamond itself dating it back, with documentation, to 1876.

"So do you wish to purchase this ring?" the old man, finally, asked.

"I do."

"And how do you wish to pay for it?"

Daniel Shays set 9x13 bubblewrap-lined evelope on the counter, "Cash."

The old man's eyes squinted, then he smiled, "You know that this transaction will be recorded? It *must* be recorded in order for the ring's value, for its reputation and credibility, to be maintained."

Daniel laughed, "I assure you, Mr. Gill, that this is not illegal money. I am, in fact, an FBI agent."

"Do you have proof?"

Daniel showed him his identification. The old man, still, seemed reluctant.

"I promise you," Daniel continued, "This is for a really great love."

The old man sighed, "Very good then."

The cash was exchanged, the documents were given to Daniel Shays in a moisture-resistant case, and the diamond ring, with it's uniquely artistic setting, was put into a handcarved wooden ringbox lined with deep blue velvet.

The moment it was in Jeff's possession he was overcome with a fierce sense of, 'What happens if I loose it' and so he decided to, without delay and in spite of the fact that it was already early evening, to return to the lab and deliver the ring, and the remaining money, the $455,000.00 of it, to Notoc Kachuka.

As he drove across town he thought, "I wonder if Notoc really meant it about a 10% finder's fee. $4,500.00 would be a nice way to start things off with Chloe. I mean, if we really hit it off," he delved deeper into the fantasy and the romance of the moment, "I could get her a really nice ring with that kind of money."

Daniel Shays suddenly realized that it would be odd for him to be returning to the laboratory while off duty but it didn't take him long to come up with a plan of attack: he put the ring and its documents inside the 9x13 bubble-wrap-lined envelope containing Notoc Kachuka's remaining $455,000.00, sealed it, and wrote on its tan skin, "Personal and Confidential." He signed it, "For Notoc Kachuka via Chloe Simpson in care of Agent Daniel Shays."

When he arrived at the lab he recognized one of the officers, a man who'd gone through the same class as he did but not someone he'd ever hang around with. His name was Burt Bergamot. Daniel Shays had never liked Burt Bergamot because he reminded him of all the other guys he'd known his whole life: little guys with big chips on their shoulders who take extra effort to harass anyone and everyone they get a chance at just to make sure and share their misery. Naturally, then, Burt Bergamot was the officer to ask Daniel Shays what the hell he was doing there.

"I was asked by Mr. Kachuka to retrieve this envelope from his bank."

"Has it been inspected?" Burt Bergamot asked.

"Yes." Daniel replied.

Burt took the envelope, looked at it, "What's in it?"

"Money and an engagement ring."

Burt Bergamot poked his co-agent, a man Daniel Shays did not recognize, "Another rejected scientist. Gotta love that." Then he turned to Jeff. "We're going to have to open it."

"Naturally," Daniel replied without taking his eyes away from a face-front position.

Burt Bergamot slit the top with a razorsharp blade. "Phew," he wistled, "That's a lot of money!"

"Yes Sir." Daniel said. "$455,000.00 per the said bank representative." Daniel pointed to the name he'd written.

"Chloe Simpson," Burt read aloud. "And do you," he looked at Jeff, "know what this is all about?"

"I was asked by Mr. Kachuka to retrieve this package from said bank. I was doing as he asked as my instructions are to provide for Mr. Kachuka anything and everything he asks for because of the urgent nature of his work."

"This is true," Burt Bergamot said, as he handed Daniel back the package, "so go ahead but next time you need to inform the proper chain of command and follow standard protocol procedures. This request was not properly documented and I will be noting that in my report, Agent Blook."

"Yes Sir," Daniel replied. "Thank you Sir. Now may I deliver the package to Mr. Kachuka? He's expecting it."

When Notoc saw Daniel he lept across the lab as if a Wagnerian protagonist from the tetralogy, *Der Ring des Nibelungen.*

"Show me, show me, show me," he chanted, darting his eyes over at Misha who couldn't help but be curious about Agent Blook's unexpected appearance and Notoc's much-altered behavior. Notoc waved her off, "Oh mind your own business," he chastised, knowing this attitude would sufficiently offend her sensibilities, which it did and she returned to tinkering on the fat collection chair that had been proving rather challenging.

Daniel Shays whispered to Notoc all that he'd learned about the ring, handed him the package and was utterly shocked when Notoc handed him bundles of money totaling $50,000.00.

"What are you doing!" Daniel exclaimed.

"I said I would pay you a finder's fee."

"But the ring was only $45 grand, that wouldn't even be five thousand to me."

"You and I see things differently that's all. Now go away. I want to propose to my future wife." Notoc smiled, slapped Jeff's shoulder and sort of hovered, like an airpowered boat atop water's skin, to where Misha, still curious but not wanting to admit it, awaited. But before Daniel could even make it out of the laboratory he heard a loud meeting of skin and Misha yell, "You Pig!"

Burt Bergamot couldn't resist a final dig at Jeff, "You know," he said, "In Medieval times you would have been killed for being the bearer of bad tidings."

Daniel wanted to refute Burt's assertion "But," he thought, "To what end?" And so he quietly nodded, quietly slipped down the hallway, quietly got into his car and drove to his quiet home where he finally felt he could look at the most amount of money he'd ever held in his hands that was his. "Holy crap!" he exclaimed, then, immediately called Chloe Simpson.

"This is agent Blook," he spoke into the phone.

"I know. I can tell."

"Would you want to go out with me tonight?"

"I thought you were busy."

"All done."

"It's kind of late isn't it?"

"For who? Me or you?"

There was a slight pause, "Okay. Come pick me up in an hour."

"Are you hungry?"

"Not particularly. Are you?"

"Yeah. I haven't eaten yet."

"I'll order delivery."

Jeff's heart flipped in his chest. Could he really be hearing what she was saying? "My God," he thought, "It's been a long time."

"Are you still there?" Chloe asked.

"Oh. Sorry about that. Just daydreaming."

She laughed, "Any allergies I should know about?"

"Nope and I like every kind of food there is so you just get what you'd like and I'll love it."

"Music to my ears," she purred.

When Daniel hung up he went to the bathroom, stripped, looked at himself in the mirror, looked at his scarred up and arthritic body, sucked in his stomach, "Jesus," he exclaimed, "I look like hell!"

He didn't. For a guy his age, he looked great. But one doesn't see with age-inflated eyes—one's eyes are always naïve and when Daniel Shays saw what was in place of a washboard abdomen measuring less than 34 inches and his chest which had shrunk, considerably, from its previous 54 he couldn't help thinking, "Life's a real bitch." But that was quickly followed by a, "Ah, what's the use of worrying," and that was followed by jumping, though careful not to slip, into the shower and taking extra, extra time and effort to become squeaky clean—everywhere.

At the laboratory, Notoc approached the agents, "I want a special dinner delivered here within the hour from one of the fanciest restaurants in town. I want no expense spared."

Burt Bergamot replied, "We're not authorized to allow outside meal service. Tell us what you'd like and we can bring it to you."

"I want," Notoc used his firm, authorative voice, "A meal delivered from the finest restaurant, silver dishes, crystal service, the whole nine yards and I can pay for it so this is *not* negotiable."

"I'll have to call in for authorization," Burt Bergamot answered coolly.

"Fine," Notoc huffed, "Let me know ASAP!" and he returned to Misha and to the chair they were almost finished with.

A few minutes later the Burt approached Notoc, "You've been authorized, though we must search everything before it can enter the lab."

"You treat us as if we're prisoners!" Notoc screamed, "I'm a scientist for God's sake!"

Misha looked at the Burt Bergamot's icy eyes and firmly grabbed Notoc's arm. She knew what *that* look meant even if Notoc was unaware.

Burt continued, in the same toned voice, "You just tell us what you want, from where, and we'll make sure it is here within the hour."

Notoc turned to Misha, "Well, my love, what do you want for dinner?"

Misha did not confess that what she'd seen left her stomach turning, "Ital..," she nearly whispered, then cleared her throat, "Italian," she said a little louder. Her voice betraying a slight quiver.

"Italian it is!" Notoc boomed.

Burt Bergamot's voice remained unchanged, "Where would you like to order from?"

Notoc didn't have a clue what Italian restaurants were in Cambridge. Misha whispered, "I like The Red House. I went there before and it was wonderful."

Notoc's face turned beet red, "With a lover!"

Misha's face turned beet red, "No! With friends. Back before the days of being sequestered for science."

Notoc's flush dissipated, "Very good. The Red House it is," and he pulled up their dinner menu on the computer. "What would you like, my dear Misha?"

It took almost half-an-hour for the both of them to decide what to order. They finally settled on a poached shrimp coctail and sweet potato, apple & cheddar torte for the appetizers; baked stuffed lobster and linguini with day boat sea scallops for dinner; and for wines they chose a bottle of 2008 Pinot Noir, Montinore, Oregon for dinner and a 1990 Dom Perignon, Moet et Chandon for desert.

"Wait!" Notoc cried, "What about desert? We must have desert!"

This time the Burt Bergamot contributed, "There is a place my wife loves, it's Finale Desserterie & Bakery. I'd suggest the Fantasia. It is a strawberry tart with mascarpone mousse; a peach chardonnay torte; white chocolate flower petals fileld with butter crumb cake; lemon Bavarian cream and blueberries; chocolate basket filled with mixed berry sauce and miniature sugar cakes; orange crème caramel and cinnamon rice pudding with mango sorbet."

"How," Notoc's expression was one of shock and amazement, "Do you remember all that?"

"We go there…a lot. And we've been married for 16 years."

Notoc looked at Misha, with a sort of dopey puppy look on his face, "I can't wait to reel off, from pure route memory, your dietary preferences."

Misha laughed. This made Notoc look even dopier.

"Fine," he said to the Burt Bergamot, "You order the Fantasia."

"There's only one problem," Burt, who was now also getting caught up in the moment, "My wife's sister tried to order a delivery last-minute and they couldn't do it. They said they needed at least 24 hours' notice."

"That will not do," Notoc replied. "You call them and tell them we need it within the hour and I will make it worth their while."

Notoc grabbed Misha and kissed her, right in front of the agent, which was not typical of his usual demeanor of utmost discretion when it came to intimacy. Then he turned back to the Burt Bergamot, "Both places—one hour! You *make* it happen, do you hear me! Money is not an issue."

Notoc grabbed Misha's hand and whisked her off to the closet. He could hear, behind him, the Burt say, "Yes, Sir!"

Inside the darkened room, Notoc got down on his knee, held Misha's hand, looked at her face, literally looked, for a few seconds, then stood back up, cupped her face in his hands, kissed her, "My god!" he exclaimed, "You are a beautiful woman!" Then, as if remembering suddenly something he forgot, he went back down on his knee, "Misha Goldstein, will you marry me?" Notoc pulled the dark blue velveted ring box from his lab coat pocket, and opened it.

Misha, knelt down with him, looking not at the ring but at Notoc, "You don't want to marry me."

"You can't tell me what I want," he said, "You can only tell me what you want."

She hugged him, knee to knee. For Misha Goldstein it was a strange moment. In all her life she'd never imagined getting involved with the institution of marriage. Her upbringing, her politics, her scientific mind and cognitive focus, she just never considered marriage something she'd be likely to encounter. But here she was, facing it, in the eyes of her lover, her young, handsome, intelligent lover.

"Misha, you're killing me," Notoc cried. "Say something. Yes or no, but give me an answer. I don't like the unknown."

She kissed his ear, cupping the back of it and pulling it to her mouth, like a trumpeter to his horn's mouthpiece, "Yes," she whispered.

"Great!" Notoc exclaimed, pulling away from her to get the ring out of its box. Suddenly Misha's whole person changed, like a blue sky suddenly grayed with clouds of rain.

"What are you doing?" she asked.

"Giving you your ring."

"I don't need a ring to be married."

"Yes you do," Notoc's confusion was obvious.

"No. I don't." She ripped the ring from Notoc's hand, "You see this," she cried, pointing to the diamond. "Do you know how many people suffered because people like you decided it was a prerequisite for love?"

"Misha," Notoc pleaded, "I just wanted to get you something special. Something beautiful, like you are."

"It's not beautiful, Notoc! Human suffering is *not* beautiful!"

"Oh God, Misha! I don't want this to be happening. I wanted everything to be so special." Notoc stood up and pulled the jeweler's documents from his pocket, "You see, this ring is a piece of art. The diamond is old, here's its provenance, it's history."

Misha stood up, "You're damned right it has history! Enslavement, exploitation, and misery. Is that really what you want to adorn me with?"

"Fine!" Notoc shouted, "Let's just forget the whole thing!" and he stormed out of the closet, leaving Misha holding the ring, only to have the agent rush up, with obvious excitement on his face, "I got it all. Just as you wanted. The dinner and desert. They'll be here within the hour. Mind you," he sighed, "It's going to be pretty expensive but you said 'Money is not an issue' so I went ahead and ordered just as you said."

"Thank you," Notoc replied, sullen and detached.

"Is something the matter," the agent asked.

"Nothing."

Notoc went back to work on the chair. Time went by. Notoc could hear the agents talking in the hallway. One of the deliveries had come and was being searched. It was the desert. It arrived before the dinner. Notoc harumfed, "Naturally! The story of my life." But it wasn't much earlier, and soon the laboratory was filled with the exquisite smells of very fine food. Misha did not come out of the closet and Notoc decided, come hell or highwater, he was *not* going in after her.

He instructed the agent to set up a table by the window. The dinner came. Notoc down and began to eat. Occasionally, he'd glance at the closed closet door, but Misha did not come. Every stir, every sound, his head raised and looked at the closed door and every time she did not come to the table he swore, in his mind, at her and at himself for being so stupid as to think things with her could ever work out. "We're just too different," he said to himself, over and over again. "Everything is a fight with her," he ranted in his head, "I don't think I could survive 16 years of this," he raved as he finished the last of his dinnerr and gulped a glass of wine, not even tasting the glory of the feast before him. Then, suddenly, there was that particular sound, the sound of a latch opening, of a spring, tensioning, of metal slipping over itself: the door of the closet cracked. Notoc's heart raced a marathon at that one small sign, but stopped himself short, "It's not good enough! Too little too late." And he remained, unchanged and fixed, sitting at the dinner table.

A few minutes later Misha slowly, with head hung low, like a just-scolded animal or a branded cow, trod the laboratory's floor and came to Notoc's side, knelt before him, with cowered eyes, "I'm sorry."

His eyes were crying. He'd never seen such defeat, it ripped his marathoning heart from his chest, "If this is what victory means," he cried to himself—but aloud to her—"Then give me defeat! Love, love, love," he cried, "Stand up tall and proud because you are driving a stake through my heart!"

Misha stood but something in her eyes had changed, a spark, a glint, she threw her arms around his neck, "I love you, Notoc. I want to marry you, please forgive me."

Notoc looked at her hand. The ring was on her finger. Notoc grabbed it, trying to pull it off, "No Misha. That ring will not due for you!"

"But," she cried, with tears streaming down her cheeks, "That's what's so hard…I sat in that closet looking at your ring. And I'm ashamed to say it, but Notoc, it's the most beautiful thing I've ever seen."

Notoc shook his head. "I don't understand."

"How can I find it so beautiful, knowing what I know, and yet it is. With the curvy swerves, like a woman's figure, and the way the diamond sets in their midst, like the pregnant fruit of love's perfection. It's beautiful, Notoc, really. It's no less so than the art I've seen at the Louvre and even though I know the truth of it, I want to keep it. I want to wear it. I want to be your wife and for this," she held out her hand to Notoc, "to be our symbol."

Daniel Shays climbed in his car and drove to the nice part of town. As he drove he thought about the last time he'd been with a woman. It had been a long time. Being a government agent meant making Government number one: everything else took their respective places. Even when he was younger, when he was new to being an agent, Daniel Shays wasn't the type of guy to hang out in bars, he didn't go to church, and didn't go in for social clubs. He had one pastime, working out, and he did it religiously. For Jeff, working out wasn't just about weights, equipment, and physical fitness; it *was* his social life. In fact, as he was driving, he remembered that the last woman he'd been with had been a lady he'd met at the gym, though lady wouldn't have exactly been the adjective he would have applied to her. A nymphomaniac with hyper-flexibility would have suited her better. Daniel had only gone out with her once, which was all it took for him to know that she wasn't the woman he was looking for. She was an aerobic instructor at the gym, she taught "Megayogacardio."

The gym was a sort of sanctuary for Daniel Shays. A place where he could rediscover his own strength, feel his heart beating, push himself and overcome obstacles, and where he could unwind, relax, and socialize not just with women but with other men. Being an agent meant being close-lipped. Agents weren't big talkers. They were succinct and utilitarian. Daniel Shays realized, after working for the government, that he actually enjoyed human language and that other men, men that didn't work for the government, had a colorful way of not only expressing themselves but of seeing the world, perhaps because of their expressions. That was why Daniel looked forward to the sauna and hottub, so much, after a strenuous workout, because he could visit with men who did different kinds of work—in other words, he made friends at the gym and, over time, would greet them, warmly, just as they would greet him, and it felt, to Daniel Shays, like a small community. There was the banker, the fireman, the minister, the postal worker, the elementary school teacher, the police officer, the carpenter: all of which Daniel Shays got to know as well as any guy he'd ever known and each, seeing and talking about the world, in very different ways. Their language even, the words and phrasings they used, brought Daniel Shays a tremendous amount of joy. These were just some of what was missing for Daniel as a result of his work and its required dedication and this is what made the government's announcement to its agents particularly hard on Jeff.

"An outbreak of antibiotic-resistant staff infection, or *Staphylococcus aureus*, has been found to be a significant risk to our government agents, therefore, all agents are to abstain from visiting or frequenting public restrooms, gymnasiums, health and fitness centers, or any type of sport facility as well as any form of water-based communal structure, such as a pool, hottub, sauna, which includes all form of public massage until further notice. However, all agents should consider this edict as irrevocable because this issue is pervasive and, very likely, permanent. Any agent found disobeying this direct order will face immediate termination and prosecution."

Daniel Shays wasn't the only one in the agency to take this news badly. Other agents, such as the national powerlifting and gymnastic champions that Daniel Shays did not know personally, took it so hard that one quit the agency and was never seen again and the other committed suicide. They were the only two extreme reactionaries, everyone else, including Jeff, simply adapted.

Daniel went down to the fitness equipment store and bought himself a commercial-grade, multi-station freeweight/weight-stack machine with Smith bar/squat rack combination, a heavy boxing bag with a stand, a windtrainer for his bike, and a treadmill. It wasn't the same, but it was as good as it got.

As Daniel Shays drove to Chloe Simpson's house he thought about the last time he was with the yoga chick, about how aggressive she was, how it was all about sex. And even though it had been long enough ago that "just sex" sounded pretty good, Daniel hoped for something more with Chloe, though he didn't know why. He told himself it was because he was getting older, because he wanted to settle down, but inside him he knew there was more to it. It was as if a spark in her touched a spark in him, "Like cells or genes or something" he said to himself. He wondered, "Could she be the one?"

"Are you hungry," Notoc Kachuka asked Misha Goldstein.

"No," she replied, "But I have a surprise for you."

"You do. What?"

She put her ringed left hand in his right and led him to their closet. Inside, she had arranged a small bed of blankets on the floor, and had set up a Bunsen burner.

"It's not much," she said, her cheeks flushing, "And I wish it could be more, but we really don't have the capability here, in the lab, for romance."

Notoc pulled her to him, "You're all the romance I need," and he kissed her. "And you said 'Yes,' which means I'm the happiest man in the world. What more could a person want than this."

Misha began to answer. Notoc put his finger to her lips, "It was a rhetorical question."

She smiled. She grabbed the flint striker to light the Bunsen burner but Notoc motioned her to stop. "You'd better not," he said, "Not in here. Besides, I think I've developed nightvision. My phalanges have mapped you, too the tee, and created a topographical map called "Misha" in my brain."

Misha laughed as she stripped naked and climbed onto their blanket-bed, "You sure know how to charm a girl."

Notoc, already lying down, fully clothed, guided Misha to rest her head on his chest. "Are you cold?" he asked.

"I'd be warmer if you were naked with me."

"Then strip me."

She smiled.

"I heard that," Notoc said.

"What?"

"Your smile."

Her small hands undressed his body. Her small mouth kissed where her hands undressed. His hands stroked her body, whether she was kissing or touching him, and for the rest of the night, they made sweet, tender love.

Daniel Shays rang the doorbell of Chloe Simpson's apartment. He waited, each second his heart raced thinking he heard the door opening, but there was no reply. He rang the doorbell again, stepped back an inch and waited: 30 seconds, 40 seconds. He began to worry he'd gotten the wrong address but he was sure. He rang the doorbell again but this time put his ear to the door and listened. Just as he thought, "The doorbell is broken." Daniel Shays knocked on the door and within less than 5 seconds Chloe Simpson opened it with such a smooth and easy pull that Daniel instantly thought, "Butter."

"You're late," she scolded.

"I'm sorry. Your doorbell doesn't work."

She laughed, "I was just teasing. You're right on time. Hungry?"

"Sure," Daniel replied making sure to look her in the eye even though he could see, peripherally, she was wearing a sumptuous dress.

"Come in the kitchen and we'll see what I have to offer," she winked.

Daniel watched her walk in front of him, watched the emerald colored satin gown with spaghetti straps made of rhinestones shiver over her skin as she sauntered and noticed that nothing interrupted its movement; no lines of any kind. He smiled. The dress' back was cut in a deep swoop that lay just atop the crest of where her back met her ass. Her back was strong, well-muscled, he liked that.

In the kitchen Chloe Simpson pointed to three bottles of wine, "White, red, or champagne?"

"Oh, I don't drink. Not anymore," Daniel answered.

"Recovery?"

"Excuse me?"

"Are you an alcoholic?"

"Oh no," he laughed, "Just getting old. My body doesn't seem to recover like it used to and my job requires me to be tip-top."

"I see. Do you smoke? Drugs?" Chloe leaned over the solidwood butcher block standing in the middle of her kitchen on which the wine bottles remained standing and unaccosted.

"Is this a job interview?" he teased.

Her eyes flashed, impishly, "Yes."

Daniel Shays couldn't help himself, it was something in the way she looked at him, something in her tone, it was absolutely uncharacteristic of him, but he went up to her, from behind, pressed his hips to her, and kissed her between her shoulder blades, directly on her spine and kept his lips there, like a child playing the game of "Guess what I'm writing on your back" except it was his lips, "N" he spelled with kisses. "O" he pressed them to her flesh and made a circle. He put his hands to the side of hers and braced himself on the butcher block. He braced himself for either her submission or retribution.

She whispered, "Good answer."

He smiled, pulled himself away from her and leaned back on the counter behind him, putting his hands on the counter in an absolute position of vulnerability. She turned, facing him, "You're different," she said.

"I think we could be something," Daniel replied, hardly believing those words came out of his mouth.

"Me too. It's just a feeling."

"I know," he said but before he could continue Chloe pressed her body against his, pressing her cheek to his chest and taking in a deep breath. "You smell so good," she sighed.

Daniel kissed the top of her red, red hair and breathed in too, "So do you."

"Let's get to know each other better," she purred.

"Just what do you have in mind?"

"I want to see you naked."

Daniel raised his hands, put them on her shoulders and pushed her away from him, "Hey, I think that's going too fast. I just want to take some time."

She laughed, "Isn't it me who's supposed to say that!"

Jeff's playfulness stopped, instantly. "I'd better go," he said. "This was a mistake."

"But I thought we were meant for each other," Chloe was still teasing.

"Hey, if all you want is sex, I'm sure there are lots of men who would be happy to oblige. I just thought there might be something more, something special. I'm not interested in a good time for a night is all I'm saying."

Chloe's demeanor became very serious, "I was hoping you'd say that."

"So you were testing me! I was being totally honest with you and you were messing with me?"

"I had to know, that's all."

Chloe leaned back against the butcher block, "Are you still hungry?"

"Not really," Daniel smiled, "I don't know what the hell is going on."

"Exactly," Chloe smiled, "Me neither."

"So now what?" Daniel asked.

"I say we get naked and talk."

"What's with you and getting naked!" Daniel boomed, feigning indignation but actually embracing the playfulness that Chloe seemed to be infecting him with.

"I figure if two people can be naked together, without having sex, then when they talk they'll be honest."

"Hmm," Daniel contemplated, "Well *that's* a new one."

Chloe laughed, "But of course!" and she, gently, took his hand and led him to her bedroom.

The lighting was subtle, cream-colored. The walls were varied: one was Red Fox, it had French Doors leading out onto a terrace. The two sidewalls were Muted Gold, and the wall with the door was Sugar Wafer. How Daniel Shays knew this was that, in very fine black script, at the top of each wall, the names were written.

"That's strange," he said to Chloe, pointing to the titles.

"I like the names too, not just the colors," she replied, letting her emerald green slip to the floor as effortlessly as water falling over boulders worn rounded over time.

"You're a complicated person," Daniel replied, trying to keep his eyes at her eyes but finding himself uncontrollably looking at her body. "You are," he stammered, "very beautiful."

"Your turn," she smiled, pointing at him.

Daniel looked around the room. Everything was just as he hoped his life would be if he'd ever had a life to share with someone. The bed, the very bed he'd dreamed of, a deep, heavy wood sleighbed with matching nighttables, a dresser with a beautiful scrolled mirror, and a chest of drawers. There was also an antique armoire with two mirrored doors. In this Daniel could see himself standing. In this Daniel could see himself undressing. He felt anxiety begin deep inside him, somewhere in his guts, "I don't know," he hesitated, unbuttoning his shirt, "if this is a good idea," he said.

"It's the only idea. It's okay. You're more than your body."

Daniel smiled, "I used to be in a lot better shape."

"I'm not here to judge you."

"Then why are you doing this?"

"To love you."

He let himself strip. Naked, before three different mirrors, facing her nakedness. She walked to him, put her arms around his neck, "See," she smiled, angling her face up towards his, which made his face angle down towards hers, she kissed his lips, soft and quick, "it's not so bad."

Daniel smiled, kissed her back, attempting the same speed and pressure, "Now what?"

"Tell me your favorite color," she quickly pulled away, hitting him in the stomach, not too hard but not too wimpy either, and she raced over to her bed, ripping the covers back, jumping in and frantically pulling them over herself, "But come over here because I'm COLD!"

Daniel Shays climbed into bed with Chloe Simpson but when he rolled to his side, finding himself facing her, he told her, with a very serious tone to his voice, "I don't want to have sex tonight. I want to wait."

"You don't trust me," she said, reaching a hand from under the covers to stroke his soft hair, "When you do, you won't have to say things like that."

"So you trust me, is that it? I mean you don't even know me."

"I trust in trusting. You and I will go as far or as near as we're meant to go. Regardless of what you proclaim. Love is bigger than rules. And I think you feel it too."

Daniel Shays knew what she was saying was right. He'd felt it from the moment he met Chloe Simpson, that there was something about her, something different than any other woman he'd met, something almost at the basic, animal level, like a homing mechanism that leads animals back to mating grounds they never even knew existed, as if primordial. He felt it…he just didn't trust it.

"You're right," he said, "I don't trust it."

"Well," she slid close enough to him that he could feel her body heat even though their bodies were not touching, "That's an improvement over not trusting me. So here's how the game will go."

"Game?"

"Sure, what's life if not meant to be fun—like a game. So here's how it goes. I'll ask you a question and you have to answer, no matter how awkward, but I have to answer it too."

"That's not fair," Daniel asserted.

"You're right. Okay. You ask the questions then," Chloe replied.

"Still not fair. How about we Rock-Paper-Scissor who gets to ask the *first* question, then we take turns after that."

"That sounds equable.." Chloe instantly rolled to her back and began hitting her fist into her palm, "One, two…"

"Wait!" Daniel cried, "I'm not ready yet!"

"Okay. Well, come on then!"

"Okay," Daniel rolled onto his back, fist poised above palm, "I'm ready."

"Fine then," Chloe smiled, "One, two, three!"

Daniel shouted, "Yeah! Rock beats scissors!" and, without thinking, he hit his fist against her splayed fingers.

"Ouch!" Chloe cried, clutching her hand to her chest.

"Oh shit! Did I hurt you!" Daniel leaned over her.

"Not at all," she smiled, giving him a kiss, "Hey, you want to know my secret passion?"

"I thought we were playing the question game."

"Oh we are," Chloe said, jumping out of bed and quickly going to the armoire, "I just thought you might like to know this, because I wouldn't think you'd think of asking about it."

"Yeah, but you could have asked *me* about it and then I would have asked you."

"Too complicated. Life shouldn't be that hard. So," she beamed, opening the doors to reveal shelves of trophies where Daniel Shays had expected to find clothes. "I'm a powerlifter!"

"No shit!"

"Yep. National champion but I only let me closest friends know because most people think it's really strange."

Daniel shook his head, then put his hands behind it and smiled, "Chloe Simpson, you are a pretty weird, amazing, and surprising woman."

Chloe closed the door, ran to the bed, and jumped in, "I know. Now let's play that game."

"Do you like me," Daniel asked.

"I do. Do you like me?" Chloe asked.

"Yes. Now it's your turn."

"Okay," Chloe suddenly seemed to get shy, "But the rules were that I could ask *any* question. So here it goes: do you now, or have you ever, had a sexually-transmitted disease?"

Daniel laughed, outloud, "Well it's funny that you should ask that. In fact, all agents working for the New Government must be tested for *all* testable sexually-transmitted diseases every four months."

"You didn't answer my question."

"You're right. The answer is, 'Yes.'"

"What!"

"Yep. When I was in high school my girlfriend of 3 years cheated on me."

"And she gave you an STD?"

"Chlamydia. I took antibiotics and that was that."

"Anything since then?" Chloe asked.

"Nope. Clean as a whistle. Now you're turn."

"No STDs but once I had an abortion." Chloe's mood grew dark. "I thought I was

in love. But it didn't work out."

"That's terrible," Daniel pulled her to him. It was the first time their naked bodies had touched. He cupped her head to his chest and stroked her hair, "You don't have to tell me if you don't want to."

"Do you want to know me?"

"Of course I do," he kissed the top of her hair. He could feel her body shaking. She was crying. He noticed that her voice slightly deepend when she cried.

"I was fifteen. He was two years older. We'd been dating since junior high school. He was a football player, like you."

"How did you know I was a football player?"

"It's not hard to tell. Your physique, your scars."

This time it was Jeff's mood that darkened. Chloe could feel it in his body. "What's the matter," she asked.

Daniel was about to tell her about his football-ending game when she lept out of bed, "Let's take a bath," she said.

"Okay," Daniel replied, climbing out to follow her.

The bathroom was done in Atlantic Sea and Calico Blue with a Regency White trim and it had everything a bathroom should, especially a 2-person soaking tub. Chloe turned the hot water on, "I hope you like it hot," she winked.

"The hotter the better," Daniel tried to wink back, knowing that winking had never been one of his strong suits—a fact he realized after spending significant time in front of the mirror trying to master it. Chloe, upon seeing his wink attempt, sniggered.

"What!" Daniel cried.

"Oh nothing," she laughed.

Daniel noticed there was no toilet in plain view, "Hey," he said, "Where's the bathroom?"

"You're in it," she teased. "Oh," knowing fullwell what he meant, "Through there," she pointed to a door at the back of the restroom. Inside, Daniel was amazed at how much room there was. He'd been in detached toilets before, but they were always sort of closet-like. This could have easily accommodated a wheelchair and it had a beautiful, smoked-glass round window behind the stool as well as a mural in front depicting a pastoral scene that led to the sea and had such depth as it made Daniel feel like he was slowly, unsteadily, submersing himself into that fanciful world of greens, blues, seafoam and glittering light.

Still hearing the flushing toilet in the background, Daniel returned to the tub to find Chloe already in the water.

"That mural is something," he said.

"You like it?"

"It's great. I bet it cost you an arm and a leg. I bet this apartment does too."

"Yes on both counts, but the painting only cost me supplies and time," Chloe replied then tapped the water's skin, "Are you coming in?"

As Daniel climbed in the near-scalding water he asked, "You mean to tell me, you painted that?" He was positioning himself to sit in the tub's spot designed for the second person, the spot facing the other person's face, but Chloe tapped the water, again, "No," she said, and spread her legs, "I want you to sit here. Come on." Daniel did as he was told; he sat down between her legs, his back to her chest. She put her hands on the side of his head and gently guided it to rest on her shoulder.

"There," she said, "Isn't that better?" She took a shell, an actual sea shell, scooped the bath's water, and slowly, steadily, poured it over Jeff's exposed shoulders and chest then set it aside, reaching to the tub's side, she opened a small bottle of oil that smelled of… "What does that smell of," Daniel thought to himself… "It smells of—church." It was frankincense and myrhh. She rubbed it into her hands then ran her fingers through his hair.

"You know," she said, "You're really beautiful…between your legs."

Jeff's neck tensed. He couldn't help it. He was not used to a woman speaking to him like this. He'd never been in a situation like this. Feelings of being completely unnerved and disorientated began to make him panic. He felt himself autonomically begin to retreat from her observances and embraces, when her oily hands slid across his shoulders and down his arms, "It's okay if you want to leave. I won't stop you," she said.

Like a hiccup, a glitch, an autorestart, Daniel Shays sort of shuddered and then, with absolulte will, he forced himself to ease back into her embrace. Chloe Simpson smiled and kissed his fragrant hair. "By beautiful I meant you are quite large."

"Really?" Daniel Shays would have never admitted it, but he'd always wondered and had assumed most other men had wondered the same thing about themselves too.

"I mean, your testicles."

From the peak of the mountain crashed to the floor of the sea: "Great," Daniel Shays thought, "I *am* small!"

"You must not have taken steroids."

Feeling angry and resentful about his penis size he snapped, "Oh yeah! What makes you the expert?"

"Testicular atrophy. Number one side-effect," Chloe answered.

"Well that shows how little you know because I actually *did* take them."

"Hmm. Then you must not have taken them for very long."

Daniel Shays was filled with rage. He wasn't conscious of why, just that it was his state of being. He suddenly yelled, "What makes you so smart!" He felt a frog in his throat. Chloe pushed him away from her and stood up, water rivuleting down her figure while steam radiated from it. She stepped around him, pushed him back so that he was sitting where she'd been, stood in front of him, with her legs straddling his hips in a shoulder-width spread stance. She used her creamy white hands and slender fingertips to gently retract her prepuce and reveal a perfectly pink pintobean-sized nub of flesh.

"I thought about taking them myself but didn't because I was afraid my clitoris would get bigger and I've always thought it was too big already."

With this announcement, with this revelation, she turned her back to Daniel Shays and sat down in front of him—assuming the same position to him that he'd been in earlier with her. So, naturally, he did what she'd done. He used the same shell. Used the same oil and, in silence, tried to think of what the hell to say after what had just taken place.

Finally, as if in a warm cozy dream, he softly said, "I got upset because I think my penis is too small."

Chloe Simpson leaned her head back, took Daniel Shays's hands in her hands and placed them on her breasts, then reached up behind his neck and drew his face to hers. She kissed him. He kissed her. It was the first time their tongues touched. Chloe Simpson could feel Daniel Shays against the crest of her pelvis. She whispered, "You're wrong."

He whispered back, "I think you're just perfect…there."

She pulled back, a flash of excitement—like that of a little girl—crossed her expression, "You really think so?"

"Absolutely," his voice came lower, huskier, "But there's only one way to be sure."

She laughed, "Oh?  And how's that?"

"I am particulary good at measuring things—with my mouth."

"Daniel Shays!" she cried, "What about the whole 'I'm not having sex with you' and 'I want to go slow' and 'If you want sex then you better go get yourself another schlump.'"

"I never in my life used the word 'schlump.'  Besides, some people don't consider that sex."

"Well, surprise surprise.  I'm not like other people.  It's sex to me."

He pulled her close to him, hugging her tight, "Chloe Simpson.  I love you."

She snuggled in, wiggling as if to get every concave aspect of her to match that of his which was convex, "I love you too."

He kissed her shoulder, "I don't understand this at all.  I've never done this before.  I feel so stupid.  Like a highschool kid or something."

"What's so stupid about highschool love?  It's the most honest there is. Maybe not the most logical or best-suited love for longevity—but it's honest, and deep, and intense, and absolutely wonderful."

"You're right, Chloe.  As I'm beginning to see, you're probably right most of the time."

"Good thing you figured that out early on.  Let's go," she said, standing up, turning, and reaching out a helping hand.

"Now what?"

"You'll see."

Daniel smiled, "Somehow that makes me feel just a bit uneasy."

Chloe Simpson laughed, a full-bodied laugh, "Finally! You're getting me."

Notoc Kachuka and Misha Goldstein were so deep in the sleep only intense and intimate lovemaking can create that neither stirred when the closet door opened. Notoc and Misha both dreamt, simultaneously, of a pesty mosquito-like bee that had landed on their necks. Both, as if in a trance, experienced their hand's desire to "swat it" coincide with the inability to move. And then there was darkness for one…but not the other.

Misha Goldstein could feel her body being lifted and carried. She could feel the pressure of her weight against hands, wrists, arms. She could feel herself limp and, try as she might, she discovered she was unable to move her body. She couldn't even open her eyes to see who it was that had her. She felt cold. She felt her body involuntarily shiver but she could not open her eyes or speak. She could hear footsteps beneath her. She heard the agent, Burt Bergamot, ask, "Where are you taking her?" And she heard a voice, a man's voice, that seemed so familiar…but she just couldn't place it. If only she could open her eyes. She heard that unknown voice say, "She is needed elsewhere." And she heard Burt Bergamot, then in the distance behind her reply, "That's too bad. They just got engaged—I think."

The strong arms beneath her did not falter. She heard the man's heart beating. It was steady, moderate, regular. "Carrying me," she thought, "Is not a burden for him. He is fit." She thought of all the men she knew that were fit. There was the agent, Daniel Shays. Was it Daniel Shays that was carrying her away, still naked, down the hall? Misha could feel her cheek gently rubbing the man's chest as her limp body swayed with the movement of his gaited swagger. "No," she concluded, "Daniel Shays's chest is bigger than this I'm sure of it." Then it hit her, like 220 voltage: "Shy Locke!"

Panic raced through every nerve in Misha's body. "Shy Locke!" she screamed inside. She remembered only one distinctive thing about him: his eyes were like cold lead. His eyes were the eyes her parents and their parents told her stories about, so that she should never forget to beware of them. "Where is he taking me," she wondered first, followed, quickly, by "What has he drugged me with?"

Suddenly, she felt warmth. She heard roaring, not animalistic but mechanical. She thought she smelled something familiar. In her mind she tried to retrace the steps that had carried her to where she was, but it was no use because each time she had an epiphany, her brain stopped triangulating. Misha Goldstein had absolutely no clue where she was. She felt Schei Loch lay her down. She expected the hard ground but was surprised to find a warm softness beneath her. She *knew* that smell! What was it? She willed herself to remember. She used every bit of her consciousness to recall it. She didn't realize, at first, what was happening. Her legs had been spread. "Oh God, no!" she cried in her mind.

The first time she'd ever known a man, it had been rape. She was thirteen. He was twenty, a next-door neighbor who knew about her parents and threatened to expose them to a Cold War America. He told her that if she didn't squirm, or scream, he'd keep their secret but not before he asked her if she'd started bleeding. For all the years after she cursed herself, "If only I would have been smart enough to lie!" She told him that she hadn't. After he was done he looked at the sheet beneath her and proceeded to beat her, "You're a lying whore!" he yelled before he left her alone. It took her a few years to understand he'd assumed that because she didn't bleed she wasn't a virgin. "At least I took *that* satisfaction away from him," she said to herself. It was her own way of reclaiming her dignity.

Misha Goldstein was instantly transported to being 13, only this time it wasn't a matter of not crying out for help—it was that she couldn't. Schei Loch spread her legs. Misha Goldstein prepared herself for what was about to happen. Braced herself for him to climb on top of her, pound away at her as if she were a side-of-beef hanging on a hook in a meat locker, she prepared herself for everything but what actually happened. Schei Loch spread her legs, climbed on top of her, rested his weight on her body and began to gently, slowly, kiss her neck. One of his hands softly ran along the sides, the backs, the front of her arm. The other ran along her thigh, her hip, her side. His hands, as if a dancer's body on stage, rotated, swirled, moved at one moment intensely but at the next moment so soft she could hardly perceive it at all. Misha Goldstein had been with a few men in her life but none, not even Notoc—maybe even especially Notoc—had ever touched her the way Schei Loch was. His lips grazed her ear: first the helix then, without letting one fine hair escape his touch, he circled to the lobe where he, ever-so-slightly, touched the tip of his tongue to her skin; he kissed her tragus as if it were the nose of a child, then started his circle—again—only this time he was closer in, this time he was in the fold, the antihelical fold and used his tongue's strength to fully fill her scapha, following it around until he plunged into the fossa, snaking over and around into the Concha, and finally, slowly and steadily, he—centimeter-by-centimeter—penetrated her external auditory meatus with his pointed tongue's tip.

Misha felt a surge of warmth to her groin. "No," she thought. "He can have my body, but I am in control of my pleasure!"

Schei Loch stopped. She felt his body lift off of her. "Dear God, is it over? Maybe he got so excited it's over!" Misha had been with a few men, "It's possible," she thought. Then she felt Schei Loch roll her to her side, he climbed in behind her, she could tell he was naked, she could tell he was aroused. "Oh God," she thought, "That is going to hurt." She'd been with enough men to know.

Then Misha Goldstein felt her whole body being heaved up in one fail swoop only to be returned to her back, only this time she was on top of Shy Locke's body. "What in the world?" Misha wondered. Schei Loch bridged up, lifting Misha's body with it, then kept his knees bent. He positioned Misha's legs to rest on his, so that the soles of her feet touched and touched his penis and testicles. Her ankles and shins were pinned by his upper thighs. Only once in her life had she ever been in such a position.

She'd gone to a midwife for her annual pelvic exam. The old woman told her to climb onto the treatment table, keeping her knees bent. When Misha asked about the stirrups for her feet the old woman laughed, "Those were made by men and men don't understand women. Here, I'll show you what to do." The old woman put her hand in the curve of Misha's lower back, "Now bridge up," she instructed.

"I don't know what you mean," Misha replied.

"Use your legs and your butt to push your hips up through the ceiling then come back down."

When Misha did this, the old woman gently guided her returning pelvis into a rocked back position—like a person doing situps.

"There," the old woman smiled, "Can you feel now how much more relaxed your pelvic floor is?"

Not wanting to confess that she didn't have a clue what the woman was talking about, Misha answered, "Yes."

"Good, now I want you to bring the soles of your feet together, so that they touch like this," the old woman put the palms of her hands flat against each other.

Misha obeyed.

"There, you see, your knees naturally fall outward and all the muscles, ligaments and tendons are in a supportive but not restrictive attitude. This is how a woman is meant to be examined. When put in the stirrups, as if a cowboy riding a horse, the woman's hips are widened which causes the whole pelvis to react unnaturally, tensely, as if in preparation for the rigors of riding horses. To examine a woman, all must be gentle, open, easy and relaxed."

"But you won't be able to see as well from where you are. In the stirrups, the doctors can see straight in."

The old woman laughed, "I am not a baseball player, I am a midwife. All I need to see I can see. Trust me."

To Misha's surprise, the old woman kept her promise of seeing. But, not trusting that the woman could actually do what she believed she could do Misha scheduled another appointment with her regular Ob/Gyn, only to find the results bore out the same. "Ever the scientist," Misha thought of herself.

Misha was, to her horror, that vulnerable in the position Schei Loch had put her in. She wondered, "How does he know about this type of positioning? What is he doing with me?"

She felt her arms, limp and useless, flopping and her hands touching the floor. Schei Loch entwined his fingers with hers rendering her arm merely a reflection of his desires as if she were nothing more than a human marionette. He took Misha's other hand and tucked it in her armpit where it was held in place by him, therefore also by her.

With his one free hand Schei Loch repositioned Misha's head atop his shoulder where it was supported by the warm cushioning beneath them both. He pushed Misha's hair out away from his face and turned his head so that his lips pressed close to her exposed ear.

"You are the most beautiful woman I've ever seen." His free hand touched her clavicle. "You are the most intelligent woman I've ever known." His free hand stroked her neck like it belonged to a cat. Misha wished, with all her might, she could lift her head up and drop it back—smashing his face. She tried. She really did. But it was no use.

"You know all this don't you? But I know things you don't know. So many things you don't know." His hand cupped her breast, gently kneading it like an old woman kneads bread. "I know how to please you," he whispered. His warm breath going deep into her ear.

Misha remembered, suddenly she remembered the smell: "Oh my God! We're in the lab animal crematorium!" Misha's eyelids fluttered. She could feel her eyelids fluttering. "I'm coming out of this nightmare," she cried in her soul.

"Not yet," Schei Loch purred then Misha felt, again, the piercing probiscus of that same wasp-bee.

"Wait," Misha thought, "Wasps and bees don't have proboscides." Then she remembered where she was, how she was. She braced herself for Shy Locke's fingers to violate her. She waited as he hooked the top ridge of her belly button and steadily, gently, pulled it towards her sternum. She felt, at the very core of her, down between her legs, down at the base of her torso, a flush of relaxation. She waited for the violation but his hand traveled *up* her abdomen in the groove of her linea alba, repositioning to exactly halfway between her bellybutton and stomach.

"What on earth is he doing?" she asked herself. She felt his fingers gently massaging her fingers with his other hand as he began pressing into her gut with the fist he'd formed, rolling it slowly like a drill bore. It hurt, a little, at first. Misha would have struck his hand away from doing what he was doing had she been able to. She could, in her state, merely surrender to the pain of it. She couldn't even tighten her stomach muscles to protect herself from his strength. He droned on, rotating slowly, deeper and deeper, "My God," Misha screamed to herself, "He's going to hit my spine!" She was exactly right, he would have, had he continued, but he stopped short, stopped just where he knew to and when he reached that deep destination, his fist opened, his fingers formed a crescent moon, and he rhythmically darted in, in, in. Misha felt herself on the verge of vomiting just before a surge of, "It could not be!" She felt pleasure shoot throughout her body. He must have felt it too, he whispered, "Yes, yes." Then slowly withdrew from the depths of her guts, continued up her linea alba to her sternum and pressed it firm, steady and with absolute authority so that her immobilized body seemed to meld into his. He kissed her ear, "Beautiful love, now you are ripe" then gently rolled her off of him and onto her side. He rose up, rolled Misha Goldstein to her back, and spread her legs. A tear trickled down Misha's cheek, "I suppose crying is autonomic as well," she sniffled in her mind, "Now he's going to rape me," but then she felt Schei Loch reposition her legs so that they were straight, and almost touching each other. She felt Shy Locke's hands travel from the arch of her back to her ass, rocking it upwards towards the ceiling. "What in the world now!" Misha cried.

She could hear him positioning himself and felt his stomach's warmth against the front of her thighs. His elbows rested beside her hips, she felt his breath on her pubis and heard him inhale just before he used his fingers to guide her labia and clitoris upward just before pressing her legs tightly together with the strength of his own inner thighs clenching. Misha felt what could only be described as terror. She knew something was about to happen but didn't have a clue what. She tried to brace herself, but bracing implies one knows what to brace against, like muscle memory knowing that a full gallon of milk will require a certain amount of mucle fiber activation—when one doesn't know then one uses too much or too little and it is only through learning, through experience, that a determination can be made as to the ways in which to adequately brace. Misha was totally disorientated, totally helpless, and completely unable to prepare for what she knew, just knew, was something she knew nothing of.

Schei Loch used his fingers to slowly, gently, and rhythmically move the prepuce, the foreskin, the clitoral hood over Misha's involuntarily-hardened clitoris without directly touching it. He used his fingers to grasp the foreskin and slide it over the clitoral body, up and down, making sure to encircle the entire shaft with the soft, pliable, hood. He felt it begin to throb beneath his touch and, with each pulsing, to grow larger and denser. He tightened his legs' grip, achieving the desired effect, rigidity. He placed his lips over her glans and, in unison with his deft fingers along the shaft, retracted Misha's foreskin and sucked the head of her clitoris into his mouth and onto his tongue.

A moan escaped Misha's throat. Tears began falling from her eyes and into her ears. "Dear God, no," she cried, "No! Please no…not this!"

Three more assaults was all it took. Like Vercingetorix, the Gaul, in the battle against Julius Ceasar at Alesia—the body, the frailty and complexity of the human body, under conditions of siege warfare could only withstand so much. For Vercingetorix, his defeat came from starvation: hoping for mercy from his enemy, he sent the women and children out to the Romans so that they might be saved from such a terrible suffering by letting them pass through enemy lines to safety but Caesar issued orders that they should not pass and that nothing should be done for them. The women and children were left to starve in the no man's land between two armies: in plain view for Vercingetorix and the Gauls to witness. The end, the surrender, came soon thereafter. For Misha Goldstein, it was her very own nervous system, like those women and children who went into that land of limbo between death and the hope of salvation, the no man's land at the mercy of one's enemy, that had betrayed her warrior strength. She could never have been prepared for the onslaught of Shy Locke's advances especially because she could not fight or flee, because she was totally helpless to her own anatomy and physiology.

Misha's tears did not cease again. She felt her eyelids fluttering again only this time Schei Loch did not sting her, instead he used his forefingers and thumbs to open them wide. He was smiling, "You see, dear Misha, you are not the only expert in the world." And then, without a single warning, he violently thrust his legs between her legs, spread them wide, and raped her long and hard so that each thrust drove her just slightly closer to recovering her physical control. Misha felt her legs begin to respond to her commands, she felt hatred building in her heart, "Just a little bit more," she thought, "Just a few more minutes of recovery and I'll be able to move. I'll kill you Shy Locke!" she screamed in her mind. Schei Loch looked into her eyes, still flowing with tears, and sneered, "Oh yes, I know what you're thinking." He thrust especially hard, "But don't hope. It won't happen," he thrust again, arching his back like a cat stretching, so that his pubis drove into her pubis, "At least *that* won't happpen…but you might be surprised what will," he thrust again, as if his hips ran in a perfect semi-circle. Misha could feel her clitoris hardening, "Oh God, not again!" Schei Loch smiled, "Oh yes, Misha Goldstein…again," and he, like lightening, withdrew himself from her spread legs and placed his mouth over her, this time hard, fast, and his hands massaging her labia majora and pubic mound in large, circular, deep and rhythmic thrusts.

To her utter shame, Misha Goldstein came. Her body shuddered through the very muscles she was hoping to recover willful movement over. Then came the sting but Schei Loch wouldn't let Misha close her eyes. Instead he turned her face so that she could see the label on the machine that had given them both so much warmth, The Pheonix animal carcass incinerator. Misha Goldstein knew it well. It was located in the room attached to her dog laboratory and she had disposed of many dead dogs there. All the animal study scientists disposed of their animals there, including the bovine and equine scientists found on the crematorium's other adjoining door.

"That's right, Misha Goldstein," Shy Locke's voice had not changed one bit in tone, it was as much cold lead as his eyes, "I think you know what's happening now," and this time he climbed atop her, thrust thrust thrust, grunt, quiver and was done. Misha Goldstein thought, "I could have braced myself for that."

Schei Loch got up but before he dressed he grabbed Misha's left hand, "You won't be needing this where you're going," and so, like an old mother preparing a chicken dinner, he grasped Misha's hand and the finger joint below where the ring of Notoc Kachuka rested, and easily—with no muscular or ligament resistence—used his pocketknife to cut the attachements from the distended bones. He slipped the ring off and tossed it onto the bedding that Misha could then see was nothing more than a tarp on the cement floor. Misha's fingerless hand bled out onto it. Still naked, Schei Loch rolled Misha Goldstein's live body up like a burrito, opened the frontloading door of the Pheonix model capable of handling animals up to 1,200 pounds and closed Misha Goldstein inside of it.

Those few seconds felt like an eternity to Misha.  She thought about Notoc, first.  Thought about the ring she'd worn on her finger and, like the man who'd raped her when she was only thirteen, she declared a small victory for herself over Shy Locke, "You loose!" she cried in her silent world, "You may burn me like a witch but you have released me from my herecy!  You and your raping of me, your stealing from me an object that you think is dear to me, as the final degradation—just shows that you're NOT as smart as you think you are, Shy Locke!  Your ignorance has redeemed me!  My parents will own me now, again and my grandparents and all my inheritance because that ring was my downfall—not you!"  And, for a brief moment, just before her tears of protest were turned to salt in her eyes' punctum by the flames, Misha Goldstein contemplated the act of branding: the smell of seared flesh and the cries of cattle.

Chloe Simpson handed Daniel Shays a large, white terry robe and, for herself, she wrapped an oversized towel around her still-wet body then grabbed Jeff's hand and led him out of the bathroom, through her bedroom and out on the terrace where the wind had kicked up the season's cool air and made Daniel Shays clutch the robe's lapels to his neck, "It's freezing out here," he proclaimed, "What are we doing?"

Chloe grabbed the robe's belt, untied it and pressed her body to his.  She kissed his neck, then quickly twirled around so that her back was against his abdomen, "Just look at the view," she sighed.

It was in the darker part of night and so the lights seemed even brighter.  Some strands of Chloe's wet hair were already drying and, unlike the others wet and matted, found freedom on the breeze.  "You know," she continued, "It was this view that sealed the deal for me."

"You mean you bought this apartment?"

"Oh yes," she swirled again to face him, "It's mine.  Signed.  Sealed and delivered."

"But how does that work, in reality?  I mean, I've never really understood the whole condo/apartment thing.  You own it but not really, meaning you pay dues and you have to follow the charters, laws really, of your association. So how is that, and he made the signs for quotations marks with his fingers, "'owning' versus 'renting'?"

Chloe Simpson whirled back around, once again, facing away from Jeff, "It means that I can paint my walls any damn color I want and that I can stand out on my terrace with a lover and if my neighbor sees a tit or two I won't get kicked out. And it means I have a tax write-off."

"Is that true?" Daniel asked.

"Yes. Same write-off as a traditional," this time it was her turn to make the quotation marks with her fingers, "'homeowner.'"

"I meant about the tits," he teased.

Chloe let her towel drop to the ground, "Well, let's find out shall we?"

Daniel suddenly got very nervous, "Hey, stop that. I could get into real trouble over something like this."

"Oh," she teased, "Now who's worrying."

"That's not funny, Chloe. Now pick it up and cover yourself. Agents have gotten fired for less."

"You've got to be kidding," she scoffed, but did as Daniel demanded. "Sheesh," she said wrapping up, "Your job sounds even worse than mine. Let's go back inside where we can be quote-unquote indecent." She did not offer up the coinciding finger gestures.

Once inside Chloe grabbed the towel, holding it in one hand and ran, naked, back to the bathroom, jumping into the still-warm but not hot bathwater.

"Ahhh," she sighed, slinking down so that her whole body, neck and face clear up to her nose was submersed.

Daniel let the robe fall onto the bathroom floor, "Scoot over," he smiled. "I'm damn cold." This time they sat as the tub's design had intended, face-to-face, her right foot at his left hand, leaving all other feet and hands to touch the tub. Daniel rubbed Chloe's ankle and shin, "You have beautiful legs."

"Well thank you," she smiled. "So, tell me how you came to be an agent."

He made a small circle around the bone called maleolus, "I guess I didn't really think about where I was going or what I would do when I got there. College, for me, was all about football and when I got hurt and couldn't play anymore I just sort of drifted."

"What was your major?"

"One guess," Daniel teased, sliding his palm along her smooth leg.

"P.E."

He laughed, "And that would make you…WRONG!" He splashed her. She returned it, "Then what?" she cried.

"Business." Daniel answered.

"That's so funny. I actually went to school for business too."

"Why is that funny, you're doing what you went to school for right?"

"Not exactly. I began studying to be a vet." Chloe slid her foot over Jeff's leg, resting her toes on his cock. "Would you like to hear about it?"

"Oh yes," he smiled, noticing that her breasts, beneath the water swayed with it in a sort of gelatinous way. He thought, "Everything good is made from fat: breasts, mouths, vaginas…no wonder God wanted His sacrifices to be fat."

"So," Chloe went on, her toes wiggling every-so-often, "I was in my junior year of college when I decided I'd better get some practical experience before applying to vet schools. I contacted a vet and he said it would be fine so I showed up, all eagerness and sunshine, with straight As in school and determination in my belly, only to find myself, at eight in the morning, observing the spaying of a *very* old cat."

"If it was so old why did it need to be spayed?"

"The uterus was diseased."

"Gross," Daniel exclaimed.

"Yes. And no book had prepared me for what I saw either. The vet kept saying, 'I hate working on old cats like this, see,' he'd grab the tissue with the forceps, 'the tissue just tears apart.' And it did. Shredded really. And there was so much blood. All of a sudden I felt sort of light-headed. The vet said, 'You don't look so good. Maybe you'd better go get some fresh air.' So I went to the bathroom. I was actually dizzy. But I was determined."

Daniel laughed, "You. Determined? Nah! Couldn't be."

"But by the time," she gave Jeff's balls a little toe-flick, "I collected myself the surgery was over. So the vet, this great old guy who'd been practicing forever, says, 'I've got the perfect thing for you.' And he leads me out back where a rancher had unloaded 50 bulls. The rancher drove each one into the shoot, the vet showed me how to make the incision into the bottom of the scrotum, then," Chloe tightened her toes on Jeff, who was—in context of the story—becoming a little uncomfortable, "he slit it, pulled the testicles through the incision, inserted the Emasculator, which crushed and cut the spermatic cord, while catching the balls with a large plastic bag."

Daniel lifted Chloe's foot off his genitals. "Ouch," he said.

"It was pretty bloody. They just left it open like that. The poor buggers go trotting off, draining blood all over the floor but not before they get de-horned."

"Yuck!"

"Yeah. After the cat fiasco I was already queasy and the castrating-dehorning thing didn't help *at all*. But the final blow, what knocked me out for the count, was the branding. You see, all the bulls were driven into a crush, a pen that makes them so they can't move, and the after the vet was done the rancher used an electric iron to make his mark."

"Man it sucks to be a cow."

"Bull," Chloe corrected, "Well, at that time—steer."

"You said that was the final straw, why?"

"Well…" Chloe hesitated. Daniel lifted her foot, putting it back on his cock. Chloe smiled, "…the thing is. Those poor dumb animals stood there and took getting

**194**

their balls and horns cut off, took being penned up with their blood running out on the ground and down into their eyes, but when it came to that rancher putting his brand on them—making it known to the world that he *owned* them—well…those beasts, they…literally cried out.  And the smell of their burning flesh was…ghastly…as if it was unholy.  I just couldn't bear it!"  Chloe shuddered.  "So I thanked the vet but said 'No thanks' to vetting.  Funny thing though."

"Yeah, what?"

"That old farmer came up to me as I was leaving, held up that plastic bag filled with blood and white balls in it, and said, 'Do you want to take these?'  I said, 'No thanks.'  And he nodded, cowboy hat and all, and said, 'Your loss!' then left the clinic.  The vet came up to me and said, 'He must like you.'  I asked why he thought so.  He said, 'Because they're a real delicacy.'  That was the final nail.  I decided to go into advertising with an art minor.  Clean, neat, and no balls.  Changing my major so late in the game meant two extra years of college, but what they hey.  It was only a ton of money in student loans!"

"Very funny," Daniel laughed.

"Seriously, though," Chloe continued, "Isn't the New Government great!"

Jeff's expression grew serious, "Why do you ask that?"

"I mean, look at us.  You became a government agent and I became a bank manager.  The New Government kept its promise to give people all kinds of work."

Daniel shifted his weight.  He removed his hand from Chloe's leg.

"What's the matter with you," she tried to tease but it was no use, Daniel Shays had gone grave.  She slithered up beside him, put her head on his shoulder, "Hey," she said, her voice filled with sincerity, "I don't know what I did, but whatever it was—I'm sorry."

He looked at her eyes and for a moment he thought about Japanese comics and Manga, and cartoons, and so he did the only thing a man could do in a situation like that, he kissed her.  Her body melded.

He pulled away, "It's just that sometimes," Daniel turned his head, staring at the wall in front of them both, "I wonder why the hell they chose me to be an agent. Other than being big and strong, I don't fit the bill at all. I mean, when I was a kid we learned all about how hard it was to become FBI, CIA, NSA and now it's like I wonder what happened to all those standards I know I sure as hell couldn't have passed."

Chloe pulled his gaze back on her, "I think you don't give yourself enough credit."

"Maybe," he kissed her again, "But I do give myself enough credit to know that I've had just about enough soaking in tepid water so either we re-heat or I have a better idea, let's get back into bed!" He forced his eyebrows to go up and down a couple of times.

"Suits me."

Daniel could hear the water draining long after they'd snuggled up, naked. For a moment, it seemed to him as if they'd been together for his whole life. For a moment he had to think *really* hard to remember that they'd only just met, that they'd only spent less than a full day together, yet there they were, in Chloe Simpson's bed, her with her head resting on his chest, her with her hair draped over his arm that encircled her shoulders and pulled her close to him, her feet rubbing the length of his leg from toes to knee and her arm brushing across his abdomen and chest as she stroked his arm, side, hip and thigh with deft fingers.

"You know," she finally said, "I should be offended."

"Oh yeah. How so?"

"You seem to be implying that the New Government puts inept people into positions that once were held by more suitable candidates. If that was true, then I should be offended."

"So you're saying that you were fully qualified to be a bank manager?" he stroked her hair.

"I'm saying that once I *was* a bank manager I was able to do the job."

"So you're saying that when the New Government recruited you and told you that you'd be in bank management you went, 'That's exactly where I should be.'"

"No," she hesitated, "I wondered what the hell they were thinking but it all turned out okay."

"That's all I was saying," Daniel kissed her hair.

"Well then, I guess that's alright. How about we change the subject?"

"Yes PLEASE!"

Chloe laughed, "So what you're saying is that you'd like to change the subject eh?"

"I have an idea," Daniel volunteered by sitting up and pushing Chloe onto her back.

"I thought we understood the rules." Chloe bantered.

"You assume too much," he smiled, "But only by a little."

Chloe smiled back. Daniel knelt, spreading Chloe's legs. "Now, I want you to touch yourself."

"Excuse me!"

"I want you to show me what gives you pleasure."

"I'm not going to do that. We just met!"

Daniel sighed and motioned as if to lie back down, "But," Chloe sort of whispered, "How about," Chloe sat up so that her face was at Jeff's chest, "I touch," she repositioned herself behind Daniel like a skilled wrestler, "you...the way I like to be touched?" she ran her hands up and down his back, his ass, and hips, she let one hand travel to his neck where it cupped the base of his skull while she kissed kissed kissed, then let her free hand travel along his side, along the crest of his pelvis, and down into his hair until she touched the base of him, "See," she positioned her fingers topside then, gently, used his skin to encircle the shaft, "See," she masterfully tensioned the skin, then released, never touching the head of Daniel Shays's penis, "This is how I like to be touched…at first."

Daniel felt wetness drip from the tip of his cock and drop onto Chloe's sheet, "That's never happened to me before," he moaned.

"Don't worry," she purred, "It's not what you think, see," she reached down, touched her fingertip to it and raised it to his lips.

"Uh, no thank you," Daniel scrunched his nose.

"Oh?  It's just wetness, just like mine—it's de-lish!" and Chloe Simpson, as sexy as anything Daniel Shays had ever witnessed, slowly slid her fingertip into her mouth and, ever-so-slightly, moaned, "um."

It was just about all Daniel could take, "Okay, my turn."

Chloe plopped back and spread her legs, "I assume you'd like me in this position?"

"What makes you assume that?"

"Don't most guys like to masturbate lying down?"

"Don't most girls too!"

"Point taken.  So is this how you want me then?"

"Actually, no.  For me, I'm a shower guy."

"Great!  I love water!"

Jeff's fingers were still pruned from the bathtub, but he was telling her the truth.  On the occasions that Daniel Shays partook of that kind of pleasure, it was typically in the morning during his daily shower.

Chloe Simpson's shower had a very cool feature: a built in stool, which Daniel sat on, "You stand in front of me, put your hand on the wall…"

"Like I'm being frisked by a cop?"

"Like you just got out of bed, your joints hurt like hell, and you're trying to let the hot water wake you up."

"Got it. Like this then," and Chloe hung her head the way she imagined a coal miner might on a cold morning before going down into the belly of the earth. She let the hot water pelt her spine.

"Tighten your ass, like a hip thrust," he told her as he rested his one hand flat against her lower back while, with the other, he reached around and found that her clitoris was already erect. "I usually use soap," Jeff's voice came so low and shallow that Chloe almost couldn't hear him, "But…you're…uh…wet enough." I grasp the shaft of my cock, but I can't do that with you."

"Why not?"

"It's…logistical."

"Your penis and my clit, with regard to pleasure, react the same."

"Yeah but you're a lot smaller than me."

"It's scale. That's all. If you grab the shaft ofyour cock then use your imagination to figure out how you can grab the shaft of my clit."

Daniel used his forefinger, middle finger and thumb to grasp her, envisioning a quarter-inch length of drinking straw, then placed his fingertips as close to the base of it as he could, so that his fingertips pressed against her pubic hair. He gently squeezed and pulled, up and down.

He was utterly shocked to find that Chloe Simpson had been right, she did have a shaft to her clitoris and it was getting harder and harder the more Daniel used his fingers in the same way he used his full hand on his own cock. Chloe began to move her hips, thrusting them into Jeff's hand. Daniel felt her ass tighten and release and heard sounds coming from her throat—there was no mistaking it. She was in pleasure. Daniel knew where this was going. He felt, suddenly, torn between sticking to their deal of no sex and giving into the thrill, the possibility of being part of Chloe Simpson's climax. Chloe grabbed his hand and pulled it away from her, breathing heavy, "I can see…why you like that," she turned, facing him, bending over and kissing him, she moaned, "But I don't think we're going to keep our bargain if we do much more of this," she smiled, "So why don't we grab our robes, get something to eat, and play a game of cards."

"Cards! Are you crazy! I don't want to play cards. Come here," Daniel tried to reposition Chloe, grabbing her hips, but it was no use. She was the strongest woman he'd ever been with.

Settling down on the sofa with cups of hot chocolate, complete with marshmallows, Chloe grabbed the deck of cards on the coffee table and began to shuffle but something had shifted between them. Something had begun and it wasn't going to be stopped so easily.

"Listen," Daniel negotiated, "I just want to feel your body against mine for one second. And then…we'll play cards, okay?"

Chloe smiled, "One second?"

"Yes, just one. I promise, but I want us to both be naked."

"Then let me light the fire."

Daniel watched Chloe build a fire, from scratch: newspapers, kindling, wood. It was the most expert firemaking he'd ever seen and the moment she'd accomplished it, he laid her down on the floor, pulling the sash of her bathrobe letting it fall to the ground while disrobing himself, then he laid his body on top of hers. "You know," he said, bracing his upperbody weight on his elbows, "I have never been able to get a fire going without one of those flammable chemical logs."

Chloe smiled arched up and kissed him, "Well, I'll just have to teach you."

"You're just full of surprises…aren't you?"

She kissed him again, "You have no idea."

One second passed. Then two. Chloe Simpson's legs relaxed, Daniel Shays felt his wetness touch her wetness, his erection pressing hers, and—their bodies moved together, rhythmically in a sort of beautiful dance of moaning, of pleasure, and all while keeping their promise to each other: they did not have sex. No coitus.

No coming. Just the sheer ecstasy of physically sharing the love that was so quickly growing between them until the early hours of morning, until Daniel Shays had to leave, even though he'd been trying to leave for an hour but every time the thought entered his head it was unbearable. Until, from sheer exhaustion he cried, "Chloe! I have to go. I have to get at least *one* hour's sleep before work." And Chloe cried, "I know, me too!" but every time he tried to leave it was as if the thought of being apart would kill him.

Finally, after many false starts, Daniel Shays dressed, kissed Chloe Simpson goodbye, and watched, painfully, her door close behind him but not before both promised to see each other directly after work that day.

While Daniel Shays drove back across town he found himself spontaneously smiling. He'd done so much kissing that his lips were, literally, sore. In all the sex he'd had in his life, he'd never been that physical or that intimate with a woman. The word "love" kept creeping into his mind. He doubted if he'd even be able to sleep. But, unlike youth who can live on love, Daniel Shays found it quite easy to fall into sleeping the moment his head hit his pillow. His alarm was set for one hour's time. He thought, just before his closed eyes drifted him off to a deep deep sleep, "Man, am I exhausted."

Daniel Shays was dreaming of the sea. Of deep bluegreen warm with salt, sweet with pleasure, he was dreaming of a woman in his arms and her long red hair that swept across his chest, his throat his stomach, as her body swayed with the tides and with his own body. Her hair, growing more vibrantly fire against the ocean's cool, wrapped around him tighter as his lips pressed to hers. So tight he suddenly felt the urge to escape yet her eyes, glimmering like sunlit flicks on the water, beckoned him to stay and he wanted to. He wanted to stay with her more than anything in the world…but something was tearing him away, her hair, it was binding him it was choking him. In an instant his eyes thrust into the dark night to focus but were unable to, clearly, for a milky film. He could not move. He'd been bound. It was no dream. It was Shy Locke.

"Good morning," Schei Loch said, with deadpan expression.

Daniel Shays heard the rattling sound his breathing made.  He shook his head.  The moment he heard that distinct crinkle he knew.  Schei Loch was going to kill him.

"I want to know where Notoc Kachuka is," Shy Locke's monotone continued.

From instinct, Daniel struggled against his bindings.

"There's no use struggling.  And I think you know that.  But I don't blame you.  I would do the same.  I assure you, however, your struggle is futile.  I've been doing this longer than you've been alive and any possible flaws to my technique have long-since been rectified.  Where is Notoc Kachuka?"

Daniel felt the adhesive on his wrists, his ankles but it was the tightness of his chest that made him worry most.  It was like a woman's 19th century corset and his first thought was, "How could he have done this to me without me waking up?"  But he, of all people, knew; there were ways.

"I'm not telling you shit," Daniel replied.  "And I know what you've done already and you, of all people, should know that I know how it works."

"It?" Shy Locke's face feigned surprise.

"Yeah.  Thiopen and amytal!"

"Oh.  Those.  I thought you meant the real world."

Jeff's expression betrayed his own confusion.

"You silly boy.  That's for the movies.  It's so much easier than that and, virtually, untraceable."

Still not knowing what he was talking about Daniel shouted, "Oh yeah, there'll be binding marks."

"I hope so," Schei Loch smiled, "Otherwise it might not seem authentic."

Jeff's eyebrows pursed.

"You still don't understand. I'll teach you. You see, you are bound softly because when you went to sleep, with a mild sleeping agent…"

"But I don't take sleeping pills."

"I know. But you do. I have a prescription in your name. You eat and drink ergo you have taken sleeping pills and this particular one," Schei Loch shook the emptied and dumb orange Rx container with it's white printed top, "is a hypnotic. So your own dreams, my dear boy, helped me to comfortably and without struggle, bind you as you now find yourself. And just now," Schei Loch touched the milky colored trash bag covering Daniel Shays's head, "judging by the condensation forming inside there, you're entering into anaerobic metabolism. You remember that, don't you Jeff? From sports?"

Daniel stared at him, blankly. He could feel his head growing lighter and small ripples of nausea building.

"Oh yes. That's it. You know what I'm saying," Schei Loch continued, "You'll vomit before long. That's okay. It uses up more oxygen and that, Jeff, is the whole point. You are slowly suffocating yourself. Nothing dramatic, nothing violent. Just a slow dying. Where is Notoc Kachuka."

"Why should I tell you? I'm dead no matter what."

"Yes. You are. You're a traitor and deserve to die. And if you were brought to trial for the treachery you've enacted against our government, you'd be sentenced to death for being a terrorist."

Daniel could feel his stomach begin to spasm, "But I'm not a terrorist! I love my country. All I did was help a kid, a boy, not even a man really yet, who fell in love, like all of us want to be in love, and all he wanted was to be with her and then she was gone. He just wanted to find her. I thought, if I helped him find her and I figured she left him because she was the difficult kind of girl, but I thought if he saw the real her then he'd be more willing to fully commit to the project without distractions. I LOVE MY COUNTRY! "

Daniel Shays vomited.

Shy Locke's face stayed stone but his voice quivered a little, "That's really unfortunate, Jeff."

"I swear I'm telling you the truth. I did it for the RIGHT reasons!"

"I know."

Surprised, "You do?"

"Yes.

"I don't know where Notoc Kachuka is. I swear I don't know where he is. I'm telling the truth."

"I believe you." There was a long pause before he continued, "Because at this stage your body is doing everything it can to survive and that is the ultimate, the," he laughed, "naturopathic truth serum. Your own body won't let you lie because it takes too much energy and it needs everything you have just to stay alive a few more seconds."

"Please, Shy. Please don't kill me," Daniel pleaded. He began to cry. His nostrils flared.

"That's it, Jeff. That's the way. It will make it go faster." Then Shy Locke's demeanor changed, "I'm sorry about this. I *really* am."

Daniel sniffled. The smell of his own vomit burned his eyes but a sort of righteous indignation came over him, "They'll know it was murder."

"No. You're an erotic-asphyxiate. You and your girlfriend were deeply into it. You even have a journal on your computer detailing your adventures with her and how much you like to push it right to the limit because it gives you the most pleasure."

"Girlfriend?"

"Yes. Ms. Chloe Simpson."

"But we haven't even had sex…" Daniel began to loose consciousness. Suddenly he was dreaming of the sea again. It had been Chloe he'd been dreaming of. It was her red hair in the sea. He saw her face, now, clearly. Her beautiful eyes, her creamy skin. He kissed her lips. She pressed against him. She was naked and so was he. He felt her touching his chest, his stomach, he gasped before burying his face into her wet hair and kissing the flesh of her neck. He heard her moan before she guided him into her, he heard her…did it sound like crying…he heard her say, "I'm sorry, Jeff," before he came inside her.

Several months later, tucked away in the belly of the paper's *Local News* section, a title proclaimed:

WOMAN CONVICTED FOR THE INVOLUNTARY MANSLAUGHTER OF FEDERAL OFFICER.

In a bizarre case of kink gone wrong a local woman "accidentally" killed her lover while practicing erotic-asphixiation. Prior to the death of a Federal officer, whose identity has been kept confidential for security purposes, Chloe Simpson had sent multiple emails to the officer detailing their sexual encounters.

The last email she sent to the officer, dated the day before his death, she confesses she had had to perform C.P.R. as a result of their escapade and expressed the thrill as well anxiety this had caused her.

When asked why she'd used duct tape around the victim's chest, the expert psychologist stated that it constricted the ribcage thereby limiting lung capacity in order to facilitate slower asphixiation. "They do this," he said, "in order to prolong the length of time they experience sexual pleasure."

A distraught Chloe Simpson maintained, throughout the investigation and court hearing, that she was innocent. At today's conviction, she stated, "I am innocent. I only met (the officer) once. I don't know why this is happening to me!" But the overwhelming amount of evidence led the jury to hand over a guilty verdict."

Meanwhile, in a small midwestern town, the body of Daniel Shays—the body of a son, a brother, an uncle and friend, was memorialized. The town had two funeral homes, but the Blooks' son had played football and one of the homes was now run by Jeff's former teammate; he'd inherited the family business after his own father had passed away.

The funeral home was very chic and classically modern. The Home Collection advertisements must have held a great sway over the owner's purchasing psyche: the funeral home could have been their catalog.

Jeff's family was sat in the row closest to the casket of redish wood. There were a few flowers, there was music piping throughout the funeral home's extensive (and expensive) audiovisual system and three flat largescreen TVs displayed rotating pictures, with captions, of Daniel Shays: a whole lifetime of him flashed in 3 second intervals with intermittent glimpse of the computer-generated background of a park filled with trees, ferns and winding pathway. He was a baby. Forty-five seconds later he was an Agent. Somewhere in between he played football, drove a muscle-car, dated. The casket wasn't on the video. Everyone could see how the film ended—and that the casket was closed. They'd been told to keep it closed "due to extenuating circumstances." They'd been told that he'd been killed in the line of duty and that he had been issued an honorable medal of service. The medal, in its decorative box, sat atop Daniel Shays's casket. There was a flag also, resting there, though not fully covering the wood—as if a Victorian woman's dress, hinting that there was something scandalous, there…"under.

The family's church minister spoke about God, about His infinite wisdom, how He had called Daniel Shays back to Him and that it was not for mankind to question the acts of God. That God was with everyone, to guide them, to comfort them in their times of loss, and that none should fear evil because the Shephard's rod and staff, with its hook around a lost lamb's throat, would deliver all his flock from the ravenous gluttony of wolves.

The funeral home's finches responded to the music. Encased in a large rosewood and glass aviary a colony of finches lived their lives amidst the sorrow of death. They were quiet when people spoke, as if out of some inherent respect for the dead, but when the piped music began their rantings began also: "eep, eep, eep" they chided. Their flyings, within their glassed in world, became erratic. Some flew into the walls, others hid in their manmade, teardrop-shaped wicker nest. There was one group of babies who, upon hearing the music, stopped poking their heads out for food. Then, just as quickly as this sort of odd behavior began, it ended with the end of the tune and they'd all resume their regular flight, eating, mating, living. They were not affected by man, in general, just this one particular act of something in their environment that, no matter how they cried out against it, how they fought to stop it, it permeated. Or maybe, in their bird brains, they just knew that it was their "eep, eep, eep" and their own self-injury in fighting the "outside" that had forced the intruder, the music, to stop. Even if they had to "eep, eep, eep" and smash themselves to death on the glass, and a few finches had lost their lives in the battle to protect the nests, it was a small sacrifice to make the music stop. And the music always, eventually, stopped.

A PEOPLE'S HISTORY OF THE MONARCH (AKA: THE SERPENT)

It was called the Serpent. It was called the "Serpent" but not because it had a cloacae. It was a Biblical reference to a thing like nothing the world had seen. With the ability to possess, in computer terms, any shape. It was beautiful, really, in the way it ravaged—without mercy. It struck at the human core of terror. For whether one spoke of the medieval woman trapped within the body of a wolf or the modern views of genetic adaptation, "othering" was the noir of horror.

The experts didn't even know how to classify it: was it a virus, a worm, a vortex. What the experts did know was that they had to keep the Serpent a secret from the people for as long as they could. For if the public had been made aware, it would have been catastrophic. The financial institutions needed time. At first they needed time to try and figure out what the Serpent was. The government agreed to keep a hush on all intelligence and the media was strongly discouraged from digging too deep on the issue. But as time wore on the experts were no closer to understanding the Serpent than when they'd begun. It possessed a way to remain undetected and was so successful at doing so that all the world's Intelligence could not discern exactly when the World's network had been infected. Just as acutely as they were helpless to predict when it might end, they were unable to stop it.

At first the industry asked for time to defeat the Serpent but, after realizing the impossibility of this, asked for more time in order that they could prepare to transition their credit systems back to paper. The government gave them this and they passed legislation allowing for the fact that computerized compounding of interest for debt was no longer a viable option; the legislation allowed the industry to notify their customers of what they thought their balance should, approximately, be and then, in fine print, the customer had 1 week from the postmarked date on their bill to question or challenge that balance. If they didn't, it went onto the ledger books. If the balance went unchallenged it remained, thereafter, legally binding. No one knew whether the figures were accurate. Accuracy was irrelevant: it was legal. And the government's legislation allowed the financial institution to implement this procedure for three years before both bodies came forward and informed the public of their secret, the Serpent. Of course, it was reported as 'groundbreaking news.'

Yet the Serpent wasn't a cruel thing, it didn't destroy universally. In fact, it had a highly specified scope: the Serpent strangled to death debt and—all debt including the credit industry. This, alone, was enough to bring the World to a screeching halt. Governments reacted by banning internet use for fear of the virus spreading. The World, in effect, slowed and became, once again, a large place. People communicated only with people they had direct contact with.

Yet as the World slowed, the virus, like all good viruses, simply lay dormant. It waited for the credit signals to trigger a relapse. Which is exactly what happened: "financial crashes" spread like the flu and happened over and over again.

*All* debt ended in the Serpent's belly: mortgages, car and recreational loans, student loans, hospital bills, even tax debt—the collection industry came to a screeching halt around the world in a matter of hours. The Serpent liked, especially and with lightening speed, to attack then feed on, what fat the banks loved most: credit card debt. It was prejudiced this way even though all debt faced the same fate.

When news of the Serpent first hit, the News reported that the world was meeting with its apocalypse. Governments around the globe went into lockdown. Its existence justified applying martial law for many countries as people were told that this was just the beginning of the end. But, as life with the Serpent continued, the news reporters slowly began to hint that the earth might not be destroyed by it. There were no bombs bursting the air. No orgies of horror. In fact, the actual number of Terrorist attacks decreased. Some speculated that it was because even terrorists used credit.

Debt had been cleaved from the world's humanity, a medieval nose of adultery. The face of the world then forever wore the artefact of its abomination: it had defiled the sacred bed with which compassion had lain with human greed and spawned the hybrid whose swaggering hips bred corruption and whose thick makeup painted profit. The whore that the world had become lost its nose—there could be no more debt ever again. The Serpent made sure of it.

In the beginning the World espoused the Serpent would quickly die away. That surely, with the worlds' top minds fiercely working on a way around it, the Serpent would be defeated. But, after years and millions of retries, this did not prove to be anything more than wishful thinking. All other programs on the computers and networks worked just fine. There was no ill effect to any other form of computer interaction except when it came to credit and debt.

If a computer had been shut off for years, left in complete disuse, and then re-commissioned, everything about the computer would function perfectly but as soon as the issue of credit/debt was introduced, the system announced its impending failure with a simple phrase, "People are worth more than linen/coton." This phrase would scroll the computer's screen until it killed whatever credit/debt issue had triggered it in the first place. After the eradication, the computer would simply return to its start menu as if nothing had happened at all leaving all other programs intact and functional. It became, to the financial sector, painfully clear that no computer could be trusted in matters of credit and debt.

To real people, the understanding was condensed to, "Computers can't be trusted." Landfills brimmed with computers and prophets claimed that the Age of the Computer would go down in history as the darkest ever.

Only a few, maybe one or two, actually considered that it was the vessel of the Computer that had delivered liberation to the People because every move the programmers made, the Serpent stealthily countered.

Yet, in the real applications of the world, it did—relatively—nothing of consequence. Banks still had money. People still had land. People had cars they had to fuel and mouths to feed. Hospitals delivered babies and death certificates. The world went on and money still flowed only there could be no debt. As soon as debt was logged onto any computer…it vanished. It was as simple as that.

The Serpent first saved a man. He only had twenty dollars in his pocket when he arrived in the emergency room after a serious auto accident. He had a fractured Femur, three cracked ribs and one had punctured a lung. He was in bad shape and the hospital bill was tremendous but after the clerk had entered the charges, charges totaling into tens of thousands, her computer went blank. She tried again and again. She called her supervisor. The hospital administrator came in. The more they tried the more other accounts disappeared. It was as if a supernatural force was at work. In the end they took the man's twenty dollars and that was the end of it. The man had been laid off work. He was already on his third application for unemployment benefits and that twenty dollars the hospital took was his last twenty dollars. It was supposed to have bought him food for three weeks. But he gave it to the hospital without a fight because he owed them his life. He'd figure out the rest of it later. But even he admitted that the Serpent had given him some hope. Hope that he'd be able to recover both in body and spirit.

Then the serpent saved a woman. She'd always been an art lover. Living in the big city, her free time was spent at studios, museums, art shows but her working hours were spent behind a desk of a medical billing office until the day an epiphany came to her: "I'll open a little picture framing shop." After having read up on how to write a business plan, she invested every penny of her minimal savings and secured a small business loan with the house her grandmother, an Irish immigrant, had managed to buy (and pay off) and had left to her only surviving kin. For ten years she struggled but there were a few good, fat years. If there hadn't have been, she'd have gone under long before the knock on her office door came. It was the tax collector. The woman, the tax collecting woman, said she was to give her all her papers, receipts, accounting books for the last five years. The collection woman smiled, warmly and said "Yes" when asked if she'd like a cup of tea. The audit took three days and on the third day, the collector rose from her seat, handed the woman the tax sheet saying she owed $120,000 in back taxes because for the last five years she had marked the wrong box on her tax form and had underpaid the government. The woman, feeling like she would vomit, because she'd expected to have to pay something to the tax collector (no one got out of an audit unscathed...she often wondered where were the people who had gotten audited only to have the collector declare they had *overpaid* the government and were to receive a tax rebate—she'd never met a live person with such an experience though she heard about non-human people, corporations, experiencing audits like that). She was expecting to pay a few thousand dollars extra—not more than a hundred thousand. The collector smiled, "I understand that you're upset but I did audit only five of your ten years of employ. If you disagree with my findings, then I can request a more thorough audit and we can look into your financials over the life of your business—since I found so many discrepancies." The woman shook her head, no. The collector left. The monthly tax repayment was difficult, especially in the lean months of which the woman found herself experiencing more and more of because the economy was struggling and people were not spending their money on expensive custom framing. If they needed a frame they went to Walmart but she was still in the fight. Each month making due with less and less for herself and more and more for the business and the government until one day she found herself opening her eyes, feeling very woozy, and found herself lying on the floor. Try as she might, she was unable to lift herself up. Her vision jumped, darted, and transitioned back and forth from tunnel vision to blurred full vision. She managed to pull her cell phone from her pocket and call 911. After being rushed to the hospital and receiving a barrage of diagnostic tests, she was diagnosed with Multiple Sclerosis and was told that often times the disease manifests itself when a person is under extreme stress. She was told that now they would have to monitor her to see if her MS was the relapsing/remitting kind, the variant that would allow her to live a relatively normal life when her MS was in remission (though her employers would have to be accommodating to her when the MS was active and debilitating) or if she had progressive MS. If it was the latter then she would need to prepare for complete disability. Hers was the latter and when she finally received her medical bill, it matched the government's tax. She found herself unable to work ever again, with no income and no family to support her financially or emotionally, applying for Social Security Disability Insurance (into which she'd been paying her whole working life) but having to wait, having to endure almost a year without any financial assistance. Then, when she got her first Social Security check, the government informed her that they would be taking out, in the form of a lien, the money she desperately needed, in order to force her to repay her tax bill. The medical bill, because the hospital had once been publically funded, was cut in half "Because," she was told, "You qualify for financial hardship." She was allowed to make monthly payments on the remainder. So, in the end, her Social Security benefits, the money she needed to live on and pay for the very expensive medications she needed, was garnished for back taxes—for old debt. It wasn't enough that she was sick and that she would suffer from that day forward to her death. It wasn't enough that the Social Security payments didn't cover her monthly rent (because the bank had repossessed her grandmother's house to cover the small business loan she was unable to pay off after getting sick). But what really made her mad was the fact that the government was *purely* funded by the public: why, in contrast to the hospital, were they allowed to take and take and take? At nights she would cry at the mercilessness of it, the injustice of it, and then she would read in the papers at the library, because it was the only place she could go to for entertainment, how the big corporations, like BP gas—who'd contaminated the Gulf's water with their carelessness, with their spilled oil—how they got tax refunds in the billions…but she, she was having Social Security garnished! And she would rant to anyone who would listen, a bum, a drunk, or the volunteer librarians (because the library's budget had been cut, once again). She was the second person the Serpent saved: one day—all of her debt simply went away.

The cancer patient and she were the beginning, the first, the Adam and Eve of many.

One of the things that fascinated the top computer and network programmers was that the Serpent remained in a state of dormancy until triggered and the trigger was highly specified: debt. Everything else was unaffected. It was a perpetual neutron bomb when activated but invisible any other time. Businesses could continue to charge fees and interest and as long as the person paid their balance, in full, each month then there was no problem. It was only when "debt" had occurred, when the account, for whatever the reason carried over to the next month without complete payment being made, that the accounts zeroed out based on the assumption that the person *couldn't* pay.

Naturally, this inspired those with tendencies to figure out how to manipulate situations to their own ends. People bought on their bankcards without any intention of paying…and then, when the card showed debt, it zeroed out.

The banks responded to the Serpent by eliminating access to funds that weren't, physically, in the bank. Cash became the gold-standard form of payment. Cards were viewed with trepidation and suspicion but the world, and its people, marched on, relatively, unaffected by what many claimed was, by nature, otherworldly.

THE NATION

So, civilian relocations and transformational infrastructure continued long past the conditions which had once mandated them because those with corrupt intention quickly determined the profit in it and, in turn, made sure that every annual vote to reauthorize his dictatorship the Benevolent Leader passed, overwhelmingly, predominantly through influencing the general public who, through the Benevolent Leader's establishment of the fourth branch of government, the People's Branch, used their co-equal voting power to trigger a supermajority veto of the president's Executive Order for the dictatorship's dissolution.

EYRE PROUST

[describe how the infrastructure operates: with only 20 fortified cities all else is left to nature so roads, rails, rivers all in various stages of decay where nature has returned and where the people of the Free live in state supported/supplied anarchy— ergo no law enforcement except social norms and no prisons anywhere as the punishment for breaking laws in the remaining Cities or violating rules in Fortaleez results in either being induced into Sleeping Sickness/fat profit center or being discharged into the Free zone]

Fortaleezians were required to participate in an LP program, as were all patients who'd fallen into comas as a result of the Sleeping Sickness, but City residents typically gave their fat if they were short of money—like blood or reproductive material.

She remembered that. She'd just started fourth grade when the Benevolent Leader addressed the nation. To her, he looked sadder than anyone she'd ever seen as he declared a national state of emergency and instituted martial law. He swore he'd restore democracy the moment all the citizens living in contaminated buildings had been successfully relocated to their nearest Fortaleez; in the beginning they were nothing more than scattered collections of tents, yurts, and domes.

THE CITY: NANETTE BAKER, CREDIT OFFICER

She spent her days explaining:

Graduating high school earned a diploma, $50,000 deposited into a city bank for the graduate, and a debt free certification; failure to graduate resulted in expulsion from Fortaleez. Very few failed to graduate but those who did would never be allowed to enter the cities; they'd spend the rest of their lives being free.

A high school diploma and debt free certificate meant automatic acceptance to university where only a small amount of debt could be accumulated, thanks to legislative reform and price capping, or one could make their pilgrimage to their closest city, and try to find work.

With only $50,000 that was a perilous option because the cost of housing in the cities after the epidemic renovations had become exorbitant, jobs were scarce, and the debt laws in the cities required both employment and housing in order to qualify for debt—and without government sanctioned debt…one could not return to a Fortaleez

For Mendy the choice was easy university. At least graduating from university would add another $50,000 to her bank account in the city but she, like everyone else she went to school with, was worried what would happen to them after graduation.

Estelle was glad that the Benevolent Leader had put an end of such abuse by creating the Compassionate Reconciliation of Debt (C.R.D.) and the Fortaleez system where debtors could enjoy a high standard of living while paying off debt. She only wished other countries could do the same; nearly every day there was another headline claiming that The Monarch had struck again somewhere else in the world. She cringed every time. The interim between The Monarch's attack on computer based debt and the establishment of the C.R.D. had been a time of unparalleled American suffering.

EYRE PROUST, CITIZEN

At the age of ten the only thing Eyre Proust understood was that the Benevolent Leader was forcing her family, and every family she'd ever known, to leave their homes. When the Marine came to the door, weapon in hand, and said, "Five minutes," Eyre swore she saw fear in her mother's eyes when she told Eyre, "Quickly…grab your things." Eyre didn't know what to grab. She was deciding between a book about a doctor who'd gone to an island where he could hybridize humans and animals and the microscope she'd been given for Christmas—her parents had told her that one day she'd grow up to be a scientist; her ears perked when she heard the Benevolent Leader say from the television that had not been turned off, "Our wonderful scientists have saved us from this plague. Now our national health, perhaps even humanity itself, depends on your cooperation. I beg you, do not resist relocation. Housing and provisions will be supplied to you by our government for as long as it takes for us to triumph over this national disaster."

Her mom began to cry when she rushed into Eyre's room to find she hadn't packed a single thing. She'd never seen her mother frantic. She'd grabbed Eyre's small school backpack, dumping books and notebooks onto the ground before stuffing clothes and shoes from her closet into it. When Eyre held out the book, for she'd finally decided which to take, her mother slapped it out of her hand. "We don't have time!"

The Marine raised her visor as Eyre, her mother, and father walked past; Eyre was surprised to see a beautiful woman who smiled and said, "It's all going to be alright." Eyre's mother tightened her grip on Eyre's arm, pulling her into the street, where she saw that everyone in the neighborhood was also being turned out. As the group walked towards the governmental buses the cacophony of televisions continued the Benevolent Leader's echo, "I promise you that every property owner, whether personal or commercial, will be given fair market value for your land. If you don't vacate willingly then our Marines will forcibly remove you. I assure you that this is matter of national security."

The moment that Marine had made her feel safe in chaos Eyre decided she'd that when she grew up she'd become a Marine too, even though it went against her parent's wishes.

[Note: make sure there are no inconsistencies with her story…the following paste contains at least one]

Have her talking to other marines

She couldn't remember exactly when she'd decided to become a Marine but she couldn't ever remember a time when she hadn't wanted to be one. Now everyone who was in the military was a Marine; the Benevolent Leader created a nation united through a united service.

As a kid, Eyre liked the television specials about the Nobel Prize winning scientists because the music was good and the colors were vibrant and cared less about the dialogue touting that their discovery proved, beyond doubt, the validity of macroevolution. She also hated the stark black and white public service announcements that interrupted her cartoons at least three times per show, talking about how everyone had a responsibility to seek immediate medical help if they felt overly tired.

She stared, as if into a thousand mile void, and her mind replayed the Daily Memory—a rapid frame advance video featuring the faces of every Marine who'd been stricken down in the line of duty since the outset of the Great Epidemic. Many died from the sickness, others became sick but lived only to spend the rest of their lives as frozen invalids in a permanent state of advanced Parkinsonism, and then there were those who'd been killed by Americans who'd refused to leave their homes and businesses. The Daily Memory was so that the sacrifice of all the Marines, whether dead or comatose, would never be forgotten.

Thinking such thoughts made her head hurt. She couldn't wait to land. The inactivity and mechanical thrum triggered her mind to replay the faces of her fellow fallen Marines.

WILLIAM HENRY LITTLE, CITIZEN

HISTORY of

What neither William nor Moribund could know was that William Henry Little's wife, Page Little, wanted nothing more than to move back into a house and for her children to be fed. As soon as William Henry Little signed his name onto the P.T.P. project and he was driven away, the agents rounded up what women and children belonged to the men, had them sign their own, pink, brochure agreements, and loaded them into different vans. They were driven to a suburb of the city that was still so new that the sod hadn't even been delivered. Great mounds of browngray dirt skirted the stillfresh housepaint.

Page Little's house was a four-bedroom, two-bath, with an open floorplan, ceiling fans, a fireplace, hardwood floors in the kitchen and white carpet throughout. The kitchen had a dishwasher, refrigerator, oven/stove and a double-sink. Off the back was a wooden deck that could have led to a green backyard only the sod hadn't come yet.

In all her life, Page Little couldn't remember ever being as happy as she was the moment the agents handed her the key. They gave her another pink brochure, in case she'd misplaced the other, and a copy of the blue one her husband had entered into an agreement with, by signing his name. Additionally, they gave her two plastic cards, like credit cards, one pink and one blue. The blue read, "William Henry Little, P.T.P., 3." The pink read, "Page Little, L.P."

Though there were no beds, pots or pans; the electricity was on. The children bathed in nice, warm water for the first time in a long time and that night they all felt they were sleeping on clouds because the carpet was so much softer than the rocks and dirt below the raging traffic of cars.

It wasn't until morning that Page Little thought about how they were going to survive and this prompted her to read, very carefully, the agreement her husband had made. After an hour, Page Little realized that the only thing William Henry Little's blue card could do was to get her children food and that the card would be honored at all the fast-food chains and grocery stores.

"So," she thought, "William is working to pay off our debt. And the kids can eat burgers…fries…sodas…ice cream: food is unlimited, for them. But what about me!" She was still starving…and homeless. "Wait," she looked around the house, "We're not homeless now. Why not?" She clamored for the pink brochure.

THE NATIONAL GOVERNMENT WANTS YOU!

Need a house?

Can't afford to heat/cool your house?

Have to have health insurance?

Want food?

If you answered yes to any of the above then you are a perfect candidate for the new LP.

The LP (or lipophilic program) needs strong, healthy women who are willing to help our country. In return for your work you will receive:

Housing Credit,

Utility Credit and

Food Credit*

Plus, while you're working for the LP you will receive healthcare*.

> So what do you have to loose—except an excellent opportunity? Agents will be recruiting all over this great nation. Remember, everyone must do their part to restore the American Nation to its rightful place of honor, dignity and independence.

> *For LP enrollee only; *Limited.

"I have health insurance," Page pondered. "Isn't that a trip! And William does too. I wonder how he is. How the work is for him. But wait," she scrutinized every word of the pink and blue only to realize, "the kids don't have insurance. Oh," she sighed, "that's not so bad. I mean they're healthy kids, now. And I'm sure arrangements can be made if we should need a doctor."

The doorbell rang. Page opened it to find a nicely dressed young woman.

"Hello. I'm Bernice Anderson and I'm your governmental caseworker. May I come in?"

"Oh sure," Page smiled, "But I don't have anything for you to sit on."

"That's why I've come. I'm here to help you transition into your new position."

"Position?"

"Oh yes. You're new job."

"Job?"

"You're part of the L.P. team now. Didn't you read the pink brochure?"

"I did. I didn't see though how it was a job."

"Exactly! Isn't that what's wonderful about our New Government. They even make work seem like it's not work. So here is your schedule."

The lady handed Page a pink piece of paper denoting her name in the time slots of Monday, Wednesday, Friday and every other Saturday for 2 hours.

"I don't understand," Page said, looking between the woman and the pink sheet.

"Oh that's okay. It's all confusing at first, but trust me. This is the easiest work you'll ever do."

"But what about my children?"

"There is onsite daycare provided."

"And how will I get there? I don't have a car."

The lady pulled, from her valise, a yellow brochure and handed it to Page Little.

"I am authorized to offer you P.T.P. credit but only for necessities."

"Credit? I can't afford credit."

"You don't have to. Your husband is a P.T.P. employee and as such is eligible for credit."

"I'm not sure I understand."

The lady pointed to the bedrooms. "You can use credit to buy beds."

"But who pays for it?"

"That's why your husband is working."

"I thought he was working to pay off our old healthcare debts."

"He is. And that's why this credit is only for necessities. You must use it responsibly. Would you like me to sign you up for it now?"

Page Little opened the brochure. Inside was a list of essentials: kitchenware, clothing, personal hygiene, bedding and accessories, furniture, one government issued economical automobile, auto insurance, dependent health insurance and all medical expenses.

"What is the limit on the P.T.P. credit?"

"I can't answer that question."

"Why not?"

"Because it's not the correct question."

"Then what is the correct question?"

"The correct question should be, 'What do I absolutely need in order to fulfill my employment agreement with the National Government?'"

Page Little signed the yellow brochure and was issued a yellow credit card. Outside semi-trucks were delivering government issued economical vehicles to the women whose husbands had gone to work for the P.T.P. Bernice Anderson, Page Little's caseworker, walked beside her and explained that these cars were special. They were experimental and required weekly maintenance. And that it was absolutely mandated that all recipients faithfully take their cars to the government shops, once a week.

"In fact," Bernice added, "I will adjust your schedule right here and now. You will go to the autoshop on Tuesdays. Tuesdays. Do you understand?"

"Yes."

"Now," Bernice grew visibly excited, "Pick out your color!"

Page Little's children had followed them out. Their clothes were dingy. Their hair mussed. They were barefooted and hopped from side to side because the asphalt was melting in little black bubbles that, occasionally, popped. The youngest, the boy who'd died, Billy, named after his father, squatted down and stuck his fingers into the goo. His feet were tough as nails. Page often wondered if that was because of his birth. But the other two, Fawn, the eldest, and Mabel, the middle, both ran to their mother's side.

"Get the green one, Mother!" Fawn cried.

"No!  The blue one is best.  Get that one, Pa-LEEEZ!"

Page called Billy to her side.  "I figure, if it weren't for Billy, we wouldn't be here at all.  So, Billy, what do you want?"

"Dad," he said, flatly.  Then returned to the tar.

Page sucked in air.  As much as she'd blamed him for everything that had happened, even in spite of knowing it wasn't really his fault, she couldn't bring herself to think on him.  She just couldn't.  He had to do what was right by the family.  He had to be away and that was that.

"I like the rose one," she said and even though the girls protested, loudly, she stuck to her guns.  "The rose one, please."

Bernice Anderson opened the glove compartment, retrieved the documents therein, and walked with Page and the children back into the house.  The air conditioner kept it comfortable.  Bernice showed Page the map to the government auto shop and to the L.P. clinic nearest her.  She gave her, also, a map to the nearest shopping mall where all the shops were instructed to accept the government's yellow card.  Page was a little surprised to see how close she was to them all.

Before leaving, Bernice Anderson gave Page Little her card, "If you need me or have any questions, please feel free to call."

"But I don't have a phone."

"You can take care of that at the mall.  Good day."

And with that, the caseworker was gone.

Inside the cool house, Page sat on the ground with her three children.  They clothes had already soiled the white carpet.  "I bet you can buy a vacuum cleaner on the yellow card too," she half-said to herself but aloud.

"Let's go to the mall, Mom," Fawn said.

Page Little looked at her oldest child, who was just about to become a teenager.

"Okay."

The government car was a strange thing.  The driver's seat was pure metal but the others were upholstered.  Page was given specific instruction that even when her children were old enough to drive that the government contract was only between herself and the government and no one else was allowed to drive the car. There was no exception. But it was a strange car. It smelled new and strange all at once. It smelled of an odor Page was not familiar with. And it did not go very fast but they didn't need it to go very fast, because the mall and everything they needed was just around the corner from their house.

In the parking lot Page suddenly became acutely aware of how awful and destitute they all looked. She licked her finger and tried to press Billy's hair to one side. She looked in the mirror and wiped a smudge from her own face. She told her daughters to straighten up their clothes, in spite of the fact that no amount of straightening would have helped the rags they wore. And then, after doing everything she could to make them presentable, she resolved herself to the humiliation of parading their poverty in public.

To her delight, they were not alone. Throughout the mall were women and children just like them. In fact, some were even worse.

"Do you have the yellow card," Fawn asked. She was always the responsible one. "And the car key? And the house key?"

Page laughed, "I didn't lock them. I figured there was nothing to steal, at least not with the house. And the parking lot was full of cars just like ours, so why would anyone steal?" Fawn harrumphed. She hated her mother's lackadaisical approach to life. She was as intolerant as was typical of near-teens.

Suddenly Billy pulled on Page's arm, hard. "Over there!" he screamed and before she could stop him he ran into a toy store. Lights, sirens, gizmos, gadgets, it was a veritable fantasyland. Games, puzzles, paints, crafts, models, there was everything a child could want but Billy, instantly identified his heart's desire. It was MegaLab!

To say MegaLab was a child's first microscope was like saying a nano is a small thing: MegaLab had it all. Test tubes, prepared slides, high-powered lenses and both electrical and solar power. It came with its own book!

"Please Mom, please!" Billy begged but Page Little hushed him, "We don't have any money now put that back right this instant!"

A young store clerk came up, "Hi. I'm Melanie and I can help you."

"No. No thanks," Page mumbled, trying not to make eye contact while ushering her children out.

"But," the clerk continued, "I couldn't help but overhear your son's enthusiastic desire for the MegaLab."

Page Little blushed hard red. "Oh," she replied, "I'm so sorry about that."

"Oh that's not it. I mean. Well, if you'd like, he can have it."

"Yes Mommy, PLEEEEEZ!"

"Stop it, Billy!"

"It's covered," the girl whispered, "by the government."

Page Little looked at her with what must have been utter confusion.

"It's covered because the National Government wants all of our children to embrace science as much as they're willing to."

Fawn grabbed a book on wildlife, "What about this?"

"Oh yes. That too. Anything educational can be purchased using the yellow card."

Page noticed that when the girl said "yellow card" she lowered her voice, which was why she asked her, "Is the yellow card...disgraceful?"

"Oh no, no, no. I'm so sorry if I, in any way, intimated that it was. It's just that sometimes the mothers get a little...worried...and so I've tried to become more discreet."

"I see," Page Little replied. "But my husband is a good man. A hardworking man and I have nothing to be ashamed of."

"Oh most certainly not. Not at all. Would you like me to ring up the MegaLab?"

"Yes," Page Little replied, "And we'll take the book as well."

"What about me?" Mabel cried. "I want the paint set."

"Is that covered?" Page asked the girl.

"I'm sorry, no. Only science."

"Pick something else."

"But I want to paint!"

The clerk smiled, "I know just the thing." She returned with a book of the planets and universes that also happened to be a paint-by-numbers. "How's this?"

"Wonderful!" Mabel screamed.

The four left the toy store with a slip of paper that added $250.00 to William Henry Little's labor-debt at Fortaleez. Next came the beds, the pots and pans, the clothes, the washing and drying machines, the sofa and matching loveseat, the widescreen TV, the smelly shop filled with bathing supplies and finally the shoes. The stores would deliver it all later that afternoon: a fleet of delivery trucks was afoot.

All the shopping had made them all hungry. They went to the food court. Page Little bought Chinese. Billy got pizza, soda pop, and cookies. Mabel wanted a cinnamon roll the size of her head and milk. Fawn wanted a salad. She liked what poverty made her body look like. She'd been noticing the boys noticing her.

For the children's food, William Henry Little's blue card worked but for her own food, Page used her pink. It made her feel good. It made her feel independent. She liked that she was able to provide a home for her children and get all the comforts therein. She wondered, for a moment, how William was doing. But there wasn't time for sentimentality. They had to get home, gosh she liked the sound of that word, 'home,' because the delivery trucks were coming. They were coming and a new life was beginning.

WHL to talk about the current state of affairs for his wife and kids and the Fortaleez program from Separated/married mothers and children and single mothers with children: basically an all woman and child Fortaleez, and the Fortaleez for single dads with children, which never amounted to much, having the highest enrollment at the peak of the epidemic, when many mothers/wives lost their lives, but now has little demand, with only three operating in the entire country]

, being a security guard for the University.

He'd worked for a small, state-owned, liberal arts college in the 3rd poorest State in the country. He'd gotten the job straight out of high school from a college-graduate who'd just gotten the job as supervisor a month earlier. The security department consisted of 12 people covering three shifts: two parking meter ladies, who were both over 50, the supervisor, the dayshift dispatch lady, who was in her thirties, two dayshift officers, two officers for swing and three for graveyard. It made sense because the college kids got good and drunk just around the end of swing's shift. So graveyard got to deal with all the puke, the drunks, the thefts, the getting locked out of dorm rooms, the date rapes. Graveyard got to see the most shit, which was why William Henry Little, being the gentle giant that he was, was instantly and forevermore put onto it.

He didn't mind. The pay was better than minimum wage, though not much better, but he got to have the University's health insurance, which helped tremendously with his son's complicated birthdeath and his wife's health afterwards. But even with the school's insurance, the bill was more than his annual salary, three times over. So the Littles set up a payment plan. The doctors and hospitals were glad to do it because William Henry Little was, obviously, a decent man, a hardworking man, and a moral man—working in law enforcement.

He'd met Page in high school. She was, to him, the most beautiful girl in the world and was shocked to find out that every other guy didn't think the same thing. In fact, they said she was homely and poor. He defended her, "Her dad's poor not her." They wouldn't see the difference. But William Henry Little didn't care. She was beautiful in her green eyes, her brown hair, her skinny bones and square hips. He thought she was the most beautiful girl in the world and she thought the world of him too.

Her poor daddy gave his permission for them to marry early, figuring 17 was old enough and he could see the way they looked at each other. Being poor, he'd learned to notice things other often didn't, or wouldn't. He knew if they waited they'd have to get married. This way, it was a choice.

William Henry Little's folks weren't that much more well-off than Page's dad, but they had a small barn on their property and told the new couple they could live in it. William Little went to work on it right away. He mended the roof, patched the wall where a heifer had rushed in to her weaning calf's cries because her utter was filled to bursting. He tried to paint but the dried out old wood was beyond accepting it. He took his bed from his parents' house and a wash basin, even though the well had long-gone dry and he'd have to haul water from his parents' house, who'd gone onto the rural water system years ago. Page and William Little looked at their little home, their dirt-floored home, and couldn't have been happier. Of course, Page got pregnant right away.

William Little managed to finish his last year of high school but Page Little, in spite of being so tiny, was asked to leave school during her last semester. She'd begun to show. It was a time and a place where such things just were not done. The school's administration took the position that she'd "made her bed." Besides, it was assumed that her husband would provide for her. And he did.

William Henry Little was the ideal worker. He was early, he never complained, he did whatever it took to deal with a situation even when it meant he'd get hurt himself, like when a college student was throwing glass bottles at everyone who walked beneath his dormroom window, and at anyone who tried to enter his room to stop him. William Little rushed in, taking a shattering glass bottle to the head, and stopped the young man.

As blood ran into his eye William asked him, "Why are you doing this?"

He replied, "All credibility, all good conscience, all evidence of truth come only from the senses!"

William grabbed his kerchief from his pocket and put it on his brow, "That doesn't make any sense."

"It's Nietzsche you philistine!

William waited with the young man who, summarily, fell to weeping. The city's police came and took their report. One of the officers, a big man like William, came up and asked William if he wanted to charge the kid with assault. William said, "Heck no. He's just a stupid kid." The stitches ended up costing, even with the University's health insurance coverage, a couple hundred bucks.

William had worked for the university almost a year when the head of the security department called a special meeting. There had been some restructuring, because of the State's new budget, and the main difference was that their health insurance coverage was going to change. "But," the college graduate supervisor informed them, "The union is fighting for us and because of this flexibility over the health insurance, we're going to be able to keep our retirement packages. And I don't need to remind you that the University's retirement package is really something. We DON'T want to loose that."

William Henry Little's first child was born a beautiful baby girl. The hospital sent their bill home along with their Free baby kit. The bill was as big as the baby was small and William and Page little, couldn't have been happier. William saved up enough money for the deposit, first, and last month's rent on a two-bedroom, 696 square foot house. He wasn't going to have his baby girl growing up in a barn with no running water.

Page Little thought she'd died and gone to heaven the first time she used the toilet. Her father had been poor and William Henry Little, bless his heart, was poor too. It had been a lifetime, for Page Little, of using the outhouse. That clean, white porcelain, that fresh cool water, it was like living in a palace! The first thing Page Little did was stick her head in the sink and let the cold water run into her mouth. "It tastes better," she thought, "Because it's mine."

There couldn't have been a cleaner baby in all the world. Page Little stuck her little baby girl, Mabel, in a bath at least twice a day. Page Little thought all her dreams had come true. So did her husband, William. With each paycheck William got from the University, they fixed the tiny house up. Each month William would complain that Page was spending too much, that they needed to save. But Page Little wouldn't hear of it. "Besides," she'd say, "We'll save on the next paycheck."

Then Page got pregnant with Fawn, a healthy baby girl. Of course, William Henry Little had only just paid off Mabel's hospital bill but he'd paid it off and that's all that mattered. The hospital extended a monthly payment plan because William Little was a hardworking, trustworthy, average-American man.

When the final bill finally came, William Little was shocked to see how much more expensive babies had gotten in only two years' time. The difference in price between Mabel and Fawn was a good thousand dollars. But, he'd gotten a "cost of living" increase to his hourly pay.

Things were going along, like things do: day in—day out. William Little got a new uniform shirt. He'd worn the other out in the six years he'd worked. He was responsible for buying his own pants, shoes, and socks even though the department mandated they be ordered from a particular company and their products cost a lot. William Henry Little wore his clothes to threads because of this and, because of this, he almost lost his temper.

It was the night before Spring break and most of the kids had gone home. There were a few stragglers and they, of course, were partying. William got the call. A girl had been attacked and the police were on the way. William drove the security car to the site, just outside the library, where the lighting was poor. He saw someone running. He jumped out and ran after them. He remembered thinking, "I need to be in better shape," but he found he was gaining on what he could then see was a young man. The gap between them closed. William mustered his gigantic leg strength and leapt. He and the boy tumbled. William heard a "rip." His long arms held the squirming boy until he surrendered. Five minutes later the police came and arrested the boy.

The newspapers called William a hero. The boy had tried to rape a young Biology student who was leaving the library. The police department gave him a medal for service to the community. William was not happy. He'd torn his brand new pants, the pants he'd waited over a year to get, the pants that replaced his other pants that had worn themselves to seethrough on the inner thigh. He'd ripped his brand new pants on apprehending that boy. But when he asked his department head if they'd reimburse him, if they'd spring for a new pair, he was told, "There's no money. Sorry." And the supervisor was right. There was no money.

William Henry Little learned, a few months later, that his wife was pregnant again.  It had been four years since Fawn had been born and for some strange reason William thought he and Page were past it.  That maybe he'd become infertile or something, or maybe she had because for four years…nothing.  Of course, it could have been that they weren't really having a lot of 'relations' but William didn't give that much thought.  He had work to do and too many bills to pay.  And boy were there bills.

With Mabel and Fawn, Page Little had been young and healthy.  She was still healthy, everyone always said she looked healthy, but something in the world had changed.  Whereas the pregnancies with Mabel and Fawn were left up to Nature and God Almighty, minus the hospital births, the latest pregnancy seemed to require all kinds of doctor visits.  Plus there were tests and none of it was free.  Page Little had been told about a Women's Clinic by the checkout girl at the grocery store.  When William Henry Little got home Page told him that she'd made an appointment.

"Why?" William asked.

"Because I want to have a healthy baby," Page replied.

"Yes, but you always do have healthy babies."

"I know, but that's just the way they do it now."

William Henry Little realized that in just four, short years things could change.  Page Little went to the Clinic and they set her up on regular, monthly "Well Mommy and Healthy Fetus" visits.  It was not cheap, not cheap at all.  By the time Page Little was wheeled into the hospital, the Littles had racked up, at the Women's Clinic, thousands of dollars.  Then William Markus Little, called Billy, was born dead.

William Henry Little was in the waiting room when the obstetrician came.

"There's a problem with the baby," the woman told him.  "We had to revive him and even though he responded, we're concerned and need to keep him for observation."

"He?" William Little said.

"Yes, Mr. Little.  You have a baby boy."

"And how is Page?"

"We're concerned for her too.  She's bleeding a lot and we're having a hard time stopping it.  We'll need to keep her for observation too."

"Whatever it takes," William Little began to cry.

The doctor put her hand on his shoulder, "Don't worry, Mr. Little, we're doing everything we can."

In all, the mother and child stayed in the hospital for a week. Page Little received a full hysterectomy and Billy Little recovered just fine and William Henry Little signed his name to, yet another, payment plan but things at work were getting tough. The voters had voted down an initiative to raise taxes for higher education. The school was laying off non-essential positions and support staffs, like the school's health departments two secretaries, were split in half leaving one person to do the work of two. William Henry Little's security department was not immune. One of the parking ticket ladies was laid off. One of the three dayshift officers was too. Everyone was informed that the effects they were feeling were just the beginning of a "reorganization" of state-funded programs.

William Henry Little managed to hold on for two more years before he was let go. He went to the supervisor and told him that there was absolutely no way one person could do all the work and answer all the calls on graveyard, the supervisor smiled, "There won't be just one person."

"I don't understand," William Little replied.

"That's why I'm the boss and you're not. You see, William, I've made an arrangement with the university to make 2/3rds of the security force students who will get paid nothing except room and board."

"How can you do that!"

"Easy. You cost too much money."

"But I barely make more than minimum wage!"

"Yes, but the school pays double that in FICA, Worker's Compensation, and Health benefits. With the students, we don't have to pay *any* of that."

William Henry Little knew what he was saying was true. He thought of his family, his three kids and wife, his little house that he was hoping they could move out of because it was getting too small for five people. He thought of what his supervisor said.

"Can I ask you something?"

"Sure, why not."

"How much do you make?"

"A lot more than you did."

"How much more? A thousand, two thousand? Do you make double what I make? Triple?"

"I'm not going to say how much I make. Let's just say, you were hotter the longer you talked."

"Then why don't you leave and let the security officers stay. That way the school spends just as much money on the security department but has more qualified and mature people doing their security?"

"Because, William, that's just not how it's done."

That was it. William Little's job was completely eliminated. The students were filing into the supervisor's office the day William cleared out the last of his things, turned in his badge and uniform shirt. One, a young girl, smiled at him in a friendly way. William thought of the night he'd apprehended the rapist. His brow grew troubled. "Be safe," he said to her. "Oh I will," she beamed, "I just hope I get the job."

William Henry Little's unemployment insurance held his family afloat for six months but, because it was only a portion of what he made, there was nothing to save. In fact, when William cashed his check he would instantly take out rent, hospital bill, doctor bill, utilities and what was left over was what they lived on, which wasn't much. William went to the hospital to explain that he'd been laid off, but was told that he was already at the minimum allowable payment for the amount of his bill. The Women's Clinic told him the same thing.

William Henry Little's landlord raised the rent, only $50.00 a month, because he hadn't raised it even one time the six years the Littles had been living there. William explained his situation the landlord.

"I understand, William," the landlord said, "But these times are getting harder on everyone. Me included."

William Henry Little didn't blame the man. In fact, he'd always liked him. He was older, friendly, and always did his best to keep the place in good working order…without spending much money. Like the time William had called him about a roof leak that had ruined the carpet and the old landlord came, patched the roof himself, then put a mismatched carpet remnant down, claiming, "There you go." The Littles didn't mind. He'd been good to them, especially because William had heard that some landlords had rules about how many people could live in smaller places. William's landlord didn't seem to mind that the five of them lived in 696 square feet.

What his landlord did mind, was that William Henry Little's unemployment eventually wore out and, after two months of receiving no rent, he had no choice but to evict the Littles.

William Little had given all his money to the hospital, the Women's clinic, his landlord and the grocery store. He had nothing left. Page Little sold their stuff to neighbors for pennies because they'd never been able to afford things that could fetch higher prices. They ate that money up quick. William Henry Little and his family walked to the city, hoping that in the city William would find work. "After all," he'd say, "All those big fine companies have to have security officers too." But no one was hiring. The Littles heard of a soup dinner at a church where they heard of a bridge where others, other homeless people, congregated for shelter and safety in numbers. William Little thought, "I'll be Hobo security." He was surprised at the kindness of strangers. Especially when they saw little Billy, who'd just turned 2 and who didn't have a clue what being homeless meant and who ran around to everyone smiling, playing, and—sometimes irritating—all without judgment or preconception. Everyone loved little Billy and William Henry Little was thankful for that.

WILLIAM HENRY LITTLE'S FAMILY

Page Little thought she was living a dream. She looked around her house, with all its fine things, and the insides of her went fluttering with excitement. "Almost like falling in love," she thought. After all she'd lived, she just couldn't have imagined living the life the National Government had given her. And all she had to do, in return, was go to the LP clinic and maintain the government's car. How much easier it could be, Page Little did not know.

The LP clinic was, to Page's thinking, absolutely marvelous minus the weigh-in. That took a little getting used to. The first day, following the map her caseworker, Bernice Anderson, had given her Page Little, with Mabel, Fawn and Billy in tow, pulled into a fresh black parking lot in front of a brand new glass building. It was all curves and arches and there was a column in the front with water pouring out from the center, running down the sides, and filling a large reflecting pool. Billy was, immediately, drawn to it. But Page Little told him that he was absolutely forbidden to climb in, which was exactly what he'd had in mind.

Directly inside the door was a reception desk where a beautiful young redheaded woman sat. Her emerald eyes overflowed, like the fountain, with welcome and "What's your name?" When Page Little told her her name, the woman smiled warm as ember, and said, "Page Little, here is your form. Go right through those doors," and she pointed to two large milky glass doors off to the right of the lobby. Page looked at the form. Her name was typed in the space, Name, it was dated, and there were blank spaces.

"Do I need to fill anything out?" she asked the woman.

The woman laughed, "Oh no, Dear, they'll do it all for you. Just go inside." And she, again, pointed to the milky doors.

"What about my children?" Page asked.

The woman's smile was working harder to remain fixed, "Just go inside the milky doors. Everything is inside there." And she pointed, again.

The door handle was cold metal and, in spite of the doors largeness, the half Page Little pulled yielded quite easily. Inside the milky doors was a wonderland. Billy instantly ran to the fort, Mabel went to the juice bar, but Fawn clung to her mother.

A young brunette took Page's arm, "This way," she said.

"What about my children?"

"Oh they're already checked in and they'll be fine. We have lots for them to do. In fact, this is only the children's reception area. Through those doors," she pointed to two additional milk glass doors, "There's a whole amusement park with video games, go carts, jumping forts, and even waterslides."

Fawn cried, "But I don't have a bathing suit!"

The girl smiled, "That's okay, Sweetie, we've got one just your size. We have suits for all the kids."

Page's brow knit, "But I don't have any money to pay for them."

"They're free. It's all part of the LP program so don't worry about a thing. Oh, and the doors you just went through are secure. The kids can't get out until you come get them." The girl looked side-to-side before speaking, "Sometimes some of the kids are a *little* wild and, in spite of constant watching, are quite clever at running off. This way, there's no way they can get very far."

"I see. What about when we leave?"

"Oh. You go out another door altogether. But for right now, Page Little, you need to get to your appointment. So have fun and we'll see you in two hours."

Page Little watched the young girl lead her children off through the doors. She watched the doors close behind them. She looked to the doors she was supposed to go through and a part of her felt, a slight twinge, of…was it, apprehension? But it was all for nothing because through Page Little's doors was absolute bliss—minus the weigh in.

The weigh in consisted of stripping naked, sitting on a metal swing that dangled over a small pool of water, having a weight belt put on top of her lap, and being instructed to exhale all the air in her lungs upon being submersed in the water. She was told that if she failed to exhale all the air in her lungs, she'd have to do it again.

Page Little had never been much of a water lover and this experience did nothing to foster a change in her perspective. Wanting to do the best she could, she exhaled hard and quick. The swing was lowered into the water until Page Little felt the water cover her head. It seemed to last forever. It felt like she was drowning. She tried to stay absolutely still because she'd been told to stay absolutely still, but her legs involuntarily flinched. Her eyes jolted open. The thought, "I have to breathe!" and "I can't hold it any longer!" Panic set in, and just then, the swing was lifted out of the water.

"See," the young woman with athletic arms cooed, "It wasn't so bad."

"That was awful! I never want to do that again!"

"Oh, I'm sorry, Love. But you have to do that every time. That's part of the job. But I promise, the worst part's over now. Just go through those doors over there." And she pointed to, yet another, set of milky glass doors.

"But what about clothes?"

"Your clothes are waiting for you in the locker room. After you finish your work."

"You mean I have to work NAKED!"

"Oh my goodness, NO!" she laughed. "Once you go through the doors, they'll issue you your daily suit. Just go through those doors." And she pointed, again.

As Page Little walked to the next set of doors, she saw another woman coming in to the tank room. "Poor thing," she thought. Then Page Little crossed over to the next room.

Immediately inside the door a young blonde girl handed Page a paper suit, "Put this on, but be careful. They tear easy."

"I need a towel. To dry off."

"Oh no. I was told all you need is the paper suit and it's fine if it gets a little wet."

"Fine," Page consented and put it on, carefully.

"Now go into room 15," she pointed to a long hallway of closed doors.

"Where's room 15?"

"Down the hall there, on your left."

Inside room 15 was a metal chair and another young girl who instructed Page Little to sit down. Page did as instructed.

"Here," the girl said, handing Page some headphones, "You can listen to any kind of music you like. Or," she handed Page an electronic gadget, "If you prefer, you can read anything from our library, which is quite extensive."

Page took the headphones and the gadget, "How do I change the station?"

The girl gave her a tutorial on both technologies, but added, before she left, "You mustn't move. You must remain still while you're working. This is vitally important. If, for some reason, you are not able to remain still during your time in the LP program, then you may be removed from the program. Do you understand?"

"I do," Page replied. It made her think of William.

And, with that, the young girl exited the room. Page Little found some celebrity magazines at the library. She liked looking at the different hairstyles and fashions. She closed her eyes and listed to Jamaican music and wondered what it would be like to travel to a tropical island. She must have fallen asleep, but swore, before she did, she could smell something strange, faint but strange, like the smell of her car. Was it...cherry?

Before she knew it, the two hours were over and the young girl who'd introduced her to the room and technology returned to instruct her to strip out of her paper suit, "Dispose of it through that chute," she pointed to the wall where a metal handle, when pulled, opened up like the old outdoor depositories of physical libraries, "Then, when you exit the room, turn left and go all the way to the end of the hall, through the doors, and into the exit counseling area."

"Is that where my clothes are?"

"No, they're in the locker room."

"So I have to do the exit counseling naked?"

"Yes. They've found that it helps people to better understand the goal of the LP program. But don't worry. It's very short and it's absolutely discreet."

Page Little did what she'd been told to do. She walked through the doors to find another woman who ushered her to a cubicle lined with mirrors, a scale, and a door immediately to the back of it.

"Hi. I'm your counselor for today. Step on the scale please."

Page Little stepped on the scale.

"I see." The woman wrote on Page Little's form, which was attached to a clipboard she held. "You can step off now."

"I don't feel comfortable being naked like this."

"I completely understand but that's the policy. You see, Page Little, you just don't weigh enough."

"What?"

"You heard me. Look at yourself," she made Page Little face one of the mirrors, "Your stomach is sunken. Your ribs are showing in your sternum area," she pointed to Page's chest, "Your breasts are not full and look," she instructed Page to turn so she could see her backside, "You have very little soft tissue on your gluteals. You just don't weigh enough and this is a real problem for a woman enrolled in the LP program."

"It is?"

"Oh yes. Very serious. In fact, if you don't show marked improvement in your weight and underwater measurements by your next visit, then I'm afraid you may be dropped."

"But what about the house? Where will we go?"

"That's not my problem. That's yours."

Panic grabbed Page Little, as if by the throat, she began to choke, only it was tears, "What can I do!"

The woman handed her some handouts, "Read these. They'll tell you exactly what you need to do. To begin with, go food shopping and buy all the foods recommended for improving weight status and eat as much of them as you possibly can. Sometimes you might even feel nauseous. Just take a little break, then eat some more. You want to eat as much of the recommended foods as you possibly can by your next appointment and that should, hopefully, keep you enrolled."

"I'll do whatever it takes! I promise."

"Oh, and don't do any extra exercising either.  Just the minimum you absolutely must do in order to live a regular life.  After all, even though the National Government needs you to do your part for this great country, it also wants you to be happy and healthy."

"Oh I will.  I will!" Page cried.

"Good, now go through that door," she pointed to the rear of the cubicle, "to the locker room, get dressed and fetch your children.  I think you'll find that they've had a wonderful time."

Page Little did just as she'd been told.  She fetched her children and they all told her that they'd had the most marvelous time and that they couldn't wait to come back and that they were so happy that their mom had such a great job.  Page Little, however, could not feel so enthused.  She knew, in less than two full days, she'd be back in that cubicle and she'd have to have a better weigh-in.

"Listen," Page told them, "We've got to go to the grocery store first."

"Yeah!" they all screamed.  They liked the grocery store because, with their father's blue card, they could buy whatever their hearts desired, regarding food and they all, including Page Little, thanked God for the National Government that had made it all possible.

WILLIAM HENRY LITTLE'S FAMILY

To market, to market, to buy a fat pig!

Home with it!  Jiggety jig!

Stuff it till Christmas and make a fat hog,

Then at Smithfield Show* win a prize, jiggety jog!

Nursery Rhyme (1876); *Smithfield Show may refer to The Royal Smithfield Club (est. 1798)

Page Little led her little family—Mabel, Fawn, and Billy—into their little government car with the knowledge that she'd have to, in less than two full days, have to have a better weigh-in. She'd have to prove to the clinician, she'd complied and that she was able to gain weight. Everything depended on it.

"Listen," she told her children, "We've got to go to the grocery store."

"Yeah!" they all screamed.

They liked the grocery store because, with their father's blue card, they could buy whatever their hearts desired regarding food. While Page Little drove, she listened to her childrens' voices. She couldn't recall a time, ever before, when such excitement overflowed from them.

"Mom," Billy cried, "You have the BEST job!"

Page Little smiled, but it was a nervous, tense smile that pinched because from the fear that if she failed, the very sounds of pleasure from her children that caused her delight would be the utter disappointments she feared she just could not bear.

"Let's all," Mabel shouted, "Roll down the windows and shout, "Thank God for the National Government!"

Her sister and brother immediately followed her command. Page Little whispered, "Thank God for the National Government," but instantly flashed to standing naked before the clinician who'd told her she just didn't weigh enough to remain in the program. Page looked down at the handouts she'd place in between her seat and the front passenger's. She reached over and clutched them as if they were a Bible and, to her, they were: they held the answers that offered salvation.

At the grocery store, Page Little went through every page of the pamphlets. They suggested foods high in starch, sugars, fats and proteins. They suggested large quantities of highly processed foods and forbade whole grains with high fiber, fresh fruits or vegetables and fresh meats. The proteins were to come from processed proteins like bars and shakes but only to be used sparingly. The pamphlet said: "Don't worry. We're here to help you. We *want* you to succeed in the LP program so the grocery stores have marked all the foods for those who are in need of an *Improved Weight* result with green tags labeled "LP."

When Page Little looked down the cookie isle she saw a sea of green. The same was true of chips, soda, and candy. The cereal isle was spotty. The meat case reflected not a sign of green. The dairy case's pinks and browns were green—Fawn cried, "I love strawberry milk. Can we get some?" Page Little loaded the cart.

Mabel came back with frozen chicken strips. Seeing them, Page Little's stomach began to rumble, but she wanted to make sure it was on the list so all of them went to the frozen food section where Page Little was happy to see that it, too, was a sea of green.

At the checkout stand Page Little handed the girl her card. The girl smiled and said, "Congratulations, Mrs. Page. You've done very well for your first attempt at improving your weight."

"How do you know I need to improve my weight?" Page whispered.

"Oh, well, it shows up on our computer."

"Really?" Page asked.

"Yes. And we're instructed to encourage all the women. Did I do alright in encouraging you?"

"Oh," Page, shook her head still not quite comprehending everything, "Yes. You did fine."

The girl turned to Mabel, "Did you know that you can join the LP program as soon as you turn 13?"

"Really?" Mabel visibly grew excited.

"Yes, on a limited basis and with your mother's approval," the girl shifted her eyes back to Page, "And then, if you've been successful in the program, you get a chance to work at the grocery stores."

"How cool!" Mabel's voice overflowed.

"Yeah," the girl looked back at Mabel, "You only have to be 14 to work here."

Page's expression turned to scorn, "What about school?"

"Oh," the girl smiled, sweetly, "They work with you. Besides, the school offers a work-study program. My hours here work towards my diploma."

Page shook her head, "But how is this teaching you…"

The register beeped, "Oh, I'm sorry Mrs. Little, but I can't really visit anymore." She handed Page Little her receipt, her card, and then turned to Mabel, "If you're interested, there's handouts by the exit doors."

"Sweet!" Mabel cried, running straightaway to the pamphlet rack.

Page Little gave the girl a dirty look, "I don't find *that* helpful at all."

At this, the girl's smile disappeared and her eyes seemed as if they were ready to burst into a pool of tears.

In the car, Mabel read the entire pamphlet's material aloud then repeated the parts she found particularly exciting.

"It says here that my work would buy down Dad's debt. It says here that I would get the same credits for one hour's work as I would for a class and that the New Government wants to encourage the youth to view work in the same way as education—that both are essential for our Nation's recovery and growth. It says here that we can't get out of math or science…darn it! But that we don't have to take all the history classes, just modern history, and we don't have to take English or Physical Education or Health or any of the social sciences and not art or music either."

The more Page Little listened, the angrier she got, "Well then what the hell is the point of going to school at all!" she screamed.

"It says here…"

"I don't give a damn what it says!" Page yelled, "You're not doing it!"

"It says here that even if your parents don't agree, that you can—legally—enroll in the program when you're 16."

"Well you're not doing it and that's final!"

"Oh yeah," Mabel yelled, "What are you going to do to stop me!"

"You still have to live under my roof! That's the law too."

"Well it says here that the New Government will let me do exactly what you're doing—when I'm sixteen."

Page Little stopped the car. She stopped the car right in the middle of the street, turned around, ripped the pamphlet from her daughter's hand, turned back around and drove home. Nobody said a word but it was clear, Mabel was crying.

The minute they pulled into the driveway, Mabel ran into the house.

"You two, carry in the groceries," Page Little softly said. The fight with Mabel had taken the last of her strength. The two small children muled: carrying bags in, coming out empty-handed—like little honeybees. Page Little sat down on the concrete, pulled her knees to her chest, let her forehead rest atop them, and cried. She thought about William Henry Little, and how she could really use one of his hugs just then. She thought about what the LP clinician had said about not excising, about how she had to make herself eat all that food—even if it made her feel like vomiting—and she suddenly had no appetite at all. What was she going to do if she failed? Billy sat down beside her, put his 10-year-old-sized arm halfway round her back, "Don't cry, Mommy. It's going to be okay."

Fawn sat down on the other side and leant her head on her mother's shoulder, "Mabel is so mean!"

Page Little put her skinny arms around her children, pulled them to her bony sides, and kissed the tops of their heads, smelling the sweetness of the clean they'd become, "I'm going to take care of you."

"We know, Mommy!" they squealed, and kissed and kissed and kissed her.

Inside the house, Mabel had locked herself in her room. Page Little plopped down on the couch, opened four different types of cookies, had Fawn pour her a large glass of soda pop and opened four different bags of corn and potato chips. For the next hour Page shoveled food down. At first she went quickly, because she was hungry, but that sensation went away and remainder of time was spent in fighting an increasingly intense urge to vomit.

At one point Page Little thought, "I can't eat one more bite," but she fingered the pamphlets she kept beside her, and determined, "Yes I can." With that she forced another bolus down. "I'll do whatever it takes!" she cried, to herself. It wasn't much later when Page Little was seized with an urgent need to use the restroom.

Sitting on the toilet, Page Little sobbed, partly because of the pain she felt from the crampimpg but mostly because she just knew that all that food had gone straight through her: she had diarrhea. She searched the pamphlet for an answer. She knew that if she couldn't get control of it, there would be no way she'd be able to gain the weight she needed, but the pamphlet provided nothing.

There was a knock on the bathroom door.

"I'm in here," Page cried.

It was Mabel, "I'm sorry, Mom."

"It's okay," Page cried, she was seized with another cramp and moaned.

"Are you alright?" Mabel asked.

"I've got diahrea."

"Isn't there medicine for that?"

Page Little, almost as excited as Mabel had been over the idea of working in the grocery cried, "That's it! Go ask one of the neighbors. Maybe they have some."

"But Mom," Mabel began protesting.

"I need it! Now go!"

Mabel heard an urgency in her mother's voice that wasn't altogether explained by her physical condition so she, begrudgingly, walked to the neighbor's house whose lawn, like theirs, was no lawn at all yet, and rang the doorbell. She was looking at the dirt when the door opened, turning around, she found herself standing in front of one of the most gorgeous guys she'd ever seen! He must have been at least 16, tall, blonde, blue eyes and built. "Wow!" was her first thought and this thrilled her stomach into butterflies but then she remembered *what* she was there for and this made her stomach very very queasy. She just couldn't ask him for diahhrea medicine! It was too much!

"Can I help you," he asked in a voice light and creamy like butter.

"Uh, I, uh, is your mother home?"

"May I ask why you want to see her?"

He sounded so mature. So refined. He sounded nothing like the other boys she'd known when her family had lived beneath the bridge, before the New Government had saved them.

"A-hem," he cleared his throat.

"Oh, I, well we, we live next door and my mother sent me over to talk to your mother."

Just then a tall, blonde woman with blue eyes stood behind him, "What's going on?" she asked.

"The neighborgirl's mother sent her," he answered.

"Well don't be rude," she scolded, "See her in."

With that, Mabel was welcomed in. Their house was, in many ways, exactly like hers. The floorplan was identical but there was something different. Maybe it was the lack she noticed. There was no bigscreen t.v. and no fancy couch. There was a diningroom table with four chairs and, along the wall, there were four piles of neatly stacked books. The mother motioned to Mabel, "Come sit down," she said. "Would you like something to eat or drink?" she asked.

"Oh no thank you," Mabel replied.

"Okay," the woman answered, "How can I help you?"

"It's my mother," Mabel looked at the boy, who was standing beside his mother, "but I don't think I can talk about it in front of…"

"Oh," the woman smiled, "I see. Fred, will you excuse us?"

"Yes mother," he replied and left them both sitting at the table.

"Now, first things first: what's your name?"

"Oh I'm sorry. I'm Mabel Little. My mom's Page Little and I have a brother and a sister, Fawn and Billy."

"You mean your sister's name is Billy?" the woman laughed, "I'm just teasing. An old English teacher's joke. By the way, I'm Marian and that was my son, Fred, that you met earlier."

Mabel looked at the woman more closely. She looked tired, sort of worn out like some of the books resting on the tops of her book stack, as if they couldn't bear the weight of the other books on top of their spines.

"What does your mother need of me?" she asked Mabel.

"She's sick. She needs medicine and was hoping maybe you'd have some."

"I believe I do. Does you mother need me to come to your house?"

Mabel thought for a moment, "I don't think so."

"Maybe I should, just in case."

Without ever admitting it, Mabel was glad the matronly-looking woman came home with her. She was, in fact, a little scared that her mother was sick, especially because she didn't know where her father was or how to get hold of him.

When Marian stepped inside the Little's house she put her hand to her neck and exclaimed, "Oh my!"

"What is it?" Mabel asked.

"Oh nothing. I just wasn't prepared to see so much…luxury."

Mabel's smile sprung ear-to-ear. It was the first time she could ever remember someone using the word "luxury" in reference to her family. But then, all of a sudden, Mabel thought about the lady's house—with nothing in it—and flattenend her smile, immediately, into a drawn set of lips because she didn't want to hurt the lady's feelings, the lady who'd been so nice.

"I assume your house is like ours so, is your mother in there?" Marian pointed to the closed bathroom door.

Mabel nodded then ran over to the couch where Fawn and Billy were watching cartoons, eating chips and cookies and drinking colas.

Marian gently knocked on the door, "Hi. I'm Marian. Your neighbor. Your daughter came to my house for medicine and I've brought it."

"Oh thank you," Page Little cried but her voice was weak.

"I'll put it right here by the door then?" she asked.

"That would be…" Page Little did not finish her sentence. Marian O'Reily could hear pure fluid hitting the water.

"Will you be okay?" Marian asked.

"Yes. Fine. Thank you. I'll get the medicine down me and I'll be fine."

"Very well," Marian replied, "I'll just leave it here by the door." To the children she said, "If you need me," but she stopped. They were totally engrossed by the images on their widescreen t.v.

When Marian got home Fred asked what was going on. She told him that the new neighbors' mother was sick, just like she'd been, when they first moved to Fortaleez, the year before.

"I'm sure she'll get over it soon. It's a big adjustment, the diet I mean, being in the L.P. program."

Fred put his arm around his mother's shoulder. He'd worried about her this last year. It seemed that no matter what she ate, or how much, she never gained a single pound. In fact, if he absolutely had to describe her the two words that, much to his hatred of them, snuck into his mind were: wasting away.

Marian O'Ryan went into the kitchen to fix supper.

"No," Fred said, grabbing her arm, "Let me."

Marian smiled, "Okay then. What's for dinner?"

"Well, what's on your diet?"

"I think tonight is frozen fried chicken, instant mashed potatoes with butter and sour cream, and green bean casserole with mushroom sause and cheese."

Marian O'Ryan looked as if she wanted to gag, but smiled.

At the Little's house, Page finally made it to the bathroom door, finally managed to get to the medicine and, eventually, got to take some. By this time the water running through her guts was mixed with blood and stung when it rained. It was dark by the time she managed to walk, crouched like an old woman, out of the bathroom to find the tops of her three children's heads barely visible in a completely dark house except for the glow the television cast upon them. Page went and gingerly sat down on the couch, holding her stomach.

"Are alright Mom," Mabel asked.

"I'll be fine. Thank you for getting the medicine."

"You're welcome. Do you want something to eat?"

Page Little was surprised that, in fact, she was actually hungry. "Sure," she replied. Then forced a smile to her face, for her daughter was growing up before her eyes, "Any suggestions?"

"Oh," Fawn piped up, snuggling into her mother, "The cookies are WONDERFUL!"

"Which ones?" Page asked.

Billy cried, "ALL of them, Mom!"

"Okay, I'll have some cookies. And," she looked at Mabel, "do you think you could get me a glass of soda?"

"We'll all have more soda!" the three children cried, jumping up and bouncing around with bottled-up energy. Because, you see, it hadn't been just Mabel who worried. The younger ones sensed it too—a feeling of inherent unsafeness, as if every egg in the whole world rested in the nest of their mother and her three little chicks.

With much protest, Page Little sent the children to bed. It had been a helluva day. She wanted to go to sleep, she knew she needed to go to sleep, but found herself quite unable to make her eyes close and stay closed. They darted as if electric trollys on city streets delivering her passenger-thoughts from one destination to another, then back again. She thought of the L.P. program only to find it dropped off at the feet of the last image she held in her mind of William Henry Little, the day he loaded onto the bus, the day she confessed—only to herself—she was glad to see him gone because it meant she and the kids would live better.

But the train was too fast to stay there. It sped to being sick, to the voice of the neighbor, to her children, to being sick, to worrying about how everything was going to get paid off, to William Henry Little. And it seemed as if it was all speeding up somehow, into a great whirlwind of mass transit, as if her head was spinning and the only thing that would make it stop was to force her eyelids open, sit up and declare herself to be "wide awake." It was as if she was drunk. And thus, the night wore on for Page Little.

For Billy the night began with an absolute feeling of pleasure to feel his small feet rubbing against the softness of his clean sheets. He pushed his head into his soft pillow. Bounced his butt up and down a few times, to make sure his soft bed was real and then—crash. He was out like a light.

For Fawn, she lay on her back looking at the ceiling for a while. Of the three, Fawn had been especially close to her father. Unlike Mabel, who was quite "girly," Fawn was a "tomboy" but more specifically she was tomboy for her dad. Anything he did, she wanted to do. One of her most special memories was when her dad came home from work, for lunch, which never happened because he always took his lunch with him—to save on gas money—but this day he'd forgotten, or her mom had, and so William Henry Little came home for lunch. As he ate he said, "I figure it would be just as much money to eat out as it would be to drive home, so what better way to spend the extra dough than to come home and see my beautiful kids," and he kissed each one on the top of their heads.

When lunch was over, as he was getting up to leave, Fawn ran to him, clutching his legs in her 8-year-old arms, "Take me with you, PLEASE!"

It was summertime and instead of what she expected, what Page Little and Mabel expected, which was the "Sorry, I can't" he said, "Let me ask." He called his supervisor on the radio and, to Fawn's elation, his boss said "Sure." William Henry Little turned to Mabel and asked her if she wanted to come too but before she could answer Billy yelled, "I do! I do!" William Henry Little patted his head, "Sorry, Billy. Not yet. Someday, when you're a little bigger." Billy's crying was instant and unmercifully loud. William Henry turned to Mabel, "What about you? Wanna come?"

Mabel hemmed and hawed, finally saying, "Thanks, Dad, but I have a lot of other stuff I need to do. I'm helping Mom."

William Henry Little smiled. He loved that each of his kids were so different. "Very good then. We'd better be off, Fawn."

Fawn Little lay in bed thinking about that day. The way her dad's car smelled when the warm sun pelted its vinyl. The way she could see glints of stubble when the sunlight struck his neck and where he'd missed a patch shaving. She watched his hands on the wheel, his eyes on the road, and snuggled up close beside him while they drove, listening to the radio.

Mabel Little went to bed with one thing on her mind: Fred O'Ryan. She'd never, in all her life, seen such a scrummy guy. He was tall. He was blonde. He was beautiful and he was old! "I bet he drives," she thought. "I wonder if he likes me," she hoped. She envisioned him saying, "Mabel, even though you're only in junior high and I'm in high school, you're the most prettiest girl I've ever seen. Will you marry me?" To which she watched herself throw her arms around his chest and professing her love and devotion.

It was, for Mabel Little, a fitful beginning to sleep but before she knew it she was dreaming and not of Fred O'Ryan. Mabel Little had fitful dreams, nightmares, of being in a car on a road running beside the sea, ran along the edge of a high cliff top and Mabel Little could see out the window to the crashing waves far, far below and the road was curvy, oh so curvy, back and forth, being slammed in her seat, as if her mother were driving way to fast, and Mabel could see the tires beginning to lose contact with the road, begin to lose tread on the gravel shoulder with each turn her mother made, until finally—the turn was too great, the speed was too great, and Mabel Little watched her mother's hands trying to correct the steering wheel only to find she was unable to keep the car on the road—and the car, with Page Little driving and Mabel Little riding, floated right off the road. Down, down, down it feel and Mabel knew, even in her dream, that the crash was coming in just a moment. Just one more moment of living. And so she braced. Braced for impact…and felt the impact…throw her body onto the rocks and in her bed she sat straight up, covered in sweat.

Wiping her face, Mabel Little lay back down. "It's just a dream," she said to herself, feeling so exhausted that all she could do was go back to sleep, and—to her horror—found that all she could do, that night, was have the same dream.

When the morning came Mabel Little looked as wiped out as Page Little. Billy and Fawn were their antitheses: perky, peppy, and ready to "do something!"

"We're bored sitting around. Can't we go to a playground or something?"

There was a knock on the door. Mabel answered. It was Fred O'Ryan.

"My mother wanted me to check and see if your mother was alright."

"She's fine, thank you," Mabel replied, trying to cover her exhaustion with smiles.

"Are *you* okay?" he asked her.

Mabel smiled bigger, showing her teeth, "Sure. Great. Couldn't be better."

"Oh, and Mom wanted me to remind you that you need to register for school."

"Okay," Mabel smiled. "Thanks."

"Okay," Fred replied, "See ya."

School. School! The last thing Mabel Little wanted to think about was school. There was another knock at the door. It was Fred again.

"I'm sorry. I completely forgot. My mom wanted me to invite you all to my basketball game this Friday night."

"Cool."

"It costs $5.00 to get in but you can use your card if you want. And when you register for school, then it's free."

"Okay. Bye." Mabel started to shut the door then called out, "Have a good day at school."

Fred turned, smiled and waved. Mabel Little's heart fluttered. She was in love.

## WILLIAM HENRY LITTLE'S FAMILY

Page Little drove her family to the LP clinic. Mabel, Fawn and Billy ran ahead of her. Page watched her children disappear into the glass building's curves and arches. She listened to the cascading water of the fountain as she walked past it but did not give it much thought. All she could focus on was the hope, deep inside of her, that she'd made the weight.

At the reception desk a beautiful brunette girl asked Page for her name. Once given, the girl pointed for Page to go inside the milky glass doors off to the right of the lobby.

Page Little did not see her children inside. "They must be off having fun," she thought but her longing to see where they were made her eyes dart from the playground fort and juice bar to the doors leading to the amusement park and video games, go carts, jumping forts, and waterslides.

Page Little knew she needed to get to her appointment on time. So she forced herself to stop searching and forced herself to march through the doors before her—the doors she knew led to the underwater weigh-in.

Naked, Page Little sat on the metal swing. The weightbelt, on top of her lap, felt very very heavy to her. More heavy than it had the last time. "Exhale" the woman commanded. Page Little complied. Down she went, into the water, down she went...she thought it seemed to last forever. Then she was up in the air again, "Very good, Love," the lady said.

Page Little walked her naked frame through the doors, was handed her daily suit by a young girl who told her to put it on and go into room 17 where a metal chair awaited her. Page Little did as instructed but opted not to listen to music or read. She was still feeling queasy, and nervous. The smell of cherry made her increasingly nauseous such that she was ever-so-thankful to see the girl come in to inform her that her two-hour session was over.

Page Little threw the paper suit into the disposal chute and walked, once again naked, to the counseling area where a blonde-haired older woman pointed to a scale on the floor, "Hi. I'm your counselor for today. Please step on the scale."

The woman wrote on Page Little's form, which was attached to a clipboard she held. "You can step off now."

"How did I do?" Page Little couldn't help it, she had to know.

"You're exactly the same," the woman replied. Her forehead knit.

"Oh my God!" Page Little cried, "I've been eating everything on the list and I've been sick as a dog! I don't know what I'm going to do if I can't gain weight I'm going to get kicked out."

The woman put her hand on Page Little's shoulder, "Now, now. You're getting yourself all upset for nothing. The first week, or so, we don't expect to see a whole lot of gain."

"But the other lady said…"

The woman interrupted, "Don't worry about what the other lady said. You just keep doing what you're doing and we'll see how you're doing on your next appointmnet. But try, as hard as you can, to gain weight okay?"

"Oh I've been trying so hard! But I'll keep trying," Page Little began to cry, "I really want to be in this program. I really *need* to be in this program."

The woman patted Page's shoulder, "Now go and get dressed. See you next time."

The kids, once again, did not want to leave but did. After all, it was Friday and they all were planning to go to Fred O'Ryan's basketball game. "But first," Page Little announced, "We need to stop off at the school to see about registering you guys." In unison the three cried, "Awww!"


but after those first days of P.T.P. enlistment, where women and minor children were enrolled in L.P. programs at separate Fortaleez, his wife, Page, had made it clear that she no longer wished to have a relationship. Divorce was an option they'd not taken because Page would lose her enrollment in the L.P. program unless she was married to a man co-enrolled in the P.T.P. So they remained married, officially, framing the distance as occupationally. They'd agreed to a common answer when asked why they hadn't divorced: the children. Theirs was a conspiracy engaged in by many who understood that being in the Fortaleezian programs, whether P.T.P. or L.P. was—in fact—the best thing for the children born to parents who were not wealthy City dwellers.

William Henry Little's face lit up. He'd known Notoc Kachuka since he and his family had been transported from the City; they'd been living in a tent city beneath one of the bridges for months. William Henry Little's debt, accumulated through the neonatal care his youngest child had needed, qualified him for the Debt Relief Program, or the flagship Fortaleez system, and his twenty-year experience in university security perfectly positioned him to lead security at his assigned Fortaleez.

He thought back on the first time he'd met Notoc. It was before the first generation structures to be issued by the newly-declared dictator, the Benevolent Leader. Notoc was in charge of helping each community transition to the newly-engineered living structures, and away from the makeshift chaos of temporary erections utilizing whatever resources could be found that were not infected with the mold suspected to be at the root of the Sleeping Sickness epidemic, but William found that what he remembered most vividly was how many people resisted change. It didn't seem to matter that they were trading tents and cots for fully independent units designed for comfort and ease or that they didn't have to take extra food from the store for fear there would be none later. Their years spent in abject insecurity made it nearly impossible for them to accept that the Benevolent Leader would not let them down, that they would not have a basic life handed to them with one hand only to have it torn from grasp by the hand of a different political agenda. It would take time and a great deal of education and patience to get them to calm, to settle, and to feel secure enough to allow their minds to set aside, even slightly, the fear such long-borne burden drives deep into the heart.

For the first few years of the Fortaleez, between supervising multiple national research projects and interacting with heads of state and industry, Notoc Kachuka visited each Fortaleez. The types of town-hall meetings enabled inhabitants to ask questions, technical and otherwise, but it also gave him the chance to inspect how his designs were working in terms of security and longevity.

Little asks Notoc what got him involved with the government

Notoc: shares MIT,LP. Program, Misha

## ESTELLE ECHEVERRIA, CITIZEN

Estelle's senior project had been on the Benevolent Leader as a visionary for realizing the forefather's goal of direct democracy through the utility of technological infrastructure while protecting from mob rule by endowing the people with checks and balances through the Senate and House.

Estelle liked facts but loved that the moment the Benevolent Leader had finished his swearing in he declared a state of national emergency and seized domestic with the promise he'd relinquish it the moment the People's Branch had become constitutionally ratified—which he did. He'd stood against every established politician and political group and stood up to the wealthiest in the world, saying, "No more! You will not pass legislation that excludes our citizen's right to self-rule." To Estelle, and many others, he was not only the People's president but a hero. And in spite of The Monarch's devastation of the financial sector and the plague of Sleeping Sickness that leveled almost every city resulting in the largest relocation and resettlement program since the days of the Native Americans under Manifest Destiny, the United States had never enjoyed such prosperity—each decade following yielding reduced deficit, increased gross domestic product, and greater international trade.

People in white clothing mulled through the crowd. The training facilities where the time they spent in training was determined by the job they were qualified to do.

her debt qualified her to participate in the Fortaleez program for seven years; she'd been at Fortleez for ten without noticing a significant reduction of her debt, for which she was exceedingly glad.

all Fortaleez citizens were required to actively participate in the People's branch of the government by voting on no less than three legal proceedings, whether state or federal legislation, or weighing in on Supreme Court cases. The government also provided incentives for people who, like Estelle, wanted to become debt-free as quickly as possible by providing debt credits for all legislative or judicial participation beyond the required minimum.

## MENDY VITCH, CITIZEN

Mendy's dad worked on the Pneumatic Tube Project (P.T.P.). He'd come home, after being gone less than an hour, and complain that nothing ever got done. He'd been a construction worker before the terror attack and because of their own mortgage and credit card debt they qualified for the initial P.T.P. Fortaleez program.

Mendy loved to hear his stories of how when they first came they were pioneers living in yurts while they constructed the houses, domes, and city wall. He'd reminisce, as if those were the good old days, but her mother would hiss that it was the worst thing they'd ever gone through, especially since they'd been relocated in the middle of nowhere and the climate was either frigidly cold or swelteringly hot. And then she'd chastise him by saying, "And then you got sent off to God knows where, doing God knows what." To which her father would shake his head and explain, yet again, to Mendy that he'd never wanted to leave her or her mother but after the epidemic, all men trained in construction were required to go to the cities and tear down contaminated structures. Then he'd wink. "I might add that by enlisting, the government assured me a lifetime debt status and I should think that would make your mother happy considering what our other options would have been."

Mendy knew he was right. A lifetime guarantee of Fortaleez was like winning the lottery, especially now.

USED IN ABOVE—SO CONDENSE AND PERSONALIZE(Graduating high school earned a diploma, $50,000 deposited into a city bank for the graduate, and a debt free certification; failure to graduate resulted in expulsion from Fortaleez. Very few failed to graduate but those who did would never be allowed to enter the cities; they'd spend the rest of their lives being free.

A high school diploma and debt free certificate meant automatic acceptance to university where only a small amount of debt could be accumulated, thanks to legislative reform and price capping, or one could make their pilgrimage to their closest city, and try to find work.

With only $50,000 that was a perilous option because the cost of housing in the cities after the epidemic renovations had become exorbitant, jobs were scarce, and the debt laws in the cities required both employment and housing in order to qualify for debt—and without government sanctioned debt…one could not return to a Fortaleez

For Mendy the choice was easy university. At least graduating from university would add another $50,000 to her bank account in the city but she, like everyone else she went to school with, was worried what would happen to them after graduation.)

There were five main recruiting branches: healthcare, military, pleasure, engineering, and education. Each branch not only negotiated varying debt but program completion payout, which meant that although the doctors received huge debt markers and substantial completion payouts the nurses deals were no better than the elementary school teachers and they were not substantially better or worse positioned than the engineers. To Mendy, and the average citizen, the remuneration system didn't make sense but the citizenry had been assured, by the government, that because of breakthroughs in quantitative easing, they were able to provide the greatest level of opportunity for every citizen.

MYKA THORNFEIST, EARLY FORTALEEZIAN DEBT OFFICER

The Charity Prohibition Law had been enacted shortly after the Fortaleezes had become fully operational in response to the discovery of that there were some who'd learned to game the system. Each Fortaleezian living space had been designed to limit possession of physical items because beyond every basic need provided to them by the government while in the program participants could purchase additional things or experiences that would be added to their debt balance; the design was such that no one could purchase at a rate higher than their physical space limitation compared to the debt reduction rates of their occupation.

Gaming occurred through "donations to the less fortunate in the Free Zone" by, latently, establishing permanent Fortaleezian residency. Although there were some, like Eyre Proust's parents and William Henry Little—those displaced during relocation or the early debt program enrollees who'd built the first Fortaleezes— who'd been offered permanent residency in the program, everyone else would, eventually, become debt free and would have to take their pilgrimage to the city where their bank accounts and new lives awaited them.

The law was enacted shortly after the Fortaleezes had become fully in response to the discovery that there were some who'd learned to game the system. Each Fortaleezian living space had been designed to limit possession of physical items because beyond every basic need provided to them by the government while in the program participants could purchase additional things or experiences that would be added to their debt balance; the design was such that no one could purchase at a rate higher than their physical space limitation compared to the debt reduction rates of their occupation.

Gaming occurred through "donations to the less fortunate in the Free Zone" by, latently, establishing permanent Fortaleezian residency. Although there were some, like (Eyre Proust's parents and William Henry Little)—those displaced during relocation or the early debt program enrollees who'd built the first Fortaleezes— who'd been offered permanent residency in the program, everyone else would, eventually, become debt free and would have to take their pilgrimage to the city where their bank accounts and new lives awaited them.

In the early times of the Fortaleez there was not the uniformity that there is now.

NO—must be uniform for each Fortaleez.